No Apologies

Andrea Jenelle

Copyright Information

----

and all material for the training, incorporation, assimilation or appropriation of artificial intelligence. The story, all names, characters, and incidents portrayed in this production are fictitious. No identification with actual persons (living or deceased), places, buildings, and products is intended or should be inferred.

Book Cover by Booked Forever.

Character Art Illustration by Roxolana Krywonos, dba Illustrated Cliterature.

Digital ISBN: 978-1-962123-45-7

Paperback ISBN: 978-1-962123-46-4

Dedication

YOU'LL NEVER FEEL LIKE you're enough for the wrong people, but you'll always be enough for the right people and when you let your guard down with them you don't have to prove anything.

Zak Hazlett, "The Outdoor Therapist", Marriage and Family Counselor

If you have Spotify, you can listen to it here:

Chapter One: What You're Running From - Jamie Grey

Chapter Two: Matches - Jonah Kagen

Chapter Three: What They Say- Lily Fitts

Chapter Four: Troubled Waters - Alex Warren

Chapter Five: Crooked the Road - Mon Rovia

Chapter Six: Brave-Riley Pearce

Chapter Seven: Sunshine-Davina & the Vagabonds

Chapter Eight: Cold Little Heart- Michael Kiwanuka

Chapter Nine: Sweet- MO, Biig Piig

Chapter Ten: A Cut This Deep- Ike Dweck

Chapter Eleven: The Other Side- Michael Marcagi

Chapter Twelve: Little Bit More- Suriel Hess

Chapter Thirteen: Wherever I Go- Noah Rinker

Chapter Fourteen: Who Was I- Chord Overstreet

Chapter Fifteen: River-Myles Smith

Contents

Chapter One: What You're Runnin' From...

Luz

CHEESE PUFFS LITTER THE backseat and the baby poop smell of Bradford Pear trees floods the vents and blends with the sharp, fizzy aroma of cherry coke. Rico thought it would be funny to torment his sisters, so he shook up the can right before he opened it. The girls were squealing and complaining about the sweltering heat, and the sticky residue on their bare legs, until we rounded the bend in the road and our new home came into view.

Late spring in Virginia is so humid sometimes it's hard to breathe. The shadow of the mountain makes it less stifling, but there are two things I can't ignore: the only air conditioning is the stale breeze ruffling my hair through the half-open window and the windshield is covered in pollen and bug guts. Both of those things are reminders of the state of my bank account. I haven't been able to scrape together the money to fix the air or get decent wiper blades

The moaning and groaning stopped and now all three of them, including Rico, are just oohing and aahing.

There's a reason the kids are oohing and ahhing around their powdery orange mustaches. I don't know what I expected when Dex encouraged me to apply for the Willow Creek Fire Department vacancy and offered me one of his lake rentals. I know it wasn't this sprawling log home. It looks like one of those cozy-cabin-beside-the-tranquil-lake pictures from a Kinkade calendar.

All my kids swim like they were born with fins and I knew they'd miss being near the ocean more than anything. Being so close to the water will make it easier for them to adjust.

"Mom, is this where we get to live?" I can hear the awe in Rosie's voice. She's old enough to remember the trailer and the crappy apartments before we moved in with my parents so I could get my certification. It looks like paradise compared to the burned out shell of our seventies era trailer with the shag carpet and the roach infested hovels.

"It is. Make sure you thank your Uncle Dex when you see him for giving us a place to live." I'll be thanking him too. This cabin could become the first real home we've ever had as a family, and the hope makes my throat close up.

"Will I get my own room?" Rico sounds skeptical. He was sharing a room with both his sisters at my parents' house that was crammed with bunk beds and one closet.

"Your Uncle Dex said there are four bedrooms. So that means each of you gets your own space."

Rosie and Rico fist pump and then high five each other.

"But Mom, what if Rubi has nightmares?" Rosie pipes up. She insists on sitting in the pop-up back seat of the vintage station wagon I bought from my dad. I'm a worry wart - especially on the interstate, so I wouldn't let her switch seats until we were on the lake road.

"What if I'm scared, Mommy?" My six-year-old asks. She and Rosie have shared the bottom bunk for the last four years, since she turned two. The idea of a bed all to herself probably feels like the end of the world.

Rubi is a legacy of the last chance I gave Ben to show us he wanted to be there. Even though she was an accident, she feels like my biggest blessing.

"You can climb in bed with me." Rosie tells her. I'm grateful for Rosie's uncharacteristic patience with her little sister.

I put the station wagon in park and turn around to face them. "Si, Rubi. You can sleep with your big sister if you have a nightmare when I'm on shift at the firehouse."

"When will we see Uncle Dex?" Rico asks. He's my older brother's biggest fan, and is even more pumped than usual because Dex asked him to be his best man when he marries Mari in November.

"We're going over to his house for dinner tomorrow."

All three of them whistle and whoop.

"Uncle Dex told me he and Mari cook out a lot. Is he going to make us hamburgers?" Rosie asks.

"I love hamburgers," Rubi says with a dreamy look on her face.

"I'm sure Dex and Mari will make something you'll love," I reassure them. "Maybe save the special requests for next time, though. Your uncle has done a lot for us and we need to be grateful and appreciative."

We didn't bring much with us. We lost all of our furniture in the fire ten years ago when Rico and Rosie were still toddlers, and long before Rubi was here. I finally broke it off with their father for good after his shenanigans four years ago, and we were all living with my parents in Florida until I got my firefighter and paramedic certifications.

The cabin Dex is letting us live in is fully furnished, and he gave the kids a virtual tour of all the stuff he and Mari got for their rooms. I think they were the most excited about the bean bag chairs.

Willow Creek is the only place I applied, because I knew Dex and Mari would be a support system. I've learned the hard way that when you're a single mom you need people you can depend on who will be your life-raft, your pinch-hitter, and even your Mrs. Doubtfire when you need them. The fire chief didn't seem happy about hiring me, but Dex told me no one else applied and he was desperate. Since I graduated at the top of my class, Ian Montgomery couldn't dispute my qualifications.

Once I drop the kids off at school I'm stopping by the firehouse on Monday to fill out all the final paperwork.

I was able to enroll them online, thank goodness, and all I had to do was send over certified copies of their transcripts and vaccine records.

I park the car on the side of the garage because the movers will be here tomorrow. "Okay, banditos," I say as I lower the rear view mirror so I can see all of them. "Grab your backpacks, and we'll leave the rest for the morning. It's a hot dogs and nachos night, and Uncle Dex said there's a big screen tv in the family room."

They break into cheers.

"Mom, can you find Mr. Snoozy?" Rubi asks.

She can't sleep without her stuffed elephant. "Didn't you put him in your backpack this morning?"

"I helped her pack her bag, and I don't remember seeing him," Rosie says.

Oh, no. The last time we lost Mr. Snoozy, aka Rubi's security blanket, was two years ago. Also the last time they spent a weekend with their absent father. She left him in Ben's trailer and my ex-husband couldn't be bothered to drop off his youngest daughter's safety net. It was a week before I could get over there and re-trieve him. A week of bedtime meltdowns and sleepless nights. A week I can't afford to have repeated- not when I'm starting at the fire department on Monday.

"Let's grab all the bags we brought with us so we can go through them while we eat dinner."

After I've set the hot dogs to broil in the convection oven (because Rubi says they're too mushy to eat if I boil them), we dump everything on the living room floor.

I comb through the piles of clothes and toys with growing desperation.

Rico's Marvel figurines he insists he doesn't play with any more? Check.

Rosie's Barbie she keeps because she says it's the perfect way to practice braiding? Check.

Mr. Snoozy, the purple stuffed elephant? Nowhere to be seen.

Rubi is frantic. She's crawling around on the floor, shoving aside all the piles of clothes again. She has that look on her face. The breakable one. The one she had on her face the last time I picked her up from Ben's and her best friend got left behind.

I asked my trauma psychiatrist about it, because I was worried about her attachment. She reassured me and said to let Rubi cope the best way she could. That if talking to a purple elephant helped her get through her parents' divorce, I should let her keep him.

But this is why I wanted to wean her away from that obnoxious elephant. Because she doesn't have the tools to soothe herself to sleep without him. I know all the kids have abandonment issues from Ben's apathetic parenting, but his absence has affected Rubi the most. He was there at the hospital when she was born, and was her biggest fan. And then he got bored when her baby cheeks started to thin out. By the time he stayed away for months at a time, she'd stopped asking for him. Mr. Snoozy was her replacement for fatherly affection.

"We'll look for him tomorrow. Maybe he ended up in the moving van," I say as I heft her into my arms.

"Mommy, I need him!" She wails as she drops her tear-stained face to my shoulder.

"I know you think you do, sweetie. But why don't you sleep with mommy tonight, instead?"

"Will you read the caterpillar?"

"Of course, baby," I tell her. I've read the book about the caterpillar that eats everything and then turns into a butterfly so many times, I know it by heart.

"Sorry, Mom," Rosie mutters into my ear as she hugs me good night.

"Yeah, sorry, Mom," Rico echoes as he slides an arm around my waist in an awkward embrace. He turned fourteen in October, and now he thinks he's too big for displays of affection. The last time I kissed him on the cheek in front of his friends, I thought he was going to murder me.

"You're both on find- Mr- Snoozy duty tomorrow once the movers get here."

Once Rubi's snuffling softly beside me, I ease out of the bed and head for the dock I know is only a few hundred yards from the back porch. I've been scraping my toes against the canvas of my shoes since the water came into view. Once I reach the weathered gray planks, I slip off my shoes and dangle my legs over the edge. The cool ripple washes over my wriggling toes and it's like I left yesterday instead of almost seventeen years ago. When I tip back my head, the stars are right there on top of me. So close I could reach out and touch them. The chirp of tree frogs and locusts fills the air, and the croak of a lone bullfrog echoes in the silence. Everything is still and quiet and a wave of nostalgia fills my heart.

I was stupid and crazy in love and ignored everyone's advice about Ben. Even my older brother's advice. He's never judged me for it, but I could always tell Dex thought Ben would bring me nothing but heartbreak.

My older brother was right.

We skipped prom and ran away instead. Ben showed up in his granddad's El Camino and we took off like Bonnie and Clyde, with me laughing and pressing down the tulle of my skirt so I could close the door. I tossed my bag in the backseat and never looked back. Until now.

Ben used to tell me all the time that Willow Creek was too small to hold him and if he was going to make something of himself he needed to get out. And I would follow Benito Alvarez anywhere when he told me I was his little light. The sparkle in his eyes when he said it made my panties go up in smoke.

(They went up in smoke a lot back then. Usually against my better judgment.)

His dreams were nothing but smoke too. Just like this song that used to be stuck in my head about people who talked trash and never did anything about it. Blowin' smoke and goin' broke.

Somehow we ended up in a trailer park in Florida. I had Rico when I was barely nineteen and waddling around the diner I waitressed like a stuffed turkey. Ben wasn't there when our son was born- he was working a commercial construction job two towns over and said he couldn't get away.

It was like that for most of our adult relationship. He was always gone on a job or out running around with his slacker friends.

We never had enough money for groceries but made too much money for stamps and he was always spending what I scraped together on one of his stupid get-rich-quick schemes that made us worse off.

We didn't get married when I had Rico. I wouldn't have been eligible for WIC if we had - even though we were working poor. I wanted to breastfeed, but we needed my income from waitressing. So formula was the one and only option.

After Rosie came along, we finally got married at the county courthouse. I had to pump with her, and I would sit on the low commode in the staff bathroom that reeked of banned cigarettes with the pump attached like the most painful nipple clamp ever created, and fill two four ounce bottles at a time.

Getting married was a mistake. Ben seemed to think it gave him permission to act however the hell he wanted. After we tied the knot, everything fell apart. He started spending every weekend at the bar playing pool with his buddies. When he was home, he was gaming with a bunch of people he'd never met.

When we found out Rico was on the spectrum and required counseling and meds, and I was at the school almost every day because he was being sent to the principal's office on a regular basis, that's when I knew Ben didn't have the capacity to be a decent spouse or a good dad. Because he didn't step up at all.

I was taking one night class a semester, trying to get the credits for an associate degree in business, and waitressing on the weekends when Ben could watch the kids. After I came home and found him passed out on the couch with an empty bottle beside him, while the kids ran circles around him, I asked for a separation.

We couldn't afford a divorce, but it worked a lot better. Until one night we were both feeling nostalgic and had sex without a condom.

So now, here I am. Divorced. With three kids and literally living on a prayer because I just used my last thirty dollars for gas, a bag of generic cheetos, a fountain drink, a box of knockoff cereal and the stuff for hot dogs tonight.

I'm praying Willow Creek is going to be what we need to get on our feet. I landed my dream job with the town fire department - the most money I've ever earned. All of the nights waitressing at the truck stop for two bucks an hour finally added up to something good. The best part of all is that my big brother Dex is here to give me and the kids a safety net if we need it. Rico looks up to him and I'm hoping the attitude he's had lately will get smoothed out when he's around his uncle.

***

The glass is sweating in my hand, but the ice is still a cold compress against my cheek and forehead. Dex is impatiently tapping his foot against the side of his camp chair. I finally take a sip to end his agony. There's a hint of pear, and something floral. The pilsner is crisp, clean and perfect for a late spring afternoon.

We spent all day unpacking and looking for Mr. Snoozy. We finally found him stuffed in the box of spatulas and silverware. By that time, Rubi was beside herself and I was ready for a week's worth of happy hours (even if it meant they consisted of nothing but my brother's pathetic microbrew attempts) or sneaking away to smoke a joint (which I can't do because my new job has random drug testing.)

"Your micro-brewing skills have vastly improved," I tell him with a nod of acknowledgement. "I needed them. We couldn't find Mr. Snoozy last night and Rubi was on the verge of a meltdown."

Dex's eyes widen over the rim of his beer. "Did you find him yet? I know Rubi's borderline obsessive about that stuffed elephant."

"Obsessed is an understatement," I say as I remember the way she clutched him to her chest when we finally found him. "He turned up in a box of kitchen stuff when we unpacked the moving truck this afternoon. I still needed this beer though. And for once it doesn't taste like dog piss."

My brother laughs. "I hope you've never tasted dog piss, little sister. I had to up my game because Mari was getting ready to sell all of my equipment on Facebook Marketplace. She said she wanted her garage back."

I wave my bottle toward the shed. "Is that your man cave now?" He bombarded our sibling group chat with pictures of it.

"Yep," he says proudly. "And I just got more equipment."

"Mari's going to kill you."

"Oh, she knows. She doesn't mind because I paid the toll. For every new brewing thing I buy, I have to build her a bookshelf."

I shake my head in disbelief. "I never thought you'd become a bigger romance reader than Perdita and me."

"You should definitely take credit. Mari and I talked about Outlander on our first date and I think that's what sealed the deal."

I salute him with my bottle. "You're welcome."

He salutes me back. "You should join The Willow Creek Wantons."

"Is that the book club you guys won't shut up about?"

"It's kind of a substitute for couples therapy here."

I lift a brow. "As much as I love them, romance books shouldn't be a substitute for therapy."

Dex shrugs and tosses me a sheepish smile. "They aren't. They're just a way to help my friends and I learn emotional intelligence."

"You were always emotionally intelligent, Dex. A casualty of being the only boy," I grin. "Perdita and I couldn't let you grow up to be a chauvinist asshole."

"Mari says I'm a secret cinnamon roll."

I roll my eyes, because he is my brother. But Mari's right. Dex might be this burly guy who always has a five o' clock shadow and grease under his fingernails, but he has a giant heart of gold. "You shouldn't believe everything she says," I teasingly warn.

He takes another gulp of his beer and gives me a knowing look. "I don't have to. She lets me know in other ways too."

"Ooh," I say. "I wish I had something to throw at you. I do not want to talk about your sex life."

"Does that mean we can talk about yours?" Mari asks as she plops on Dex's lap and snakes her arms around his neck.

He presses a kiss to her flushed cheek and I bludgeon away my jealousy.

"There's nothing to talk about."

"Well, there should be. There are a lot of decent single guys here - you should let us set you up."

Now I'm rolling my eyes in Mari's direction. "No single guy wants a single mom with three kids."

She tilts her head. "You're too cynical. Why don't you let Willow Creek work its magic?"

I can't hold back my laughter. "The magic? What is this? Stars Hollow?"

Her shrug surprises me. "It may as well be."

Dex pulls her head to his chest. "She's right, you know. I've learned she usually is. You should just wait and see what happens."

"I don't think I'll have time for that stuff - even if I wanted it. Which I don't," I emphasize with a slice of my hand through the air.

"Even firefighters get time off, Luz. And you need something for yourself, too."

I can tell from Dex's tone that he's worried about me. "Not something like that. If I need a new hobby I'll learn to macrame hanging flower baskets. Or join your book club."

"You're joining the book club. I just finished this month's pick, so it's yours," Mari's tone brooks no argument. "I'll be right back," she says as she hops off my brother's lap and pecks him on the cheek.

He swats her butt as she walks away and the look she tosses over her shoulder promises retribution.

"You're in trouble, big brother."

He winks. "I can hold my own, little sister."

When we're getting ready to leave, Mari shoves her tabbed copy of *Bombshell* by Sarah Maclean under my arm. Dex pulls me into one of his bone-crunching hugs and I swat him on the shoulder with my free hand. "What's that for?"

He grins. "Because you're awesome and I know you can hold your own against Ian Montgomery. You're a badass, Little Sister, don't let him intimidate you."

I step back and frown. "What aren't you telling me?"

"I heard through the grapevine that you might have your work cut out for you. Just don't forget you're a Martinez and I've got your back."

Mari slips up beside him. "So do I," she fiercely chimes in.

"Now I'm even more nervous."

Dex awkwardly pats my head. Like I'm twelve again. "You don't have anything to worry about. You earned this."

Chapter Two: If You Try to Chase the Sun You're Never Gonna Catch It

----

Ian

MY OWN HOARSE SCREAMS woke me up last night. The roar of the fire filled my ears and I could feel its heat on my skin. The loose rocks pelted my nape and I could feel my boots sliding on the uneven surface as I scrambled to snap open my emergency shelter and crawl underneath it. I could hear the crash of trees all around me, just outside the perimeter my crew and I had cleared. I knew in my gut it wasn't enough - that the flames were coming for us and we'd be nothing but ash on the forest floor.

When my alarm jolted me from sleep, I was yelling for Justine when she panicked and left her shelter. Screaming as I watched the falling pine shove her to the ground and consume her in its flames.

It's been five years since I lost half my crew in a fire everyone underestimated. Five years since I stuffed a ring in my pocket I never got to slip on my girlfriend's finger. After I lost her, Tristan moved out and went to live with her sister.

The first and last time I saw him after the memorial service he broke my heart all over again. "I don't ever want to see you again. You were supposed to protect my mom. You promised. Instead, you killed her."

I got up and made a pot of coffee because even five years later, the nightmares won't let me fall asleep again, and a fourteen year old boy's angry words echo in my head.

The career I chose means I'm going to lose people. And I have. I just thought the loss and the guilt would end when I came back to Willow Creek. I was a fool to think it would. Most days, being the chief of a small town fire department is nothing like being the lead jumper or the one in charge of getting a team up a mountain, but trauma has still rocked our tight-knit community.

Just before my mentor, Chief Sullivan, retired three years ago, he took me aside to tell me the job was mine if I wanted it. I told him of course I wanted it and he warned me about the mantle of responsibility I was about to take on. He'd laid his hand on my shoulder and said, "I don't doubt you can handle it, son. Hell, given the fires you saw out west and some of the crazy things I know you've had to do, you're probably better prepared than anyone. But if you say yes, don't say no to everything else. Don't let this job eat you alive and spit you out once you're nothing but gristle and bone."

I should have paid attention to what he wasn't saying. I let my ambition and Virgo sense of responsibility speak for me and the decision I made that day gets tested on a regular basis. The canyon fire should have taught me a lesson. When I care about things too deeply, and try to juggle it all because I can't stand to delegate and I don't trust anyone else to do what I know needs to be done, things start to unravel.

It's been happening for months now, and I just keep shoving away the panic. I keep picking up, and showing up, and hiding the cracks. The ice started breaking last October, when we got called out to a house fire on the edge of town. Fire was already crawling all over the old farmhouse like it was nothing more than kindling, but the neighbors said there were still kids trapped in one of the upstairs bedrooms.

I sent in Jacobi and Grayson.

As soon as they radioed they were up the stairs, there was a giant whoosh and the roof collapsed. We watched it crush and burn them and there was nothing we could do about it because the water pressure was almost non-existent. I blame myself because I'm the chief and I should have known the condition of the building and the strength of the flames.

It's one of the many reasons I didn't want to hire Luz Martinez. If I make a mistake, she has too much to lose and her kids could be the ones paying the price.

I've been buried in paperwork all day, trying to fill out the monthly reports and get everything ready for her to sign. I asked her to come in tomorrow to finish up her paperwork and meet the rest of the team.

I just put the finishing touches on the virtual sexual harassment workshop I'm making all the guys take. I don't think any of them will be a problem, but I want to head off any issues before they boil over.

"I'm heading out, big brother," Jack's voice startles me. When I lift my head he narrows his eyes. "When are you going to call it a night? I saw the schedule and I know you're off duty."

"Just getting stuff ready for our newest team member."

He nods. "I think it was a good idea to develop the training. I don't think they'll try anything, but you can never be too cautious about stuff like that. You need to finish up though, so you can go with me to mom's for dinner tonight. You've missed three Wednesdays in a row and I know she's worried about you."

"I'm almost done. Let me finish up the benefits package I have to give her tomorrow and then I'll see you there."

"Promise? You know how relentless Grace Montgomery can be when she thinks her children are avoiding her."

I wave him away. "Go. I promise I'm right behind you."

He pow pows me with his thumbs like he's the Lone Ranger and gives me a salute. "Good. I need someone to take the heat off my back. Both her and Ness are trying to set me up again."

Ness and Mom gave up on trying to set me up once I turned forty. I haven't dated in almost four years because I'm too busy and I don't have the patience for stalkers who fetishize my calendar photos. Three years ago when we started doing an annual calendar to raise money for the department, I thought it was a good idea. That was until I realized that women are just as capable of objectifying us as we are of objectifying them. After the tenth date that resulted from that calendar I got tired of feeling like a piece of meat.

If I'm meant to be with someone, I'm going to let it happen organically. My schedule and my responsibilities make it hard to meet people, so fate is going to intervene if I'm meant to have a happily ever after. I'm almost forty-four, and I gave up on pipe dreams. If there's a fairy godmother out there somewhere granting wishes, maybe I'll get the happily-ever-after my sister Ness found last Christmas.

Against my will, my mind drifts back to the final virtual interview I had with my new hire. Two weeks before I offered her the job after agonizing over the decision. She'd looked so young and fresh-faced and eager over the screen - even though I knew she was almost thirty-three. Even though I knew she had three kids. What we do is one of the hardest, most dangerous jobs there is. We see death and destruction on a daily basis and I didn't want it to warp her. Or take her away from her kids.

Objectively, I'd acknowledged how pretty she was too. Too pretty to be stuck with a bunch of guys for twenty-four hours at a time who can be really crass. It's why I asked for Trevor's help with the sexual harassment training - the force has three women on it now and he had to do the same thing.

I staple the last packet together and slide it into the folder on the edge of my desk. When I stand and stretch it feels like every bone in my body is cracking in half. I need to go for a swim in the lake to work out the cricks, but I don't know if I have time. I bought five acres on the point two years ago and I just finished building my two-story cabin. I've been living there since I framed it up because it's far enough out of town the sirens don't wake me up.

Jack knows I blame myself for what happened to Jacobi and Grayson and he keeps telling me I need therapy to deal with the trauma I carry around from both the U.S. Forest Service and being the chief here. It just feels like admitting my fear will give it space I don't want it to have in my life.

***

Mom rises to her tiptoes and pecks my cheek as soon as I hang my coat by the door.

The smell of basil and garlic curls into the room and I inhale. "You made my favorite," I say as I give her a peck back. "I'll wash the dishes for you."

"I made lasagna because you've been working too hard. Your brother said you never make the time for lunch. I bet today was no exception."

I grimace. "He should worry about himself."

"I worry about both of you. I don't think either one of you is ever going to settle down."

Turnabout is fair play. If he's bending her ear about my eating habits, I'm going to nark on him about his latest dating fiasco. "Did Jack tell you about his latest date?"

Just like I predicted she would, she whirls in his direction with shining eyes and clasped hands. "Will you see her again, Jackie?"

He frowns in my direction and flicks his middle finger at me. He hates it when Mom calls him that and he hates the fact she's focused on his love life now. "No, I won't be seeing her again. She blocked my phone number."

Ophelia Daniels was the friend of a friend of a friend, and Jack was nervous about the date. Something happened he still hasn't told me about. He just said he was intrigued and wanted to see her again. She didn't feel the same and I think it's the first time in his life a girl's had the audacity to ghost him.

I volunteered to wash the dishes after dinner. Once Mom gets tired of Jack's one word answers, I know I'll be at the receiving end of a line of third degree questioning. I can avoid it if I'm stuck in the kitchen.

As soon as I volunteered, my sister Ness's new fiance Alex jumped in to help. He said he'd take drying duty. He must have something to talk to me about, because he looks nervous. We haven't spent a lot of time together since Jack and I strong-armed him last Christmas to find out exactly what his intentions toward our sister were.

"Hey," he nods in my direction when I hand him one of Mom's linen towels.

"Hey," I say as I return his nod.

"So I was wondering if you wanted to help coach the freshman summer team?"

"Wouldn't my cousin be a better candidate? I mean he was an MLB player."

Alex shakes his head. "I already asked him. He said he has his hands full with coaching a traveling team this summer, and pointed me to you."

"How'd you get roped into it? Aren't your kids teenagers?"

"My oldest is graduating and wants to beef up his college resume. He's the assistant. I was a football player, not a baseball player, so I'm onboard to help him out but it's not really in my wheelhouse."

"I haven't even played at the college level."

"No, but River said you could have."

I shrug. "Maybe. There were recruiters. It just wasn't the path I wanted to follow."

"Maybe Ness and I can have you over for dinner next week so we can hash it out?"

"That depends on what's on the menu. Your chili recipe needs a lot of work." I purposefully keep my expression bland so he can't tell whether or not I'm serious.

He snorts. "Winning the cook-off trophy the last five years doesn't make you an expert."

"Oh, I think it does."

He shakes his head and tosses me a rueful grin. "Maybe everyone's just too scared of you to give first place to anyone else."

"The judges are sworn to impartiality."

He shakes his head and picks up the towel to dry the casserole dish I just washed. "I'm not buying it. My chili was way better than yours. Even your sister thought so."

I snort in disbelief. "My sister's allegiance has changed and her opinion can no longer be trusted."

Chapter Three: Can't Find the Ground

Luz

"It's LATE FOR YOU to be face-timing me," Perdita says as she covers a yawn.

"I know, but I just put the kids to bed," I explain while I prop the pillows behind my head.

"Rosie sent me a picture of her hamburger that made me jealous. If there's one thing Dex learned from Dad it's how to grill the perfect burger."

I nod enthusiastically. "The burgers were really good and our brother's beer making skills have improved too."

She sighs. "I'm definitely green over the two of you being there together while I'm still stuck here in Florida with Mom and Dad."

"You're not just there for them. You're married to your library."

She chuckles warmly. "True. Maybe someday I'll branch out and actually open up my bookstore - but that day isn't today."

"So Dex gave me a pep talk, but I need one from you."

She points a finger at me through the phone. "You overthink things. They hired you because you're a trained professional. You don't have anything to worry about."

"I don't think the fire chief wanted me onboard. I think I'm here because there wasn't an alternative."

My older sister shrugs. "So what? You're there now, so who cares how it happened? Just kick ass. I know Dex and I showed you how."

"What should I wear tomorrow?"

"Does the town seem old-fashioned? Maybe you should wear pantyhose."

I wrinkle my nose. "Ugh. I hate them. If I have a pair stuck in my suitcase, I'll wear them. So you think I should wear a skirt?"

"You know you have great legs. Why not show them off? I inherited Dad's monster calves and I'm jealous."

"Maybe I shouldn't remind him that he hired a woman? He didn't seem too happy about it when he offered me the job."

"Luz, wear the skirt. Maybe he'll be so busy enjoying the view he won't be a hardass."

I take a deep breath. "Okay. I'm off to find an outfit and the wrinkle release spray because I have no idea where the ironing board is."

She blows me a kiss. "Sleep well, little sis. And let it go. You're there and you're starting over. You've worked hard for this and that's all that matters."

After we hang up I scrounge around in one of my battered suitcases. When I find my matching navy blue jacket and skirt, I breathe a sigh of relief. There's a pair of panty hose wadded up in the net bag too.

***

I had two pep talks last night, and this morning Rico shoved his lucky tigers' eye marble in my hand and pecked my cheek before he whispered, "Good luck, Mom. You don't need it, because you're awesome."

The marble and the pep talks haven't helped. I'm still a bundle of nerves. They're like crawling snakes underneath my skin as I smooth my sweaty palms against my skirt and knock on the half-open door.

"Come in," a deep voice commands.

I push the door all the way open and step inside. And immediately smother a groan.

He's a mountain behind his desk and the tiny screen he filled during my interview didn't do him justice. His dark auburn hair has a cowlick that's cutting through the middle of his left eyebrow. It almost covers up one of his insanely bright green eyes. His full beard is lighter than his hair, more like the color of a sunset streaked with little swirls of deep golden honey, and there's a splash of freckles across his nose.

Mom was obsessed with Robert Redford and made me watch the movie *The Way We Were* so many times I have a thing for gingers too. When my friends were fantasizing over Chad Michael Murray and Orlando Bloom, I had a bedroom plastered with pics of Prince Harry.

His arms are crossed over his chest and he's already glaring. Like my very existence offends him.

"Sit down, Ms. Martinez," he waves toward the ladderback chair in front of his desk.

Once I clasp my hands in my laps and cross my ankles, I look up. He's still glaring as he shoves a red folder across the scratched metal surface of the barrier between us. "You're fifteen minutes late," he says grimly. "I hope that's not a habit."

I remember what Dex said. *Don't let him intimidate you.*

I clear my throat. "It's not a habit." What I don't say is that there were at least five meltdowns this morning. A bowl of soggy Cheerios that spilled all over the floor, the quart of orange juice that joined it, a finger paint picture from Rubi that left Rosie's favorite t-shirt streaked with green paint that required a wardrobe change, and neither of my older children could find their school backpacks. I retrieve a pen from my purse and hope it still has ink.

My new boss is making me feel guilty about things I can't control. His hostility makes no sense because I'm not even starting today - I'm just here to sign benefits paperwork.

"Good. Because that's the difference between life and death in a firehouse."

I glower and point my pen in his direction. "I'm not on shift yet."

His palms flatten on the desk. "No, you're not on shift yet. But your tardiness is disrespectful because you're taking up time I can't afford to rearrange. It's important I keep to my schedule."

I roll my eyes. Another disrespectful reaction - but he's being ridiculous. "Well, excuse me. I thought you allotted an hour for this."

"And we need every minute. Sign the paperwork so I can introduce you to the guys."

I click the pen so I can scrawl my signature on the lines marked with arrows. Of course it's out of ink. "My pen's not working."

He sighs in exasperation and slides a bright red ball-point toward me. "Keep it," he growls.

I nod, because I don't trust myself to answer. I need to hold my temper in front of my new boss.

I don't know why I listened to my sister. I yank down the skirt Perdita told me I needed to wear over my knees to cover up the run in my nude pantyhose and focus on the health insurance documents. She's the one who told me to wear them too, and now my cooch feels like someone hotboxing their last cigarette in an alley. Hot and uncomfortable. And probably pungent.

My new boss is looking at me like I'm a bug that he wants to squash and smear across the window with one of those electric zinger things.

To top off all the breakfast accidents, Rubi spilled grape Kool Aid down the side of my blouse when I dropped her off at my brother's and I'm pretty sure Ian Montgomery has x-ray vision and can see the stain on the white blouse underneath my blazer.

He just crossed his arms again and he's still scowling at me from behind his woolly mammoth sized desk. It doesn't help that the virtual interview that landed me here didn't do him justice. His craggy face was hidden by the weird lighting then, not front and center in harsh relief like it is now. His dark auburn hair looked brown, and the way he was sitting you couldn't see the jagged thin line of snow white that starts just behind his left ear and disappears into his ruthlessly clubbed nape. He looks stern and foreboding. Like the dark sunset version of Robert Redford without the laugh lines.

The gray and green flannel he's wearing makes his eyes look like the postcards my best friend sent me from Ireland. The green doesn't just pop - it saturates. His lumbersnack fantasy- inducing shirt is stretched across his shoulders and chest like it's painted on there with decoupage.

I can't believe I thought the run in my hose would be the end of my morning disasters. A full-blown, panties in a twist, all-consuming crush on my new boss is a disaster of apocalyptic proportions.

"I didn't want to hire you."

I snort, and grip the pen so hard it leaves a mark on the side of my thumb. "I figured. You haven't exactly been great at hiding it."

His brow furrows and I swear he glares even harder. "What's that supposed to mean?"

"You haven't exactly broadcasted your approval of my presence."

He leans forward. "All I'm saying is you have big shoes to fill, Martinez. This job is dangerous."

"I know this job is dangerous. And I've been trained to deal with that danger. But my training doesn't matter, does it? Because you're already convinced I won't be able to do it. Why do you have such a problem with me being here? Because you're a male chauvinist?"

"I'm not a male chauvinist, Ms. Martinez. People die in this job and I don't think you understand what that means."

Now I'm pissed. "I understand exactly what that means. We should always have fear. Fear is human. It doesn't mean we can't do a job. I might not look tough, but I've seen my share of the crap life likes to throw at you when you least expect it. I know how to pivot and I'm resilient."

Chapter Four: Locked Inside My Head

Ian

THE VIRTUAL INTERVIEW AND weird office lighting didn't do her justice and I know in my gut I'm going to regret hiring her. Deep brown eyes spark at me from across the desk, like she's already plotting how to plea bargain the charge for my murder down to manslaughter. She was squirming in her seat five minutes ago, flustered and anxious, trying to find a way to cover up the run in her hose. I wanted to tell her she needed to stop fidgeting with it, because I couldn't give two shits about a run in her hose and it was drawing attention to her legs. Which I shouldn't be noticing. It didn't take her long to forget she's afraid of me and now she's nothing but flash and daring.

She's tall. A lot taller than I expected, but I'm tall too. I think if we both stood, the top of her head would be even with my shoulder. And I can tell she's strong. Her legs are long and sleek but muscled too. She has a lean runner's body except for her chest and hips. Which I am not going to focus on.

Her hair isn't sheer black like it looked through the computer screen. It's more of a dark chocolate brown - the same color as her eyes. I can see the family resemblance to her brother Dex, but she doesn't have his Roman nose. Hers is cute and freckled and a little snubbed at the end.

Everything in her job application indicates she'll fill the shoes Hank Atkinson left behind.

I'm still not happy she's here because if I make the wrong call and something happens to her, I don't want it on my conscience. But we desperately need a paramedic on the team and her qualifications are exemplary.

She might look a little frazzled, but she still exudes competence. I know she graduated at the top of her class, but our jobs are dangerous and I've made mistakes before. She's not going on the fire roster until she's shown her mettle.

The deaths that have been my fault- both on the side of a mountain in the San Juan Range in Colorado and here in Willow Creek, haunt me. The roar of the fire and the sound the roof made when it shuddered and buried them beneath smoking rubble. The eerie wail of the sirens and the silence full of the shock and hopelessness it left both magnified and filled. I have more control here than I did when I was jumping from a plane and pulling a parachute cord, but not much.

"Being surrounded by real smoke and fire, in an unstable structure with people depending on you to save their lives, is nothing like your training."

"Was your training any different than mine?"

"Not for this. But before this, it was much more rigorous. I fought wildfires for almost eighteen years out west before I came home to Willow Creek." What I don't tell her is that fire brings death and destruction and I've seen it firsthand in a forest full of scorched pine and the charred bones of a house.

"What brought you back here?"

"I had obligations." To my mom, to my Dad after his heart attack. Leaving the fire department almost crushed him and I can't forget the way his face lit up when I announced I'd applied to the department and I was staying.

She adjusts her pose before she flutters her lashes. "So it was time to be a grown-up," she sniggers. "Must be nice to have the luxury of finding your way like that."

I'm offended by her dismissal. "What's that supposed to mean?"

"It means that even though I've never fought for my life in the middle of an inferno, I know what hard choices are. I know what loss is. And I'm ready to do the job you hired me to do and be there for this community."

She's in for a lot of disappointment and despair. Because this job is full of highs and lows. The adrenaline of crisis and the boredom and crossword puzzles in between. I cross my arms. "I don't think you're ready for this. For the expectations and the weight and the things you're gonna have to sacrifice. But I needed a paramedic and you were the only qualified applicant."

She tilts her chin defiantly and clenches her jaw as she slips the pen into her black handbag. It's neat and tidy, just like her shoes. But I think that neat and tidy exterior is a disguise and she's anything but demure and obedient.

"I expected I'd have to prove myself. I'm ready for it and someday I'll make you glad I was your only choice."

She thrusts her chin out even further as she makes her vow -like she just entered the boxing ring. I admire the strength of purpose and hope she sticks to it. I don't want to see her crumble and break. I can't afford to let that happen - and I don't want it on my conscience.

"Come on," I tell her. "Let me introduce you to the guys that are here."

Of course Jack is the first one we encounter. He's peering at the coffee maker like it has three heads.

"This damn thing is broken again," he mutters when he hears me enter the break room.

"No, it's not. You're just not used to using anything besides the ancient pot that was here before we installed this one." It's a state of the art Keurig that Blake Armitage donated to the department at Christmas. Jack still hasn't figured out that you need to press the brew button after the cup is in the holster.

A crease mars the smooth line between his brows when he turns around, and he looks so much like our dad it's jarring. As soon as Luz steps forward and holds out her hand, the crease disappears and his eyes light up.

"I'm Luz Martinez, and I look forward to working with you."

He grabs her hand and shakes it heartily. "Jack Montgomery. The ogre behind you is my older brother."

I glare when he keeps her hand in his, the sting of something I refuse to admit is jealousy, burning in my gut. "I'm not an ogre. She'll find out soon enough how hard it is to keep your antics to a minimum."

She laughs, and I wish I could see her smile. "Jack, I'm the younger sibling too. I know what it's like to be on the receiving end of an older brother's judgment. I have a feeling we're going to have a lot to bond over."

He finally lets go of her hand. "Let's talk over coffee some time, Luz Martinez."

I shoot him another glare and subtly shake my head. Letting him know there will be no flirting or fraternization with the newest recruit.

He gets a delighted look on his face, like he just realized something juicy.

"I don't date, Jack." Her dismissal of his offer is softly spoken, and the rejection shouldn't make something bright and sharp bloom in my chest. Women, besides his recent ghosting experience, usually find my younger brother irresistible. He's all easy fun and sparkle - the affable playboy who's always down for a good time. I'm the exact opposite - I get stuck in my head and I carry too much on my shoulders to ever let go like that.

He shrugs. "I'm okay with a non-horizontal relationship. Let's be friends, Martinez."

"That sounds great," she says. The warmth in her voice makes that weird thing happen in my gut again.

I shoot my brother a glare and tip my head toward the doorway. "We'll catch you later, Jack. I'm going to introduce her to everyone else."

She waves a hand in his direction before she follows me down the hallway. The rest of the guys are lounging in the living area in front of the big screen tv. They're watching the recap of last night's hockey games on ESPN.

They all stand when they catch sight of her standing behind me. Romero and Sheffield stride forward first.

"Carlos Romero," the most recent hire says as he extends a hand. He's a kid, fresh out of training four months ago, and hasn't quite found his place on the team.

She takes his hand and gives him a bright smile as she drops it.

"Sheffield," my dad's best friend gruffly says as he steps forward. He should have retired when Dad did, but he told me as long as he could run a hose he was hanging on. He lost his wife to cancer three years ago and doesn't have any kids, and I know the department is all he has. That's why I haven't forced him into retire-ment yet.

Whitaker is the last one to approach her. He just made the rank of captain and he's the quietest guy on our team. "Evan Whitaker." He introduces himself but doesn't offer his hand. Instead, his grip is tight around the paperback he's carrying.

"Don't mind Evan," Jack says from behind us. "He's not very sociable and gets lost in obscure Russian Liter-ature."

Flags of scarlet flash over Evan's cheeks. "Sorry," he mumbles and tips his head in Luz's direction.

"I don't mind. It's lovely to meet you." Her gaze scans the room. "It's lovely to meet all of you and I look for-ward to working with you."

"Let's get you fitted for your gear," I say to break up the cozy vibe.

I put in a purchase order for smaller coats, boots and trousers when I hired her, and it was all delivered yes-terday.

"I'm not optimistic," she grumbles as we walk away.

"I wouldn't leave you high and dry like that, Mar-tinez. I made sure I ordered stuff that might fit you."

"You mean stuff I won't swim in? Still not optimistic, Chief."

She has no reason to be optimistic and I know this. But. "I know you took a chance on this job, and even if I'm skeptical, I'm not going to put you in that position. I take care of my team," I gruffly inform her.

"Well, I'll definitely need suspenders."

"Maybe. Maybe not. But if you do, we have plenty on hand."

I take the carabiner off my belt loop and unlock the supply closet before I wave her forward. "Why don't you see what we have on hand before you make snap judgments."

She gives me a disbelieving look as she brushes past.

The fire-retardant trousers and jackets are all hanging, and the boots are stacked in a row on one of the benches in the corner.

She heads for the boots first and I hold my breath. I did some research into the average size worn by women and guessed she would wear a women's size eight. I ordered a pair of men's size six and seven.

When she plops onto the floor and takes off her heels, I look away. All I can see is endless miles of those legs in her panty hose. Even with the run, it's sexy as hell. Probably sexier because it makes her just a little imperfect. She slips on the left size six boot.

I hold my breath when she laces it up and stands. I can tell she's wiggling her toes against the seam when she turns to me. "Good job, Chief. I think these will work. They're a little loose, but I'll be wearing thick socks."

I exhale in relief. Hopefully my guesses on the rest of her gear were just as close. "I'll leave the room so you can try on the trousers. I ordered medium tees for you and they're already in your locker."

She laughs softly when I step out of the tight space. "I should thank you for thinking of everything, but we're not quite there."

I hear the rustle of her clothing as I exit and lean against the wall.

There's a muttered gasp and a curse and I resist the urge to ask if she needs any help removing her clothing. My imagination is already stimulated enough by the thought of her rolling the nylon down her hips and calves.

Five minutes later, after I've clenched my hands so hard my ragged, blunt nails have left divots in my palms, she comes strolling out.

When she tosses her head I catch a whiff of coconut. "Okay. What do you think?" She asks as she twirls in front of me.

The pants gape around her waist, but it's not bad. "If you use the suspenders, I don't think they'll fall down."

She nods curtly in agreement. "That's what I think too."

"Why don't you try on the small coat I ordered? It's at the end of the row."

Her response is a thumbs up as she disappears again. This time I grit my teeth instead of clenching my fists.

When she emerges, she's enveloped in the fire-retardant canvas. It obscures her so completely, she could be twelve instead of thirty-three.

"It's not ideal," I admit.

She braces her hands on her hips and that helps. It at least gives her figure some definition. "I agree. It's not ideal. But I think it will work."

"When we go out on a call, you'll have several layers underneath it."

"If you'll ever unbend enough to let me tag along."

"I hired you to do a job, Martinez. As much as I was against the decision in the first place, I can't dispute your training. And we need you. Your skills will fill a void on the team."

And I'm going to do my damnedest to keep you out of harm's way, I think.

"That's good to know," she says with an inscrutable expression. Like she doesn't believe what I'm saying. "I know I'm the first woman on the squad ever and I know you probably have a lot of justification you need to do both for yourself and for the town council you answer to."

I shake my head. "It's not that, Martinez. I worked with female firefighters out west. I know women are just as capable as men when it comes to this job. Some of the smokejumpers I worked with were absolutely fearless."

"Then what is it? Because there's something you're not telling me."

"It doesn't matter. They're my own personal demons and they have no place here."

"You can tell me when you're ready. Or when you finally trust me."

Never going to happen, I think to myself.

***

I don't usually show up for dinner at my parents' table unannounced. Especially lately when I prefer to be in my own head. But meeting Luz Martinez in the flesh was overwhelming and I need a distraction.

Jack's truck's already parked in their driveway and I steel myself for the spotlight I know is coming. He's stepping out the door when I hang my helmet.

"You only ride your bike when you need to put things in perspective," he observes.

"It's a nice day and I wanted to feel the wind."

He smirks. "I'm not buyin' it. You were warning me away from our newest hire in the breakroom today. I've never seen you stake a claim like that."

My scowl must be scary, because he throws his hands in the air. "Message received. I'm going to enjoy watching you try to keep your distance."

"I'm just trying to protect her - like I would any employee. We don't need anything messy happening at the station - and I know how you like to love 'em and leave 'em."

Something flickers in his eyes, but he shakes it off. "Just waiting for the right person, brother. Not all of us are lucky enough to find someone like that when we're twenty."

"I may have found her, but the universe had other plans." I don't regret the place Justine once held in my heart - even though it's full of sadness now. Jack deserves to experience that kind of all-consuming, ride-to-the-edge-of-the-world love too. Maybe I'm being too harsh. "I'm sorry you haven't found your forever yet."

The look he gives me is full of disbelief. "You must be mellowing out in your old age because I think that was an apology."

I thump his shoulder with my fist. "I'm only a few years older than you."

He thumps me back. "According to mom, we're both gathering dust. I'm going to make sure you get the heat tonight instead of me."

Chapter Five: The Crooked Road

Luz

EVEN THOUGH I'VE HAD a long day and I'm exhausted, I accept Perdita's Facetime request.

"You have raccoon eyes. You should be sleeping instead of answering the phone."

I cover a yawn with the palm of my hand. "I'm fine. What's up?"

"I'm just calling to see how things went and get the scoop on your new boss."

I flop backward into the mound of pillows, groaning. "It's so bad."

"So he's even more of a hardass than you thought he would be?"

"It's worse than that. He's a hot hard ass."

"How hot? Like you wouldn't mind if he gave you a hot spanking or when you see him it feels like you're wading through a field of lava? Or both?"

"Both. When he frowned at me he got this tick in his jaw. Like he was grinding his teeth. It shouldn't have been so sexy."

***

I've been on the job for just over a week when the dispatch alarm goes off. I barrel into the common area. "What's going on?" I ask Miller.

"A car tried to pass a tractor on one of the county roads. There was a head on collision and it sounds like there were fatalities. We're going to need you on this one - I don't care what Montgomery says."

"What does Montgomery say?" I carefully ask, holding my breath. Whatever I'm about to hear is going to explain why I haven't been out on any calls.

"That you're too green to go out on calls."

"I'm gonna stay green if I don't get any experience."

"That's exactly what I told him. Suit up and you can ride with me."

Our chief is off for the next two days after working a straight twenty-four hours. When he gets back to the firehouse, I'm going to confront him about his high-handed behavior.

***

The older model Chevy sedan is lying on its side down a steep ravine. The front is either crumpled or gone completely, it's hard to tell from the road. One of the local deputies is already by the car, and Miller hitches a belt around my waist so I can rappel down to the victims.

The deputy's face is grim when he helps me land and unhitch the belt. "It's bad," he murmurs quietly. "I think the mother is gone. There are two kids in the back, and they look really young. We're trying to get them out now."

There aren't any flames yet, but the scent of gasoline is heavy in the grass and it mixes with the dense fog creeping down the hillside and rising from the creek just below us. We don't have much time to extract them before we lose visibility. "Let's get them out."

I make my way to the car and drop to a couch, squatting so I can peer inside the interior of the crushed car. "Are you here to help us?" The little girl on the far left asks in a squeaky, broken voice.

She's about Rubi's age, and my chest tightens. "That's exactly what I'm here to do."

There's a diagonal gash across her temple, with a thin line of blood - probably from flying glass. But her legs don't look crushed and she's still conscious. "Can you wiggle your fingers and toes, for me, sweetie?"

Her brow furrows in concentration. "Okay, I wiggled them. Can you help my little brother first? He's been really quiet and I'm scared. And Mommy hasn't said anything since she whispered she loved us."

"I need you to hang on. We're going to get your brother out first and then I want you to crawl through this window behind him."

I stretch my body through the jagged glass, grateful for the thick canvas material of my jacket that protects me from cuts. The little boy is no more than two, and his breaths are thready and shallow. I carefully unclasp his carseat and lift the yoke of it over his head. He stirs, and one of his thumbs twitches as his eyes flicker open. "Mommy?" He asks.

My eyes cloud with tears. "I'm not your mommy, sweetheart, but I'm here to help."

He starts crying, soft whimpers that barely lift his chest.

"I think he hurts," his big sister says worriedly. "That's the sound he makes when he's chasing me and he falls."

I move more swiftly. I run my hands over his body, and nothing seems to be broken. But he could have internal injuries I can't see. "I'm going to finish breaking the glass in the window. I'll be right back."

When I ease backward, someone catches me around the waist and pulls me the rest of the way out. "I should have let you come sooner. You're a great paramedic, Martinez."

My boss's reluctant praise ruffles the hair at my nape and sends prickles down my spine. "Yeah, you should have. Are you here to help or apologize?"

"Help," he replies and hands me one of the rubber mallets we use to break glass. His fingers slide against mine when I take it, and his touch lingers on my wrist for a handful of seconds before he lets go. "Sorry," he mumbles.

I nod to let him know I accept his apology and crouch in front of the window again. I reach into the interior and meticulously knock the glass from the inside out, so it lands on the ground instead of onto the kids. When I'm satisfied I've gotten it all, I slide forward again.

The little boy is quiet again, but I can still hear his breathing. There's no gurgling, so I start praying his lungs aren't crushed and there's no internal damage. "What's your brother's name, sweetie?" I ask the little girl.

"He's Cody and I'm Briony."

"Okay, Cody, I don't know if you can hear me or not. But we're going to get you out of here now so someone can take care of you." I lift him into my arms and close my eyes at the fragile, birdlike weight of him. I start praying again as I tuck him into my coat to protect him from scraping against the edges of the window as we slide through it.

Ian's touch is secure around my waist and eases me to the solid ground. There's already a stretcher behind me, and I set the little boy on top of it. His eyes flutter open again and his thumb curls around mine. "It's okay, Cody. I'm going to check you out."

"We've got him," a man says. When I turn, there are two paramedics in navy blue uniforms standing there.

"Thanks. I'm going to get the little girl out now."

I crawl back through the window and hold my arms out to Briony. She's already unlatched herself from her carseat, and she's fiddling with the straps.

"I'll help you, little one." I tell her as I loosen the straps and pull her into my arms. She bites her lip, and her snaggle tooth and the fear and determination in her face break my heart all over again. Her face hardens with that determination only kids have. She immediately reaches behind my neck and buries her head in the crook of my shoulder. Her fingers are like tiny cold claws on my skin as I ease her through the window as quickly and carefully as I can. One of the other firemen, Miller I think, is extracting the young woman in the front seat through the driver's side window. There's not much room between it and the ground, but I know he's trying not to jostle or move her further than necessary in case medical attention is still needed.

"Please help my mommy too," Briony whispers in my ear as I'm setting her on the ground.

"I'll do everything I can, sweetie. Is there anyone you and Cody can stay with once we get you checked out at the hospital?"

"Our Nanna."

"Okay. We'll make sure someone lets her know what's going on."

When I lower her to the ground, her eyes are brimming with tears. Ian drops to a crouch beside me. "Let's get you cleaned up sweetheart, while we take care of your mommy."

A female paramedic takes Briony by the hand. "I'm going to clean up that cut. Do you want a *Little Mermaid* bandaid or a *Cinderella* one?"

"I want an Ariel one," I hear her shyly respond as she walks away.

"Is their mom gone?" I ask Ian once she's out of hearing.

"Yeah," he gruffly says. He sounds weary and defeated. "The paramedic said it was internal bleeding. I know this is the first time you've been in a situation like this - how are you?"

I take a deep breath. This is what I signed up for, but it doesn't make it any less overwhelming. "I think I might need a hug."

When he slides an arm around my shoulder, I rest my head against his solid frame and sigh. It feels natural, and he doesn't shake me off. "I hope this isn't inappropriate," he murmurs.

"No, you were right. I've been through the training, but facing death in real time is nothing like taking a class. Thanks for being here - even if you're supposed to be off shift."

He clears his throat and I can feel the vibration just under his shoulder blade, where my head is still laying. "I'm still off, but I heard the call over my radio and thought you guys might need me."

"My shift officially ended an hour ago."

His embrace slips away and he clears his throat. "I'll let you get a shower and some rest. You need to wind down and spend time with your kids. I'll see you in a couple of days when we're back on the clock together."

He drops his arm and touches his fingers to his brow in a cursory salute. "You did a good job, tonight, Martinez," he grudgingly tells me.

I watch him climb the hill and a part of me wishes I'd asked him to carry me up because my gear, especially my boots, feels like it weighs a thousand tons. Every other part of me still feels the flicker of his touch, and the comfort of his arm around my shoulders.

I'm too exhausted to take a shower when we get back to the station. When one of the guys drops me off, I fall in bed as soon as I shuck everything off but my t-shirt.

***

Yesterday was my last shift until the weekend, and I need something to take my mind off the accident. I can't stop thinking about those two kids and questioning the career path I've chosen. I know it could have been anyone in that car. I know there are a thousand ways the world could take me away from my kids. My throat's still raw from crying and jangled nerves.

After I picked them up from school, I brought them here, to the local dog rescue. I don't think they're ready yet for a furry family member, but one of the guys mentioned the kennel is always looking for dog walking volunteers. Slobbery dog kisses will ease my heart and make my kids over the moon happy.

Thirty minutes later, I'm watching Rico and Rosie throw a frisbee to a Boxer mix, and Rubi is sitting on a blanket cuddling a tiny puppy. I'm lost in thought when I feel a light touch on my elbow.

"Are you guys going to adopt?" Mari asks as we watch the kids chase around the Boxer mix that kept the Frisbee instead of bringing it back.

I shake my head. "A dog is a lot of responsibility and I don't know if they're ready for that yet. Rosie couldn't even remember to feed her goldfish."

Mari throws her arm around my shoulders. "You should seriously consider it. I know Dex wouldn't mind.

We're getting one too, so our dogs could have play dates." She points to a German Shepherd mix, and I notice my brother for the first time. He's kneeling in front of it as it licks his chin and the sight makes my heart happy. My older brother was pretty broken after the war, and it's only since his reunion with Mari that I've seen the Dex I knew growing up.

"Is that the one you're getting?" I gesture toward the German Shepherd who just knocked my brother to the ground. They're wrestling around in the grass and Dex is laughing.

Mari smiles fondly. "Yeah. We had a dog just like him, Muggles, in our platoon over there."

"What happened to him?"

Her expression closes and she swallows. "He was killed in a mortar attack. Along with his handler - my brother Ramon."

I slip my arm around her waist. "Dex never mentioned what happened. I know Ramon was your brother and Dex's best friend, but there's so much he doesn't talk about."

She gulps and her eyes flood with tears. "Sometimes it hits you out of nowhere, you know?" She asks as she swipes her cheek. "I think he's always tried to shield you and Perdita from what actually happened over there."

I nod solemnly. "I know he's been in therapy for years. He was a mess after he got his prosthetic and I'm just glad he's in a better place now. And that he has you."

"Dex doesn't know - just because I don't know if he'll ever be ready for it. I think a part of him still blames himself for what happened. But, I sneak away every six months or so to Arlington and visit Ramon's grave. I wouldn't mind some company if you ever feel up to it."

Now my eyes are clouded with tears too. "I'm honored you'd ask. Of course."

Dex lopes toward us and I can sense Mari's gladness for the interruption.

He scans Mari and frowns at me. "You made her cry," he accuses.

Mari sets her hand on his forearm. "She didn't. It was just memories. I'll be fine."

"Do you need anything?" Dex asks. I can hear the thread of anxiety in his voice.

Is this what I want? A partner who handles me with kid gloves? I know Mari is just as resilient as I am, but she's letting herself lean on my brother. I can't help remembering the way Ian Montgomery wrapped his arm over my shoulder after I rescued Briony and Cody.

Mari shakes her head. "Just you. Unless Peanut Brittle is ready for us to take him home?"

My brother smiles. "He'll be ready next week."

I point to the brindled dog sprawled in the grass. "Is that Peanut Brittle?"

They exchange a smile. "It is," they say in unison.

I'm grateful again for my brother's healing, and that he found Mari again. That the body shop is flourishing and they're living in the house he finally let her decorate. That they're getting a dog.

I'm jealous too. Because most of the time it feels like I'll always be stuck raising my kids by myself. That there won't ever be anyone to ask if I'm okay. Not like that anyway.

"You'll have to invite us over for his welcome home party. Maybe the kids will stop pestering me if they can spend as much time as they want with your dog."

Mari clapped her hands. "I love that idea! We can ask Emma to make him a doggy cake."

I shake my head in disbelief. "I didn't even know there was such a thing."

Dex laughs. "If there isn't, there should be."

"What's a doggy cake?" Rubi asks.

Dex scoops her up. "It's a cake just for dogs."

My youngest daughter scrunches her face. "Dogs can eat people cakes - why can't people eat dog cakes?"

When Dex throws me a bewildered look I grin, because I'm used to Rubi's chaotic questions. "People don't eat dog cakes because they have things in them we might not like."

"Oh. Like liver and onions, Mommy?"

"Exactly like liver and onions," I assure her.

Rico skids to a stop just in front of us. "Liver and onions are disgusting," he says as he makes a face.

"I bet you ate plenty of them living with Nan and Pap," Dex observes.

Rico grimaces in disgust. "Nan makes it all the time. She says Pap loves it."

Rosie joins us. "Pap might like it, but he's the only one."

"Come on, kids. We need to head home and so do Dex and Mari."

"We're not having liver, are we Mom?" Rico asks.

"No, we're not having liver. We're having the home-made chicken and noodles I put in the crockpot earlier today."

Rosie and Rico high five each other.

After Dex sets Rubi down, he throws an arm around my shoulders. "I know you're still settling in, Sis. but you should get a watchdog. This is a pretty safe community, but you and the kids should think about finding Knocks 2.0 now you have the space."

Chapter Six: In the Cold

Ian

I HEARD ABOUT THE accident on the radio, and even though I was supposed to be off-duty, I had to go. Just in case the squad needed me. Helping Luz Martinez rescue those kids, watching her calm them and get them out safely, reassured me. She's competent and keeps her head in a crisis situation.

I felt her body trembling against mine when I wrapped my arm around her shoulders - despite the fact she prevailed in the face of danger. I wanted to do everything in my power to soothe away her fear - and that's why I left her at the firehouse and asked one of the guys to chauffeur her home. Because feeling this way, wanting to protect her at all costs, my heart in my throat as I watched her put herself in danger, compromises my survival.

I tip back the tumbler of bourbon and savor the peat-fire taste, and the way it numbs my thoughts. Luz Martinez is not someone I can want and I need to banish the rightness of her head laying against my shoulder. I need to forget the scent of rain and citrus and salt that clung to her skin and filled my lungs when I took a breath as she nestled in the curve of my arm.

When my phone rings, and the caller id shows it's my meddling younger sister, I'm tempted to ignore it. The only problem is I know she'll fill my voicemail with obnoxious messages and put my number on dive bomb repeat like she's a mosquito on the hunt for first blood if I ignore her. So I click the accept button.

"Yeah," I answer.

"Is that any way to greet your beloved younger sister?"

I snort. "No, this is exactly the way I should greet a pain in my ass. Why are you calling me at ten p.m. on a Friday? Shouldn't you be out celebrating with your new fiance?"

"I'm calling you because it's been a week since I've seen you. You didn't come over to Mom and Dad's Sunday for dinner. Are you hibernating again?"

Vanessa and I weren't close growing up. The four year age gap was just enough that I thought she was annoying and wouldn't let her follow me around. But she's the one who worries about me the most since I moved back to Willow Creek. "I'm fine, sis. I just wanted some time to decompress. I went over for dinner last Tuesday, remember?"

There's a pause on the other end of the line. "Are you sure you're okay? Jack said you've been more quiet than usual. You shouldn't be left alone to brood. Alex said he asked you over this week to talk about tee-ball."

I groan. "I know you worry about me, but I promise I'm fine. Shouldn't you be planning your wedding instead of checking up on your oldest brother? Or trying to arrange his summer? You're as underhanded as Mom."

"Alex and I just want to get married on a beach somewhere in the Caribbean, but Mom refuses to even entertain that idea. I pinky promise to keep her off your back if you can convince her to stop meddling with my wedding plans."

"I don't think any of us stand a chance. Since she started helping with production at the local theatre, she thinks everything has to be the event of the decade."

"I know," Ness wails. "She's driving us crazy. When I tried to talk to her about the venue, she patted me on the head and reminded me that neither of her sons seems at all serious about settling down and this may be her only chance."

I laugh. "She totally guilt-tripped you."

"She's such a pro. Every time I go to say something she makes puppy dog eyes or talks about Dad's heart condition."

"Dad's heart condition was amplified by the stress of being a firefighter and his refusal to slow down. According to Doc, he's much better now that he's puttering around the house and taking care of Mom's flower garden."

"That's the other thing," Ness says and sighs. "She insists on doing all the flower arrangements herself. She said she'd reach out to that wildflower farmer out on Kincaid Road if she needs help."

"You're gonna have to set your foot down, Ness. Remember this is your wedding and it should be about what you and Alex want."

"Mom wants a huge church thing like we're getting married at Westminster Abbey or something. Alex and I would be happy with a simple ceremony at Sunset Lavender. Roxie said there's no cost for family."

"Well if it was up to Dad, that's what he'd pick. Because he's a cheapskate."

"I wish it was up to Dad, but he's such a pushover since he retired."

Our mom has always been a force of nature, but since Dad left the fire department and settled in with his newspaper and slippers, she's determined to control every aspect of her life and her children's lives. Deep down we all know it's because Dad's heart attack scared her and this is her way of coping. But it's still driving us nuts. "Maybe we should all sit down and talk to her. You, Jack and I. We love her, but her intensity has been a little too much to handle lately."

"You're the oldest. You have to request the meeting."

"I'll ask her if we can all talk right after the ice cream social." The Willow Creek Ice Cream Social is our town's official summer kickoff. It's always the second Saturday in June, after the kids have been out of school a couple of weeks and have a routine. This year, there's a barn dance afterward, Sadie Hawkins style. The women will be choosing their dance partners.

She groans and I can hear the exasperation. "You're going to make me wait two weeks?"

"Yes, because she's helping organize it this year. Which means she'll have other people to boss around for the day and she'll be in a good mood."

"Is there a reason you and Jack need to set boundaries too?"

"We're both tired of her trying to set us up on blind dates. You saw what happened with the last one she arranged for Jack. I've never seen his confidence take such a beating."

"I find it very hard to believe Ophelia Daniels is the first woman to ever ghost him."

"He swears she is. And I can tell he was really interested."

"What about you?"

"She hasn't tried to set me up- not since I turned forty. But she won't leave my singlehood alone - even though she knows the craziness I dealt with after the first calendar came out and that losing Justine broke my heart."

"You never bothered to bring her home - so none of us realized how much she meant to you until it was too late. I wish I could have met her."

Her sudden wistfulness turns the conversation more somber. "I do too," I say past the lump in my throat. Maybe if she'd met my family that would have been the thing that kept her from leaving her shelter. Maybe if I'd already popped the question she would have stayed put.

"Has she asked you about Luz yet?"

I groan. "Jack's been running his mouth."

"I don't know if he's told Mom anything, but he told Alex the sexual tension between the two of you was ready to boil over."

"She works for me." I hope she hears the finality in my tone.

"And that's going to stop you from feeling something for her? If you're attracted to her, and respect her, it's only a matter of time before it becomes something more. Haven't you ever heard of forced proximity?"

"I have. Because you talk about romance tropes all the time."

"You need to read the Wantons' book club pick this month. It's all about what happens when you deny what you're feeling because you feel guilty about something that happened in the past you had no control over."

"I don't think I'm ready to read that book."

"You should. I have an extra copy," she wheedles. "Alex got one of his own because he said I was reading it too slowly."

"I'm not joining your book club, Ness."

"You say that now."

I can tell she's sticking her tongue out at me. "Enough, little sister. Go snuggle with your soon-to-be husband and let me get some rest."

"Fine. But if anything happens between you and Luz, you have to spill the tea with me first. And you're coming to our house for dinner Thursday night if I have to drag you kicking and screaming."

***

One of the first-grade classes is at the firehouse for a field trip, and I can't help smiling when I spy Luz kneeling in front of a little girl with crooked braids. The kiss she presses to the waif's forehead gives away her identity. We always let the kids explore the trucks, and this time is no exception. Under the watchful eye of Sheffield, who's a grandfather at least seven times over, they clamber over everything. When one of the kids starts clamoring for the bathroom, my squad and I decide it's time to herd them back into the building. I'm turning away when a little girl clears her throat. When I pivot back around, it's Luz's daughter. She's standing on the top step with her arms outstretched. I lift her down and she latches her hands behind my neck. They're a little sweaty and a little sticky. Another reason to herd the kids back inside.

"Mom fixed bisketti last night," the little girl confides into the crook between my neck and shoulder.

I think she means spaghetti, but her mispronunciation, and her lisp, are cute and her big brown eyes and little snub nose with freckles remind me of her mom, so I don't correct her. I think correcting kids is pompous and obnoxious anyway. "That sounds good."

She nods vigorously. "I even ate all the garlic. I asked Mom what the word hard ass meant, because I heard her say it to my uncle, but she wouldn't tell me."

I set her on her feet and crouch. "Probably because it's a word little girls shouldn't use."

Her brow scrunches in exasperation. "Then she shouldn't say it in front of me."

"She probably didn't know you were listening."

She rolls her eyes and sets her hands on her little hips, just like her mother does when she's trying to make a point. "I'm always listening."

"You shouldn't listen if you think your mom's having a private conversation."

She scoffs. "It wasn't pwivate," she lisps. "She was drinking a beer and we were playing frisbee right in front of her."

The way she mangled the r, and the thought of Luz unguarded like that, makes me chuckle. "Well, maybe just ignore what she's saying when she uses words you think might be bad."

"I don't know what that word means."

I rise to my feet and tweak the end of her braid. "It means you shouldn't pay attention."

"That's silly."

She's silly, and precious, and the spitting image of her mom. Right down to the freckles on her nose and the tiny gap between her teeth. "It might be silly, but you should try. Now, if you're hungry, I think there are snacks in the firehouse for you and your friends."

"Yay! I'm hungwy!" She squeals and waves her hand behind her as she scampers off.

I'm pretty sure I'm the hardass her mom was referring to, and I wonder what the context was. I've been trying to keep my distance since the accident, because the weight of my arm around her shoulders felt too natural.

***

Once the kids are loaded back onto their bus, I find Luz in the kitchen.

"So you talk about me with your family and friends?"

I watch the flush creep up the back of her neck as she shrugs. She gives whatever's in the pot a hearty stir before turning to face me, the wooden spoon dangling from her hand. "It's kind of difficult not to," she says defensively. "I mean we're cooped up here for days on end. And besides your chili, your cooking is shit. So of course I'm going to talk about you."

"You think my cooking is shit?" I'm not going to let her brush me off.

She rolls her eyes. "You know it is. You either burn it or undercook it. How did you mess up sloppy joes the other day? They have to be the easiest meal on the planet to make."

"I thought if I used a little less water in the recipe they'd be more hearty."

"Instead, they were more burnt. You're hopeless. If cooking isn't something that's instinctive, you shouldn't try shortcuts or make alterations."

"She's right, big brother," Jack chortles as he steps up behind me and slaps my back.

"It was a logical assumption. I would have checked earlier, but I got distracted."

"Yeah, you were holed up in your office fretting over your damn spreadsheets!" Yells Jack. "You were actually creating a fire hazard. It's a good thing the rest of us keep a watch out whenever you decide you're going to cook."

"Maybe the reason he frets over the spreadsheets is because he has no idea how to use them," Luz observes.

"I know how to use them," I protest. "They keep us organized."

"I know they keep us organized. But you spend way too much time on them. Why don't you just use formulas and pivot tables?"

I know what formulas are, but I'm still trying to figure them out and I don't want to admit I'm scared of using pivot tables. I'm afraid I'll mess something up. I cross my arms defensively and exhale before I try to explain. "Even if I'm slow, it's still way better than using paper. At least I can email stuff instead of tacking schedule changes up in the break room and hoping you guys remember to look. That's how they did stuff before, and things were always falling through the cracks."

Luz waves the spoon in the air. "Yes, it's way better than using paper. But you've moved from the Stone Age to the Bronze Age. You need to adapt to business in the twenty-first century."

"Whatever. The spreadsheets and the cooking are completely unrelated."

She gives me a look of disbelief. "They're not. You haven't been patient enough to learn either one of them. You're so particular about everything else, it's surprising."

I shrug."I don't see the point in learning stuff that won't do me any good. Especially when I can just eat the chili I make or *tack up the spreadsheet.*"

"Well, you need help with both."

"So do you want the job or not?"

She raises an infuriating brow."Which job? Cooking or spreadsheeting?"

"Both?"

"You can teach yourself to cook - that's what recipes and Youtube are for. But until you learn to make something besides chili, we're voting you out of the firehouse kitchen."

I snort. "You and what army, Martinez?"

Jack starts laughing hysterically. "She's right, brother. The rest of the squad was probably too afraid to say anything to you." He walks past me and holds his hand out to Luz. "I volunteer to be part of your army. The other guys will too. When we want chili, we'll draft him, but otherwise he's not allowed anywhere near the stove."

I'm a little embarrassed, but I'm relieved too. Cooking anything but chili stresses me out. "Fine."

She smiles. "I expected an argument. As for the spreadsheets - I'll help you with them on one condition."

"Name it." I don't care what it is - I'm tired of wrestling with them.

"You have to let me teach you how to actually use them."

I groan and palm my face. I thought I was going to be able to turn it all over to her and never look back. "Ugh. Why can't you just take it over?"

"Because it's really easy and it's better if both of us know how to use them. You'll thank me later," she says and turns back to the pot.

"It's almost the end of the month- can we start tonight?"

"Why tonight?"

"Because Wednesdays are usually quiet. You're already making dinner for everyone, right? So you'll have time afterward."

She sets her hands on her hips. "I'm not just making dinner, I'm making gumbo. At Jack's request. He said he thinks I'm the only one who can beat you in the next chili cook-off but he needs to be sure."

My younger brother is shameless. "It was his turn to cook. He bamboozled you."

"I didn't bamboozle her," he protests. "I told her I'd do all the cleaning-up and I got all the ingredients she said she needed. After she made jambalaya for the rest of us while you were off, I asked her what else she was known for."

"Why didn't anyone save me a bowl of jambalaya?" I grouse.

"There was a bowl in the fridge for you, but someone took it home after the shift."

"Probably Romero. He's living in an efficiency with a barely functioning kitchen and he has fourteen stomachs - like a cow."

"Yeah, it was probably Romero, he has no couth."

Luz shakes her head at me. "You look like someone backed over your bicycle, Chief. I'll make it again if you're that sad about it."

"I haven't had jambalaya since I tackled a fire in Kisatchie. Please make it again."

"Kisatchie?" She asks.

"Kisatchie National Forest," Jack jumps in. "Ian was a smoke jumper and part of a hotshot team before he moved back home."

Chapter Seven: Headed Towards the Light

Luz

My boss is embarrassed by his brother's explanation.

"It was a long time ago," he gruffly says.

Jack slaps him on the shoulder. "Whatever. I don't know why you're so shy about it. You were a hero."

Ian recoils and lurches away. "I wasn't a hero. I was anything but a hero."

"Ian, you were doing your job. You always do your job. Nothing that happened was your fault."

I don't know what Jack is referring to, but it's making Ian uncomfortable and he doesn't agree. "It was my fault. When you're in charge and bad things happen it's always your fault. Because you should have made better decisions."

He nods in my direction and stomps away. I turn to Jack. "What was *that* all about?"

Jack shakes his head. "It's not my place to tell you. He's being a martyr again, and there's no reason for it. You should make him tell you why he feels so guilty - maybe if he gets it off his chest with someone who doesn't know him very well, it'll help."

"Has he always been like this?"

Jack laughs, a little bitterly. "Like the oldest? Taking responsibility for shit he has no control over? Yep. I think it wouldn't be so bad if he got laid more."

"I don't think that's any of my business." Especially since I can imagine exactly what that would consist of. Like straddling a mountain.

He tunnels his hands through his hair. "You're right. I didn't mean to unload on you - it's just sometimes he's so stubborn and annoying."

"I think older brothers think they have to be. Dex can be that way too."

He tosses me a rueful grin. "Maybe. But I still think you should try and get him to talk. Maybe when you're teaching him about spreadsheets tonight."

"Well, I'm not doing that until this is done. Tell the rest of the guys it'll be another fifteen minutes," I tell him and turn back to the stockpot.

There's no way I'm confronting Ian Montgomery about his hidden demons.

***

Something thumps against the wall right before I knock on the door. I hope it wasn't the computer.

"Come in!" He barks.

When I sidle through the doorway he glances up. "Good. It's you. Somehow I fucked everything up and I don't know how to get it back to the way it was. I need to put the schedules up tomorrow."

He shoves away from the desk in frustration, the wheels of his chair squeaking across the floor.

"Let me take a look. I'm sure it's not that bad."

He vacates the chair with a swoosh and gestures for me to sit.

It takes me forty minutes to find and fix his mistake. If he hadn't been breathing against the back of my neck, with his hand on my shoulder the whole time, it would've gone a lot faster. Every time he exhales it flutters the hair lying against my nape that refuses to be confined to a braid. The air is filled with the scent of cinnamon and whatever woodsy, lumberjack aftershave he's wearing. It's so hard to concentrate, the effort is giving me a headache.

When I rub my temple and sigh, he grunts. "I'm sorry. It's too late to be doing this."

I wave a hand. "No, it's fine. I've just had a headache brewing all day and I think it just decided to take over full throttle."

Before I can protest, he sets two fingers and a thumb to each temple. I groan, because it feels so good. My headache almost magically disappears as he gently massages my head. I smother my protest when he removes the bobby pins and unpins my braid from its coil. I don't like how crinkly my hair looks when I let it down at night, and I wish I had my brush so I could smooth down the flyaways that make it look like I went batshit with a crimper.

"I like your hair this way," he says like he can read my mind. "It reminds me of those punk rock videos from the eighties. Now if you just had a pair of legwarmers."

My cheeks flame and I try not to think about why he's obsessed with leg warmers and what he'd do if he found out I like to wear them when I actually find the time to do Pilates.

His hands cup my nape and gently massage the occipital muscle. The weight of my head falls into his palms and I struggle to keep my eyes open. "You're putting me to sleep."

The quiet rumble of his laughter, like a soothing thunderstorm, washes over me. "It doesn't sound like you're complaining, Martinez."

"I'm not, but I should be. I think if we had an HR department you'd be in trouble."

"I'll stop if you want me to."

I stretch my arms behind my head until I find his wrists. When I circle them to prevent him from moving away, he laughs again. "Please don't stop."

"As long as you don't feel threatened."

"No," I moan as I clench my teeth. *Holy Mother of God the man has magic fingers.* A massage is something that's long overdue. It got pushed aside just like the other things I made myself do without - like windshield wipers, air conditioning, new batteries for my vibrator and Swiss chocolate.

"I know you don't want me to stop this," his hands flex against my scalp. "But I think we should abandon the spreadsheets for now. They're probably making your headache worse."

"I found the error in the formula, and I think that fixed it. We can put it aside for tonight."

His touch slides from my hair and I grit my teeth so I won't howl in protest. "You should get some rest. Fireworks are already on sale and you never know when someone is going to try something stupid."

I push the chair away from the desk and stand, arching my back and putting my palms at the base of my spine while I stretch. "Truer words were never spoken," I agree.

"I'll save our work and shut everything down. You should take the empty bunk."

I know he's been awake for longer than I have. I took a nap this afternoon. Not that it helped much because I think my kids have chicken pox. All three of them had mild fevers when I dropped them off at Dex and Mari's and when I wavered about calling in, they reassured me that since both of them had it when they were kids, everything would be fine.

"You need it more than I do. At least I took a nap this afternoon. How long have you been awake?"

"I don't sleep much."

"That's not an answer. How long, Chief?"

He rakes his fingers over his chin and the stubble scrapes against his callouses. "I got about four hours yesterday morning."

"You know that's not enough. Especially if something happens and you need your reflexes to be sharp."

"Being sleep-deprived isn't the same as being impaired by alcohol, Martinez," he scoffs.

"That's not true. Alcohol and lack of sleep have similar physiological effects. They both make you sluggish and impact your decision-making. You're the one who needs that bunk, not me."

"I'll be fine. Stop trying to coddle me - I'm not one of your kids."

"No, you're not one of my kids. You're a grown-up who should know better and that makes how stubborn you're being about this even worse."

He crosses his arms. "I'm not being stubborn, I'm being logical. I'm the chief and I'm the one who gets to decide who takes a bunk and when."

I cross my arms too. "Well, I don't take orders from people who have impaired decision-making."

His glower packs enough punch to incinerate me. "You're not going to let it rest are you?"

"No. Because I'm right and you're wrong. You need to take that bunk before you fall down where you stand or your idiocy causes bigger problems."

Little does he know I can debate petty shit with the best of them. For as long as it takes. There's no better teacher than a terrible two-year-old who thinks it's funnier to fling their food across the table than eat it. And I've bargained with three of the little demons.

"What are you going to do if I take that bunk?"

"Exactly what you would have done. Keep an eye on the dispatch. Catch up on the logs. Make breakfast so it'll be ready when the rest of the crew wakes up in four hours."

"Those aren't the only things I was going to do."

"So, give me a list."

"I was going to swab down the locker room and the showers. And buff out the floor in the breakroom."

"I'm perfectly capable of doing all of those things too."

"You're determined."

I sigh. "Montgomery, get your ass in that bed. I'm a single mom hanging by a thread most of the time and I don't have the patience for your theatrics right now."

He raises a brow in disbelief. "My theatrics?"

"Yup. You heard me. Your melodrama bullshit. You could give Rosie a run for her money, and since she turned twelve in March she's been a drama queen extraordinaire."

"I should probably be offended that you're comparing me to a tween."

"But you aren't. Because deep down you know I'm right. What's that book they tried to ban?" I tap my chin. "Oh yeah. Go the fuck to sleep, Chief."

***

It's the last week of school before summer vacation. All three of my kids missed an entire week because of chicken pox. We had to watch them constantly because the girls wanted to scratch away the scabs. Rico was the only one who barely had any symptoms. I had to keep them out of class until they weren't contagious. Dex had one of the guys run the shop on the days I was on shift so he could stay with them. I'm worn out, and I know Dex and Mari were relieved when it was okay to send them back to school. I was finishing up the schedule for next month and lost track of time. And then I had a flat tire.

So now I'm late for after school pick up. When I get there I hear voices. More specifically, one of those voices is that of my boss. And I've never heard him sound so cold.

"What did you say to him? He's a good kid and he wouldn't act out unless he had a reason."

There's an imperious sniff and I groan. I knew this confrontation was inevitable- I was just hoping I could stave it off. Mrs. Hoffman is Rico's homeroom and language arts teacher. She made some snide comments to me when I introduced myself and I know she feels a certain way about students she thinks are immigrants because of their complexion. She's not shy about expressing her views either.

"I asked you what you said to him."

"You're not one of his parents- I don't think it's any of your business."

"She said something mean about Mom," my son confesses.

I think I hear a growl in response to that confession. "Ms. Martinez is one of the hardest working people I know and everything she does, she does for her kids. As far as I'm concerned, she's above reproach."

"Well her son is failing my class and I can only assume it's because he speaks Spanish at home instead of English."

While I appreciate Ian coming to my defense, I need to make some things clear.

When I round the corner, Ian's eyes gleam with satisfaction. Rico just looks relieved.

"Yes, we speak Spanish at home. And English. My kids are fluent in both because they need to be able to communicate with their grandparents and fit in with their classmates. I saw the way you graded my son's latest homework assignment."

"He didn't use the past participle correctly in his last essay, Ms. Martinez."

I brace my hands on my hips and glower at her. "Mrs. Hoffman, your grading was too harsh for the crime. He made a single mistake and you dropped his score four letter grades - from an A to a D minus. You will adjust his grades or I will go to the school board and report you for discrimination."

Her back straightens and she adjusts her glasses on the bridge of her nose. "I have been teaching at Willow Creek High School for nearly twenty-five years, Ms. Martinez, and I refuse to let you intimidate me. The grade stands. You may go to the school board, but your efforts to discredit me will be futile."

I'm preparing to launch myself forward so I can scratch her eyes out when I feel the pressure of Ian's hand on my arm. Restraining me. He's been quiet during the encounter.

"Mrs. Hoffman, I am certain we can find students and parents who will corroborate Ms. Martinez's account." The cold steel of his voice could freeze her where she stands.

I take strength from his determination. "Lucky for you, Mrs. Hoffman, I am going to heed Mr. Montgomery's advice. I will find other victims and, if it's a fight you want, it's a fight you'll get."

Ian wraps his hand just under my elbow. "Grab your backpack and come on, Rico," he says over his shoulder as he propels us away from the sputtering cow.

Once we're in the parking lot, I step away from his proprietary grasp. "No one's ever defended me like that," I tell him. "What were you doing here?"

He shakes his head in disbelief. "Then you've been surrounded by shitty people, Martinez. I was here because I was making sure all the fire extinguishers were in code."

"I appreciate you stepping up and coming to Rico's defense. Do you have dinner plans for tonight? It's the least I can do. Especially since you're working on your day off."

He cocks his head. "No. Are you asking me to join you?"

"Only if you like spaghetti."

"Are you sure you want to have one of your kids' favorite meals with a hard ass?" He mutters softly so my son can't hear.

My cheeks flush as I tip my head back and chuckle. "Rubi. She repeats everything she hears. Of course she told you about my bisketti and the other thing."

"So you were calling me a hardass?"

"Can you blame me?" I ask with a raised brow.

He crosses his arms and the material of his t-shirt stretches so tightly over his shoulders, I'm surprised it doesn't rip. "I can be a hardass," he admits. "But I'm just trying to maintain order and keep the mischief to a minimum."

"You know that's pointless, right? Unless they're out on a call, the guys act like they're Rico's age."

"Who's acting like me?" He asks from the passenger seat of my car. "Can you stop talking about them so we can go have dinner? I'm starving, Mom."

"We'll leave in a second, Rico. I just invited Mr. Montgomery to join us and I'm waiting for his answer."

"I'll join you. I don't feel like frozen pizza tonight."

"We'll see you at the house. You know where we live."

He gives me a sharp nod. "I'm right behind you. You can tell me why you didn't ask for time off. I don't understand, because you've already proven yourself to me and the rest of the department, Luz. You could have stayed home with the kids the entire time."

"I had it when I was a kid - I wasn't contagious."

He clasps my elbow. "That's not why I said you could have stayed home. I said it because you've earned the right and none of us would've faulted you for it."

"I've only been here a month."

He sighs. "I never thought I'd meet someone as stubborn as me. Lead the way - I'll follow you in my truck."

Once we're in the car and he's in his truck, Rico twists in his seat and scowls. "Are you going to date him, Mom?"

I've never dated anyone but their dad. I never had the emotional bandwidth, and I didn't want my kids to be confused or resentful.

"Rico, you know I don't date. Inviting Mr. Montgomery to dinner is our way of showing him we appreciate what he did for you. Mrs. Hoffman's actions toward you were wrong."

"Why don't you date? All the other kids I know with single moms complain all the time about their moms' boyfriends."

"That's exactly why I don't date. Because it would be confusing for you and your sisters, and it's hard to make space for someone new."

****

It feels both weird and like the most natural thing in the world to have Ian Montgomery sitting at the table with my kids. Rubi crawled into his lap and made him read her the caterpillar book, and Rico and Rosie are uncharacteristically silent as his deep baritone fills the empty space.

I hear him say "The End" and the thunder of feet scampering across the wood floors. Then I smell pine and vetiver as he leans against the counter. "Do you need my help?"

"No," I say, flustered. "I just need to strain the noodles." I lift the pot and carry it to the sink.

I'm so focused on him, like a hovering mountain with his arms crossed, my grip slips a little and the water splashes onto my wrist.

"Dammit!" I yelp as I try to adjust my hold.

He's there before I can tell him no. He takes the pan from me and sets it in the sink. His long fingers wrap around my forearm and he holds it under the stream of cold water.

"I can do this myself."

"I know you can. But I'm here so you don't have to. Stop being so stubborn."

"I'm not being stubborn," I say as I try to yank my hand away. "It's not even a real burn."

"Luz," he admonishes as he shakes his head. "Stop."

The way he says my name, quietly and determinedly, like he'll stand between me and the world, makes my stomach quiver. I tell myself it's nerves, not a sudden urge to cry.

I push away the tears. "This kitchen isn't big enough for both of us. Why don't you go set the table or something if you want to help me?"

His eyes twinkle with laughter and understanding as he shakes his head again. "The kids can set the table when they get back from washing their hands."

"You got them to willingly do that? It's usually a battle."

"I promised them I'd play Twister later."

Twister is one of our Friday night traditions. The thought of ending up entangled with this man across a board game is intimidating. "We usually do a movie too. The kids have been begging to see *The Wizard of Oz*."

"I'm down for both if you need reinforcements. I'll try to keep my loathing of flying monkeys from them."

"Bisketti!" Rubi squeals as soon as I set it on the table.

I smile at my youngest as I ruffle her bangs. "It's your brother's favorite and I thought he deserved it tonight."

"Thanks, Mom." Rico roughly says. This is one of those moments like the one where I kissed his cheek in front of his friends. I can tell he's swallowing back tears.

"No problem, Rico. It's fast and easy and I know there won't be any leftovers." I cast a laughing glance in Ian's direction. "Especially since Mr. Montgomery is joining us for dinner."

Chapter Eight: The Truth Ain't Cheap

Ian

I LEAN BACK AND rub my stomach after the third plateful. "Rubi was right," I say as I smile across the table at her six-year-old daughter.

"Rubi was right about what?"

"She said your bisketti was the best."

Luz shrugs. "We have it a lot because we love it."

"Can I have a standing dinner invitation?" I ask, half-seriously.

"Jack told me the two of you already have one at your parents' house whenever you want it. And I've heard

Grace Montgomery wins the baking prize at the county fair every single year."

I grin. "She might be a prize baker, but she's also a prize meddler. She's been trying to set me up and settle me down for years."

"Does that mean your mom wants you to get married, Mr. Montgomery?" Rosie asks.

"Yes, Rosie. That's exactly what it means."

She sets her fork beside her plate and props her elbows on the table so she can lean forward. "If you wait for me, I'll marry you, Mr. Montgomery. I could make you spaghetti every night."

Luz's kids are adorable, and Rosie's barely disguised crush is sweet. "I appreciate the offer, Miss Martinez, but you need to find a sweetheart closer to your own age."

"I don't want you for a sweetheart," she corrects as she picks her fork back up. "I just felt sorry for you."

So she isn't nursing a crush. I'm relieved. Because I think I might be harboring one for her mom, and that would be awkward.

Twenty minutes later, I'm convinced Rosie Martinez is a champion conniver. She persuaded her siblings that the only people who should be allowed to move their bodies around the board are her mom and I. The kids are the ones manipulating the spinner and calling the shots.

Right now, Luz is on her back. One hand is stretched over her head and the other one is between my legs. I'm braced over her with my knees spread and both my hands flattened on either side of her shoulders. I'm trying to think about my grandmother's dentures and the way Jack was obsessed with flatulence when he was thirteen so my dick will stay down.

When Rosie calls out yellow, I wince. The only yellow spot I can reach is the one just to the right of her head. I'll have to plant my face there, basically nuzzling her. When I lower my body, her hand is going to come into contact with my steadily growing erection.

I lower my body, because it's easier to hide what the graze of her hand will do to me than explain to the kids why I can't do it. Her eyes are wide, and she bites her lip as I slowly stretch over her.

I want to soothe away the indentation left by that bite. The lime and coconut scent of her shampoo floods every inch of space between us, and I want to nuzzle the loose tendrils of hair curling over her jaw and plastered to her neck. "You smell incredible," I murmur against her shoulder.

She jerks underneath me, and her hand brushes my arousal. I grunt in surprise, and get even harder. "Do not move your hand," I hiss.

There's a soft huff and her body jiggles slightly.

"Stop laughing. It's not funny."

She chuckles again. "No, it's not funny. It's hilarious. My kids have no idea what they instigated."

"I think they might have some idea. Especially Rosita."

As if she's corroborating my suspicion, Rosie drops to a crouch and critically surveys our position. "Mr. Montgomery, your hand isn't all the way in the yellow circle. You need to move it closer to my mom's head."

If I move my hand any closer, her loose hair is going to tangle around my fingers and I may as well be cupping her nape and tipping her head up for a kiss.

I narrow my eyes at the conniving twelve year old and one corner of her mouth lifts in a smug grin. She knows exactly what she's doing.

"I concede. Your mom won," I tell Rosie.

Luz's gaze flicks down and she smirks. She knows exactly why I'm calling it quits.

I haul myself slowly away from her. Cautiously. So an inadvertent graze of her fingers doesn't send me over the edge.

"Does that mean we can watch a movie now?" Rubi pipes up.

"Yeah, but Mom gets to pick because she won," Rico tells her.

Luz, wriggles upright, her face averted. Her cheeks are blazing, and I wonder if it's from arousal or embarrassment. "Fine, I'll pick. I'll do it while the three of you are changing into your pajamas and brushing your teeth. And I'll know if you don't wash behind your ears."

Rico and Rosie bound up the stairs two at a time. Rubi drops to the floor and throws her arms around her mom's neck instead. "Mommy, can we watch Dorothy?"

"The last time we watched Dorothy, the flying monkeys made you cry."

"I promise I won't cry." She tips her head in my direction and gives me a goofy grin. "Mr. Montgomery can hold my hand if I get scared."

Luz taps the imp on the shoulder. "No, Rubi. If you get scared, I'm sending you to bed. If you think that might happen, you need to sit beside your sister or brother."

"Puh-leez, Mommy. Please can we watch the witch melt?"

"Fine. But remember what I said," she tells Rubi. Once Luz sets her down, the little girl scampers away.

"The flying monkeys are pretty scary," I mutter under my breath.

"Well, I'm not holding your hand, and you're not sitting in my lap if you get the heebie jeebies." She says over her shoulder as she finishes putting the game away. She holds out the box. "Can you stick this on the top shelf where they won't find it for a while?"

I take it and give her a slow wink. "You didn't enjoy our game of Twister?"

"I was on the verge of enjoying it too much," she grumbles.

"You weren't the only one."

Her gaze flicks to my crotch. "I'm well aware."

That fleeting glance is like a match. I feel the blood rushing to that part of my body again and this time I think about flying monkeys so I won't have to resort to palming myself in front of her. "It's your fault."

She scoffs. "You're delusional. There's no way the almost spontaneous combustion incident was my fault."

The kids are still upstairs, so I step closer. "Fine, it's not intentionally your fault."

"It's not my fault period," she hisses and practically lunges away.

Chapter Nine: Sweet on the Inside

Luz

WE RUN OUT OF popcorn right before Dorothy heaves the bucket at the witch. I'm shaking the microwave bag into a bowl, when I hear Rico. All three of my kids have been sprawled on the floor, leaning against the couch, since Dorothy started skipping down the yellow brick road.

"Mr. Montgomery, do you think that would work on real bullies?"

It's quiet in the wake of that tentative question, and I instinctively know Ian's trying to figure out why my son is asking and inform him getting rid of bullies will take a lot more than throwing water on them.

"Melting someone with a bucket of water? No, Rico, it doesn't. And you can't ignore people like that either. It just makes them feel more powerful - like there are no consequences for their actions."

I breathe a sigh of relief at his answer. I don't know if he has any kids in his life, but his response is the perfect blend of acknowledgment and caution.

"So how do I get them to leave me alone?"

My son sounds desperate and it breaks my heart.

"You can't win them over. It's impossible. You have to give them FOMO so they want more than anything to hang out with you. And then you ice them."

"Ice them?"

Rico's not the only one wondering exactly what Ian means.

"Ignore them," he explains. "Let everyone be a part of your circle but them."

"Won't that make them angrier and meaner?"

I can hear the bafflement in the question.

"Maybe. But it won't matter because you'll have your own circle you belong to and you won't need their approval or acceptance."

Ian's subtle use of psychology is impressive. He's encouraging Rico to pursue his interests and cultivate his talents - so he can find common ground and make real friends. It's great advice.

"What if I want to play baseball this summer? Do you think that would help? When we lived in Florida, I was one of the best players on the team. There's a summer league here, but they can't find a coach."

"It sounds like you know what you need to do."

"Have you ever played?" Rico's voice is tentative again.

There's a rumble as Ian clears his throat. "Yeah, I played in high school."

"Maybe you could be our coach. If you have the time."

I know Rico feels lost sometimes, but I don't want him becoming attached to Ian Montgomery. It's too dangerous. For me. For our family. It will infringe on the space we've made - the space we're comfortable in.

I step back into the living room. "Rico, stop pestering Mr. Montgomery. He's one of the busiest people I know."

Ian gives me a wry grin as he runs his broad palm over Rico's head. "Your mom's right, kid. I don't think I have time to be a proper coach."

Rico straightens his shoulders, but I can tell he's disappointed. "It was worth a shot," he says as he shrugs.

"If anything changes, I'll let you know."

Rico turns back to the movie and I settle on the couch beside my boss. It's supposed to hold three people, but he's so broad and tall, he takes up more than half of it. There's no way I'm going to be able to fluff the cushions back to their original state, or keep myself from sliding closer.

I set the bowl on the floor for the kids so I can grip the edge of the cushion I'm sitting on. If I don't, gravity is going to be my downfall and I'll end up pressed against him like he's a black hole vortex pulling me into a warp between the stars.

"I don't bite."

He sounds offended, and I'm tempted to apologize. If I do that, it's like an admission that his rough whisper has the power to make me let go. Of the cushion. Of my inhibitions. Of my resistance to his magnetism.

"I know," I whisper back.

"Do you?" His tone is still low. So low it skates over the bared skin of my arms - especially when he cups my elbow in the heat of his palm.

"I do. I'm just trying not to get caught in the wake of your man-sprawl."

"I'm not asking you to straddle me, Martinez. Just stop trying to strangle the cushion."

I ease my grip a fraction. But only because it's starting to cramp my hands. "Better?"

He shrugs. "If you're comfortable, it's better. If you're not, then no."

"I'm comfortable," I grumble around my grinding molars.

"I can tell you're not. Why'd you ask me here if you're not even going to look at me? Can't we just put the awkward game of Twister behind us?"

"I asked you here because I felt like I needed to express my gratitude. You didn't have to step up for Rico like that. I'm not looking for anything, Montgomery."

His hand cups my elbow again, and this time he exerts pressure until I turn to face him. "I didn't do it because I wanted you to thank me. I did it because it was the right thing to do. Because he was being bullied and his teacher was out of line. Anybody decent would have done the same thing. I'm not looking for anything either." His gaze searches mine. "Even if I think I finally found it."

I laugh harshly. "Then the world must have a shortage of decent people. Because it's always only been me that came to the defense of any of my kids."

The deep green of his eyes pierces me, like he's mulling his answer. "Well, all you have to do if you need someone to stand beside you, is call me."

I swallow past the lump in my throat. "I appreciate the offer, but at least I have my brother and his fiancee now. It's one of the reasons I took the job here. So I'd be closer to a support system. I have a circle of people I can depend on now."

He nods, his expression still sympathetic. "I get it. It's really important to have a soft place to land when you're a single mom," his hand slips to my wrist and he strokes his thumb over my pulse. "Especially when you're a single working mom who's starting over."

I want to wrench my hand away, because his touch makes my pulse flutter like a hummingbird's and the compassion and understanding I see in his eyes is unraveling my resistance to him and making me wonder how hard it would be to rearrange the spaces in our family so he could fit in. The lump in my throat is big enough now to choke me if I let it. I'm not going to let it. "I know you didn't want to hire me."

His thumb stops stroking my pulse and just rests there. "What have I done to give you that impression? And why are you bringing it up now?"

"You won't look at me. You haven't let me go out on any of the calls since the accident. Even though this is what I've been trained to do. I'm bringing it up now because the only reason I was able to go to the accident was because you weren't on duty to stop me. I want to know exactly what your problem is."

He growls in frustration, throws his head back and runs his hand through his hair. I bite the inside of my cheek so I won't get distracted by the flex of his bicep or that rumbling sound.

He pinches the bridge of his nose and closes his eyes. "If I say it out loud I'm going to sound like a chauvinistic asshole."

I want to challenge him. "Well, aren't you one? There has to be a reason I'm the only female firefighter on the team."

He snaps his head forward, and his hands slap his thighs in frustration. His glare could easily incinerate me.

"It's not the fact you're a woman. It's the fact you're a single mom."

Now I'm pissed too. "One of the guys is a single dad and I don't see you handling him like a baby bird."

"It's different."

"It's not different. I came here to reset my life and use the certifications I worked my ass off to get. You have no right to stop me from doing that."

"I'm the fire chief and your boss. I have every right."

"Are you guys fighting?" Rosie interrupts us.

"No," I tell her as my head swings toward the tv screen again. The credits are scrolling, thank God. This conversation is too intense and now I can end it.

I clap my hands. "The movie's over. You know what that means. Bedtime. It's the last week of school before summer break and even though tomorrow's Saturday, you need to stick to your routine."

"Are you gonna make us do chores this summer like you did last year?" Rico grumbles.

"You already know the answer to that question, young man. Chores build character and teach responsibility."

"Ugh. I wish we had school all year round."

"No you don't. You just wish you could spend the summer doing nothing but kicking around a soccer ball and swinging your bat."

All three of them rise to their feet when I do, covering their yawns. "Off to bed, sleepyheads. I'll be up in a minute to tuck you in."

Once I'm convinced they're out of earshot, I turn back to my dinner guest. I've had enough of his high-handed behavior where I'm concerned. He stood while I was talking to the kids, and I stomp forward until there's only a breath of space between us. I punch him in the chest with my finger and try to ignore the solid muscle. "You're being ridiculous. I'm just as capable as anyone else."

He grabs my finger. "I know you're capable, Martinez. That's not why I've restricted you from going out on calls." His feet shuffle as he takes a step closer. "I've been limiting your exposure because I don't want any-thing to happen to you. And not just because you're a single mom."

"What's your other reason?"

"Because I can't be near you and not want to do this." One step, and our bodies brush against each other. When he dips his head and feathers a soft kiss across my upper cheek, all of my breath whooshes out of me.

"We shouldn't. It's a bad idea."

"We're not," he says as he retreats to a safer distance. "There's too much at stake. The way it will affect how we interact with the rest of the team. Willow Creek's perception of your competence. How your kids will re-act."

"Because any time a woman becomes involved with someone in a position of power her ability to do her job is immediately questioned," I bitterly observe. "And yeah, I haven't dated anyone since their dad left, and my kids would be confused."

He clenches his jaw. "Which is why I won't ask that of you." His hand cradles my cheek and he slips a loose tendril of hair behind my ear when he steps forward again.

Against my better judgment, I wrap my hand around the back of his and decide to tell him exactly what I think about when I'm alone. "Even if it's something I think I want to happen? Even if it's something I think about at least thirty-seven times a day?"

"I think about it a lot more than that, Martinez. It's why I try to keep my distance. It's kind of impossible now that you're showing me how to use the spreadsheets, because you're right there every time I turn around and my whole office smells like you. It's driving me crazy."

"Maybe you need something else to think about. Like coaching Rico's team." I shouldn't encourage him to build a relationship with my son, but Dex is the only other man I've heard Rico ask for advice. I wish someone had told me that raising a suddenly sullen teenage boy with clear abandonment issues was going to be one of the hardest things I've ever done.

"You heard that?" He asks with a grimace.

I rush to reassure him as his hand drops away. "He never asks anyone for anything. Not really. I'll keep my distance."

He groans and clasps his hands behind his head. "It's not that. I'll think about it. You don't have to keep your distance. I'd like to think I have a little more control than that."

"Then what is it?"

"I'm already so involved in the community, I want to keep some space for myself."

"You're an introvert." I shouldn't be so surprised, but it literally explains everything.

"I don't broadcast it. Everybody in Willow Creek thinks I should be the kind of fire chief my predecessor was. Gregarious. So woven into the fabric of the community pushing him away would be like ripping out its heart. But that's not who I am."

"Who are you?"

His laugh is raw. "Hell, if I know, Luz. But if everyone keeps pressuring me to fill his shoes instead of finding a pair of my own, I'll never find out."

I mash down the butterflies that erupt when he uses my first name again. "Maybe you need to work on making your boundaries more clear. No one has the right to infringe on your peace if you don't want them there."

"I've tried setting boundaries, but they're more like wavy lines and everyone keeps stepping over them like they don't exist."

I shake my head, suddenly incensed on his behalf. "That's just plain disrespectful. And intolerable."

"Tell that to my parents and my siblings."

"I think they're just trying to take care of you. Maybe they're worried about you?"

He shakes his head. "Yeah, probably. Every time there's a bad fire, my dad checks in on me." He closes his eyes. "I was a mess after the canyon fire. For months."

"The canyon fire? Jack mentioned it, but he didn't go into detail."

"Of course he did," he wearily says. "If you want the story, we're going to need to sit down."

I step forward and lay my hand against his chest. His heart thuds beneath my palm. Steady and strong. Like nothing ever makes it falter. Now I know differently. It does falter - he just never lets anyone see it. "Another time. It's late and we're both on shift this weekend. We need our rest."

His eyes flicker open and he wraps his hand around my wrist again. "Thank you for tonight," he murmurs.

"It was nothing. Like I said, I appreciate what you did for Rico today. The least I could do was feed you dinner."

"It was more than that, Luz. You and your kids made me forget about a lot of things for a while. Things I needed a break from thinking about."

"That's really sad, Montgomery." We're standing so close I can see each tiny hair that covers his stubbled jaw. Some of them are like honey and sunset, and some are pure white.

"It might be sad, but it's the truth." His lips drop to my forehead and rest there. Like a tiny benediction.

Forehead kisses should be illegal. They make you feel things you shouldn't. Fragility and tenderness and the ache to gather someone close and tell them you'll be their home. Things I can't feel toward Ian Montgomery.

I slip my arms around his waist and the voice in my subconscious comes trickling in. *What are you doing, Luz?* I ignore it because I don't know what I'm doing. I just know it feels good to have someone hug me like they're going to stand between me and acts of god and violence. I nuzzle his chest and tangle my fingers in the cotton at the small of his back. The scent of his aftershave tickles my nose and I imagine I'm walking through an old-growth forest where I can feel the crunch of pine needles beneath my boots.

He doesn't push me away or shun my touch. His hold on me tightens and he rests his chin on my head. The air stirs over the tip of one of my ears, and I wonder if he just pressed a kiss to the crown of my head. I'm wrapped up like a butterfly sewn into a chrysalis, and I wonder how altered I'll be when he lets go.

We gently sway back and forth, until our breaths synchronize and it feels more intimate than the hug itself.

"I should go," he murmurs into my hair.

"Yeah," I agree, but I don't let go. I'm like one of those barnacles that attaches itself to whales for survival, and he's going to have to pry me away.

He doesn't let go either.

"I really need to go. I have to get up early and help my cousin fix his fence line."

"I'm not stopping you."

"You aren't. I'm stopping myself because I don't want to let go. It's been a long time since I had a hug like this."

"Same here. And when we stop hugging we'll have to pretend like it never happened. That's not what should happen in the aftermath of a once-in-a-lifetime hug."

He clears his throat. "It doesn't have to be a once-in-a-lifetime hug, Luz."

"If we keep hugging, it's going to make us want things."

His laughter is hoarse and the muscle in his jaw ticks. "I already want things."

"Okay, if we keep on hugging we're not going to stop at just wanting those things." I reluctantly extract myself from his embrace and step back. "I need to go tuck in the kids. I'll walk you to the door."

He gives me a sheepish grin. "You wouldn't happen to have any leftovers?"

The bubble of laughter in my chest escapes. "As a matter of fact, I do. Even though you had three helpings. I'll make you a doggie bag."

"Woof," he says and we both laugh this time.

Five minutes later, I walk him to the door with the echo of our laughter hovering between us. He braces himself against the frame and grabs my hand. He lifts it to his lips and presses a lingering kiss just below my knuckles.

"Thanks again, Luz. For everything." The stars sparkle behind him, and for the thousandth time tonight I wish things could be different.

"It was nothing."

He shakes his head. "It wasn't nothing and I hope you know how much I appreciated it."

I watch him stride away and carefully stow the food on the passenger side floorboard. He gives me a wave through the cracked windshield of his truck before he backs out of the driveway. I wrap my arms around my waist to ward off the chill as the taillights disappear around the bend.

I know it's late, but if I know my older sister, she's curled up with a romance book. Perdita has always been my sounding board and I don't think she'll mind the interruption.

She picks up on the second ring and I recline on the porch steps so we can have a heart to heart.

"There's only one reason you ever call me this late," she says around a yawn. "Man problems."

"Well, he hasn't become a problem yet."

"I saw this hurtling toward you like a heat-seeking missile. It's your new boss, isn't it?"

"I can't stop thinking about him and the more I get to know him the more irresistible he gets. My kids even like him."

"Is Rosie trying to set you up? I'll never forget that time she set you up a dating profile on Match.com."

I cover my face with my hand. "Oh my god, don't remind me. I still don't know how she swiped Mom's phone and credit card without any of us figuring it out. Her latest shenanigans aren't quite so bad."

Dita takes a sip of water. "But there are shenanigans?"

"She orchestrated a game of Twister - and the only players on the board were me and my boss."

"Uh-oh. Horny adults should never play Twister."

"Exactly. She's way too precocious for her own good."

My older sister snorts and water flies out of her nose. "Precocious? More like too big for her britches as Dad would say."

"I think Rubi could become attached to him easily, but I think Rico would resent him. Since he became a teenager it's like he thinks he has to take the role of protector. I think he looks up to him, though."

My sister sighs. "That's going to be a mess to navigate if you decide to date him."

"I know. I've raised him to take responsibility and to look up to Dex and Dad as role models, but I always wonder if I've done enough. If I should have stayed in my marriage to Ben."

"*Benito es un culero!*" She scoffs. "He never grew up, thinking only of himself. You needed to divorce him."

"You're right. He is an asshole. But sometimes I second guess my decision. What if he decided to become a better person and turned his life around?"

"Hermanita, you can't change someone who doesn't want to change. Benito didn't want to change and Dex and I can't believe you stayed with him as long as you did."

"Dex hates him."

Dita frowns. "As he should. The fact he acts like his kids don't exist and has never sent you a dime for child support? *Un puerco...*"

"I don't think my new boss is anything like Benito, but I'm scared to let anyone in. The kids and I have made our own little functioning unit, and we know what works and what doesn't."

"Everything you do, you do for your kids, and I respect and love you for it. But you need someone for yourself too. Adult conversations and someone to take some of the weight off your shoulders."

"It's hard to let someone in like that, Dita. Especially when I don't know if they're gonna bail when the hard stuff happens. I don't want my emotions, or those of my kids, to get involved. We've had enough disappointment and sorrow in our lives and had to internalize so much."

She shakes her head. "If you bring this guy into your circle, everyone's emotions are going to become involved. It's inevitable. If you have to pick up the pieces, you'll do it. You and the kids are resilient and you shouldn't hesitate to claim a chance at happiness because you're afraid of the potential consequences."

"I know you're right, but I just can't shake my nerves. What if we start something and he doesn't understand or respect my perspective?"

"First of all, if he doesn't then that's on him and he's an idiota. Second, you don't owe him any apologies for the way you're guarding your peace and that of your kids."

My older sister always articulates exactly what I'm feeling. "I wish you were here."

She smiles sadly. "I do too. I miss you guys so much. But Mom and Dad need me here. Especially since Mom refuses to get cataract surgery. Dad said she almost backed into the grocery cart repository thing in the parking lot because she couldn't see it."

"Maybe it was in her blind spot?"

"I'd say that too except I know for a fact she always parks in the exact same spot. Somehow I have to convince her to get that surgery. She said a friend of one of her friends went blind after she had it and she doesn't understand that's what's going to happen anyway if she goes without treating it."

"I'm sorry for not calling more often."

She shakes her finger at me through the screen. "No apologies, Luz, remember? You're doing what you need to do for you and your kids. I'm keeping our ornery, stubborn, elderly parents in line."

"Okay, just call me if you need to vent? I know they can be a lot sometimes and you're single handedly running your library branch because of all the budget cuts."

She rolls her eyes. "Ugh. Every day there's a new challenge against some book we have on our shelves. It's exhausting."

"You're doing good things and giving people a place to find themselves. I love you."

Her smile is gentle. "I love you too. Take care, hermanita and keep me posted - you know I have to live vicariously through you."

When we hang up, my heart doesn't feel as battered and I'm determined to take each day at a time with Ian Montgomery and just see what happens.

Chapter Ten: Let the Light In

Ian

THE SUN BEATS DOWN on us as we set the last post. "Tell me again why you and Roxie need more pygmy goats?"

River stands and stretches. "It's not a matter of needing them, exactly."

"Then why are we doing this?"

His cheeks flush. "She has this thing about watching me cuddle the baby ones."

"This thing? If you tell me I'm here to help out your already very healthy sex life, I'm going to punch you."

"Then I won't tell you that," he says with a shrug and tries to hide his grin.

I should be happy at least one of us is getting laid, but all I can think about is the way Luz felt in my arms last night. A little green monster is burning through my stomach like an ulcer.

"Have you popped the question yet?" I know he picked out a ring months ago. Even before his grand gesture at the baseball game.

He tips his head to the side and gets this dreamy look on his face. "I have it all planned out. I'm taking her for a midnight picnic and we're gonna watch the meteor showers."

Roxie is as much of an introvert as I am - guarded and wary. You can tell she doesn't let people get to know her without a fight, and that she doesn't suffer fools. But when you see them together, it's obvious she's crazy in love with my goofy cousin.

"She'll love that. There's no way she's gonna tell you no with a proposal like that."

He nods. "Yeah, I knew I needed to do it in private. Me climbing the bleachers at the baseball game was almost too much for her and I'm surprised she took me back. She was mortified because she hates being the center of attention."

I grunt, because I know exactly how she feels. "Not all of us are prima donnas like you."

He laughs. "Oh, I know. All the attention you get from those calendars probably drives you nuts."

"Understatement."

The clap on my back almost knocks me over. "Someday, the right one will come along. What about the new firefighter? Jack said you could cut the tension between the two of you with a knife."

"She's off-limits. I'm not going to fraternize with someone that reports to me."

He narrows his gaze. "But you want to. And it's killing you. Is it because there are actual rules against it or because you're afraid of what's gonna happen?"

"I don't think there are any official rules against it. But it would be unethical. Plus, I'm afraid my judgment would become impaired where she's concerned. It's already hard to send her into something that could be dangerous - even though I know it's her job."

"I'd tell you that you're fucked, but I think you already know it."

"I'm well aware."

He takes off his work gloves and smacks them against his thigh. "We're done here - maybe a shot of moonshine will clear your head."

"It'll do the opposite - but maybe that's what I need."

***

We just finished off a jug of moonshine and the three of us are sitting on the porch watching the sunset over the mountains. Roxie's snuggled up against River's side on the swing he put up for her last summer and I'm reclining against the steps with my hands clasped behind my head.

"Jim Bunyan's white lightning tastes better every year."

Roxie's slurred observation is drowsy and I bet River will be carrying her upstairs soon.

"Jack's been trying to get him to expand his small-batch distillery but he says he's too old and he already has more customers than he can handle." I think there are other reasons for his reluctance to branch out. The old codger grew up with stories of the Great Depression, and I think he's worried about taking that kind of financial risk.

"I think Blake offered to back him," River says.

I shake my head. "I swear that guy wants to single-handedly revive the economy of the whole county." While I admire his attachment to his new hometown, we need outside investors too. And more people settling down here.

"We should start calling him moneybags."

We all laugh at Roxie's proposal because it fits. He's one of those rich guys with a heart of gold, and from what little I know about him, he had a wreck of a child-hood and does everything he can to make sure people in our community have the resources they need.

"It's a good thing the new subdivision of affordable housing is going in - there's too many people making do with dilapidated housing and living in fire-traps." The new subdivision is his doing too. And the new mayor's too. Blake subsidized the cost of the infrastructure and Zane made sure the developer is getting some tax breaks and still helping out the school district. It's a lot of new homes, over two hundred, getting added to the fire station's zone of responsibility, and that part worries me. We need two new trucks and I'm barely able to avoid assigning everyone to double shifts. Fretting over that stuff, trying to make ends meet, is the part I hate the most about my job.

"What are you frowning about now?" River asks.

"All the chaos I have to manage."

He shakes his head. "Man, give it a rest. At least for right now."

"It's hard sometimes."

"You need to learn how to lean on other people without feeling guilty about it, Ian."

Roxie's admonishment comes from a place of experience. Before River, she'd basically walled herself off from the entire town.

"I know, Rox. But I have "oldest child" syndrome and I can't help it."

"It's going to stretch you like a rubber band until you snap in half."

River's warning is dark. He never talks about the way he spiraled and we almost lost him after his injury, but I know he's speaking from a place of experience too. I don't know if I'll ever have the strength I see in the two of them.

On paper, they look like total opposites. But deep down they have the same resilience and grit. They balance each other out - despite the differences in their ages and personalities. It's the kind of relationship I wanted when I was younger, but now I've pretty much given up hope.

"Now you look like someone rained all over your parade. I'd get you blind drunk on the other bottle we have stashed under the sink, but I know you're on duty tomorrow."

"I appreciate the sentiment, but I need to get back home so I can get some decent sleep."

"Are you okay to drive?" Roxie asks.

River kisses her temple and gathers her in his arms.

It hurts to look at them. Especially when I can see his eyes shining from this far away.

"I'll take you upstairs, baby, and make Ian a pot of coffee."

"Mmmm." She nuzzles her cheek against his collarbone.

River chuckles softly. "Meet me in the kitchen in five minutes." He's still laughing when he hefts her in his arms and makes sure the screen door banging shut behind him doesn't wake her up.

I had at least three shots, and I'm going to be cautious and have some coffee and something to eat. I'm rifling through his fridge when I hear him saunter down the stairs.

"We have leftovers, or I can whip us up some bacon and eggs to help absorb the liquor."

Greasy food will definitely help, so I nod. "That would be great," I say and hand him the slab of bacon and a carton of eggs.

After he cracks the eggs and sets the skillet on low heat, he crosses his arms and leans against the counter. "So what are you going to do?"

"About what?"

"About all of it."

I sigh and lean against the opposite counter. "I'm going to propose a new two-year budget at the next town council meeting that will cover the cost of two new trucks and three more full-time hires. We need double the crew we have now, but I know that's not going to fly when everyone's afraid we're headed for a recession. Zane will support it, but getting the rest of our duly elected officials on board is going to be a challenge."

"Zane's exactly the kind of mayor Willow Creek needed. There's a lot of resistance from the council about his ideas, but they'll come around eventually. It's time we realized we have to grow in new directions if we're going to stay alive for another two hundred years."

I nod in agreement. "Hopefully it's two steps forward and only one step back."

"Is there anyone who can help you with your budget proposal? Luz Martinez, maybe?" He slyly asks.

"Why would she be able to help?"

"Well Jack told me she's handling the spreadsheets for you now."

I grimace. "He had no business telling you that."

"He wasn't spilling your business - he just mentioned it in casual conversation. He said he hoped it would remedy how grumpy you get when you're working on the weekly schedules."

"She isn't taking them over completely. She said she'd teach me how to use them better so we're both experts."

He flips the eggs with a hmmph sound.

"You think she can't teach an old dog new tricks?"

"It's not that," he says as he arranges the bacon in the iron skillet. "It's the way you talk about her. You're trying too hard to distance yourself."

"She works for me - I have to keep my distance," I say as I run my hand over my jaw.

"Technically, she works for the town. Not you. I don't know much about the way municipal administrations work, but I bet you don't have the final say in hiring or firing someone."

"I might not have the final say in that, but I'm the one who has the authority to send her into a situation that could kill her."

He's quiet for a minute while he scoops the food onto our plates. "She chose her profession, and she did it with her eyes wide open," he ponders as he hands over my food.

"She has kids, River."

He sets aside his plate and crosses his arms. "That's not what this is about. Bad things happen all the time. It's just part of life and we have to make the most of every single second we're given."

"I'm not gonna be the reason those kids have their mom taken away from them."

"You won't be. If something happens, man, she was just doing her job."

"And I'd just be doing mine. That's the problem. I have this instinct to shelter her from those situations because I'm afraid of what could happen. It's not fair to her or to the rest of the team."

"So you're keeping your distance but still acting like you're not."

"That's not what I'm doing."

"It's exactly what you're doing," he insists. "If you were actually keeping your distance, you wouldn't worry about this conundrum you're struggling with. You're already emotionally compromised where this woman is concerned."

"Emotionally compromised. Are you saying I'm in love with her? Because I'm not."

"You might not be in love with her yet, but you're more than halfway there."

"I don't fall in love. Not anymore."

"That's the most idiotic thing I've ever heard. I don't know what happened during the canyon fire because you won't talk about it, but whatever it was left nothing but wreckage."

"The things that happened there taught me to guard my heart. If I can't do that, I can't do my job."

"So what you do, or don't, feel for Luz Martinez is affecting your ability to perform your job."

"No. What I may or may not feel isn't affecting my job performance. Thinking about the fallout from the decisions I make is what's affecting my ability to do my job."

"Which is still all tied up in your non-existent feelings for Luz Martinez."

"It's not just her. It's her kids too."

"I knew she had kids, Dex wouldn't shut up about how excited he was to have them here when I took the truck in last week. But I didn't know you'd met them."

"I interrupted an altercation with his teacher and came to his defense."

"Where was his mom?"

"Running late- so I stepped in."

"Was she grateful for your intervention? Or resentful? Sometimes single working parents think you're judging them when you do stuff like that."

"She was grateful. She invited me to dinner afterward and I accepted. It was too easy to feel like I belonged at their dinner table and their game night."

"Game night, huh?"

I grunt at the memory. "Yeah, game night. Featuring a Twister match that almost got out of control."

River bursts out laughing. "Twister is not a game for horny adults. It's almost as bad as strip rummy."

"I'd never recover."

"So it's not just the fire department tying you up in knots -it's her."

"I already admitted it was. And it's not just her. It's her kids too. Rico's close to his uncle, but it's clear he has room for more hero worship. I think he's considering me as a candidate. He asked if I'd coach his summer baseball team after I gave him a pep talk." I tell him as I scoop up the last bite of egg and bacon.

He cocks his head to the side when he reaches for my empty plate. "You should do it. You were as good as I was, just not a pitcher. Colleges were chasing you down."

"I never wanted to play baseball for a living. I didn't love it like you."

"I bet you're still a great player. And you were always great at strategy. Hell, with you as their coach, they'd probably go to the state championship."

"So I should think about it?"

He places a hand on my shoulder. "You're wound too tight and you need something else to take your mind off things if you're not going to date his mom."

"I'm not going to date his mom."

"Whatever you say, dude. I don't think you're strong enough to resist her. Roxie disagrees, so we have a bet going."

"You have a bet going? I think I'm offended."

"At least the whole town isn't involved like they were with the pool about Zane and Taren."

"That would be my worst fucking nightmare - everyone watching me like I'm under a microscope."

"I think you're going to cave before July Fourth. Roxie's being generous and said she thinks you'll hold out until Labor Day weekend."

"So she doesn't have confidence in my ability to keep my distance either."

"Nope. Not after Jack described the way you two are when you're in a room together. He said the fact you don't look at each other makes it even more obvious you want to look at nothing but each other. He said if he had a match and threw it between you, he and the guys would be putting out a five alarm fire at the station."

"My little brother is a menace. I can't wait until he gets struck by Cupid's arrow."

He throws me a smug grin. "So I was right - Luz Martinez is really under your skin. Your *I can't stop thinking about her and she turns me inside out* skin. Another Montgomery bites the dust."

"I didn't say anything about Cupid's arrows," I grumble in protest.

"It's what you didn't say, cousin." He pats me on the shoulder like he feels sorry for me.

I don't bother correcting him because nothing I say will change his mind.

Once I get home, the insomnia hits. I toss and turn. This time it isn't because I'm afraid of the nightmares - it's because I can't stop thinking about the look on Rico's face when he asked me if throwing water on bullies actually works. He's fourteen, and even though he doesn't know everything about how the food chain works, he already knew the answer to that question. Asking it was his way of asking for my advice.

I should coach his team. At least it would force me to do something besides work on the house, or my bike, or show up on scene and at the station when I'm supposed to be off-duty. The only thing holding me back from making that phone call is the thought of seeing her glowing face up in the bleachers and waiting for her smile instead of paying attention to the field.

Chapter Eleven: Finding My Way Out

Luz

MARI AND DEX HAVE the kids for the weekend. They insisted because they could see how exhausted I was. Nursing three kids through chicken pox at the same time, trying to focus on work and hoping there isn't a disaster that requires me to be fully present completely drained me. After book club tonight, I'm going to sleep for at least twelve hours straight.

Ian and I have been holed up in his office all afternoon. He's finally getting the hang of the spreadsheets, and now I'm just barely leaning over his shoulder to watch him manipulate the data. "Isn't showing our response times, the severity of the fire, and the resources used much easier to compare, using the pivot tables?"

"Yeah," he gruffly concedes. "But I still just wish all this stuff took care of itself. It gives me a headache."

I chuckle. "Numbers used to give me headaches, too. Unfortunately, with the way every jurisdiction is fighting for a piece of the pie, we have to demonstrate our efficiency to the town council in a visual, meaningful way."

"Well, I'm drawing the line at Powerpoint."

"Hopefully, a full-on Powerpoint won't be necessary."

I'm going to be nonchalant. "Well, if it becomes necessary, I guess I'll have to tutor you in that too."

He spins the chair around so my knees are brushing against his and narrows his eyes. "You know, I might have strong opinions about a lot of things, but I'm not sexist. I don't expect you to carry all the admin weight just because you're a woman."

His comment is reassuring. Every other place I've been employed, that's what was expected of me. Because the men I worked with couldn't seem to be bothered with keeping things running behind the scenes. "I didn't think you did, but thanks for confirming. That's not why I offered - just like the spreadsheets, if more than one of us knows how to use them, it helps with continuity and efficiency. No matter where I've worked - even as a waitress at a diner- I've always done things like this."

"Okay. I just want you to know I'm not patronizing you."

I tilt my head to the side and tap my chin. "I think you are a little bit - the whole conversation about me being a single mom. Like I wasn't aware of how dangerous being a firefighter is when I chose it for my career. But you're trying to be more open-minded, so I'm going to give you a hall pass. Do you need some Advil for your headache? I always carry it in my purse - hazards of momming."

He grins, and the unexpected brightness of it makes my chest rattle.

"I'll take the pass and try harder. And I'll be okay once I get home- I can tolerate it until then."

"I know one way you can show me you're emotionally intelligent - and it might help your headache too be-cause a reliable source told me there will be cupcakes."

"Pretty sure I'm more emotionally intelligent than most guys you know, Martinez. The job means I have to be. But if you think it's something I need more lessons in...like cupcakes..."

I bite my lip. Shit, should I ask him? He's right about one thing - he's already shown me he isn't a caveman. "So, do you have any plans tonight?"

"Just a good night's sleep to get rid of this headache. These double shifts are murder."

"You should come to book club with me."

"Why? Are you trying to make me a hopeless romantic? Is that what women think emotional intelligence is?"

"There you go again. Making a sweeping generalization. Being a romantic just means you anticipate the needs of your partner and respond to them without having to be asked."

"I know how to do that, Martinez. It's just not something I'm going to show you."

"You're very arrogant, Chief. I don't want you to show me." I'm double dog lying. I absolutely want him to show me.

He uncrosses his arms and rests his palms on his thighs. I keep my gaze solidly pinned to his face. And not the flex of those hands. "So what exactly do you think I'm going to gain if I go to bookclub with you?"

"A greater appreciation of what women truly want. Plus, it's fun. And we can watch the two librarians make fuck me now eyes at each other."

"Some people might think fuck me eyes aren't romantic."

"Some people might. But I thought maybe you could come by the house for dinner again afterwards? I feel like I owe you one more meal for what you did for my son. Coming to his rescue like that. And the kids are with Dex and Mari all weekend, so there won't be any awkward Twister games this time."

"I told you I was just being decent. That anyone would have done it. You're not used to saying thank you, are you Martinez? That was kind of awkward."

"I'm just not used to anyone but family being there for my kids."

"Is that why you moved to Willow Creek? To be closer to your brother?"

"He's been pestering me forever to come home - telling me it's nothing like the place I left when I was seventeen. And he's giving me a free place to live that has plenty of room for me and all three of my kids."

"I left when I was twenty, went out west and attended smoke jumping school. The constant adrenaline of the job was the exact opposite of Willow Creek."

"What made you come back?"

"Something happened that sent me into a tailspin. Then Dad had a heart attack, and it just seemed like the right thing to do. Make a new start and put everything behind me."

"So the something that happened was traumatic." He carries all the signs. I should know because I went through it too after the fire. First from losing everything that made up our lives and then when Ben turned into someone I barely knew.

"Yeah. It was traumatic," he roughly confirms.

"According to Mari and everyone else I've spoken to, reading romance is a way to process big feelings like grief and trauma."

"You're telling me that coming to book club with you will help me process the things I'm struggling with?"

"It might," I say with a shrug. "It can't hurt to try."

"Fine. I'll go with you."

"Meet me outside when our shift's over at four."

***

I clocked out five minutes ago and this is the third time I've tried to turn over my car. Nothing. It's not even clicking. Which probably means I need a new alternator. Just one more thing I can't afford. Dex will try to take care of it for free, but I can't let him do that. I can't let him keep fixing things for me.

Every time I think I'm almost caught up, something else breaks or there's some unexpected cost I'm not prepared for. Next it's going to be braces, or something equally as expensive, that the kids can't do without.

The steering wheel is cool against my forehead as I close my eyes and try not to cry.

The knock on the window startles me. I was so intent on basking in my misery, I forgot I invited him to go with me. I crank down the window. "I think I need a new alternator."

"We can take my motorcycle."

You can tell this motorcycle is Ian Montgomery's pride and joy. It's immaculate and buffed to a shine that gleams through the layer of road dust. I bet he buffs it with a shammy at least once a week. "Do you have an extra helmet?"

He gives me a look "Not with me, because I wasn't counting on a passenger. But you can wear mine - the library's only two blocks away."

"You might have to take me home too, since Dex is watching the kids."

"That can definitely be arranged," he tells me in a rough voice.

I roll my eyes. "That's not what I meant, and you know it."

"I never know with you, Martinez. Your kids are the ones who made us play Twister."

He's determined to get under my skin. "Don't act like you didn't enjoy it. I could tell otherwise. And it wasn't my idea."

His rumble of laughter startles me and sends a shiver down my spine. It's futile to contradict him. "If you're sure." He nods, so I grab my purse from the floorboard and roll the window back up. When I reach for the door handle, he shakes his head. I'm not used to anyone opening doors for me, so my exit is awkward.

"Come on," he says as he takes my hand and tugs me toward his bike.

I stow my purse in one of the saddlebags and put my hands on my hips.

"What are you doing, Martinez?"

"I'm trying to figure out how I'm going to swing my leg over without wrenching my hip."

"No, you're not. First you're going to let me put the helmet on you," he says as he crouches and grabs it from the other saddlebag.

Before I can step away, he's smoothing my hair back. "What are you doing?"

"Trust me, your hair's going to tickle your nose if you don't make sure it's all under the helmet."

"Let me fix it," I say and bat his hands away. I unravel my braid and twist it all up into a bun at my nape. "Better?"

"No. I was hoping I'd actually get to see how long it is."

"It goes to my butt, Chief."

"Oh, I know," his fervent acknowledgment scrapes over me.

A flush spreads over my cheekbones and I ignore him as I turn back to the motorcycle and look at it in consternation.

"What now?" He asks and I can tell he's trying to be patient with me.

"Just trying to figure out how I'm going to get on it."

"Like this," he says and wraps his hands around my waist to lift me over the seat.

That was exactly the gesture I was trying to avoid. I know he's just being courteous, but every casual touch is like a comet trail over my skin. When he takes a seat in front of me, I lean back as far as I can.

"You're going to have to hang onto me, Luz," he says with a demonic chuckle.

"I will. I'm just waiting for us to take off." I'm delaying contact as long as possible.

He flips up the kickstand and braces us. "Are you ready?"

I nod against his shoulder.

"Arms around my waist," he commands.

I do what he asks, my heart ready to beat out of my chest. Hopefully the layer of material between us means he won't be able to feel how sweaty my palms are. The helmet puts some distance between us - at least it prevents me from giving into the temptation to lay my head on his shoulder or against the middle of his back.

The rumble of the motorcycle vibrates through every layer of my clothing when he revs the engine, and I push down my excitement. This is an only-in-an-emergency, once-in-a-lifetime thing and I have no reason to expect it will happen again. His muscles tense beneath the pads of my fingers when we take off, and when we maneuver over the curb, I clutch him even harder.

"I've been riding a long time, Martinez. I've got you, I promise."

"That's what I'm afraid of," I mutter. The rumble of the engine and the helmet muffle my response.

It's only about three blocks to the library, and there's no traffic. Downtown is usually sparse after the dinner rush ends at six thirty. He parks diagonally, right in front of the bay windows by the circulation desk. A whole cluster of people turn their heads and I want to burrow into the seat where they can't see me.

I dismount before he can help me, and stalk over to the corner of the building to remove my helmet. He follows me. "I know you're afraid to be seen with me, so let me help you get it off, Martinez. That way you can scurry inside."

I abandon my efforts to unclasp it myself. "Fine."

He shakes his head in amusement, and tips my chin up with one knuckle. His eyes on mine make me feel raw, like someone scraped away all of my secrets and shields. When he finally lifts the helmet away I remove the scrunchie and tip my head upside down to shake out my hair.

His eyes are glowing when I stand back up. "Now you know I wasn't lying about the length of my hair," I smugly inform him.

His throat bobs, and he visibly gulps. "Yeah, now I know. And I can't unsee it. Fuck my life."

I wonder what exactly he can't unsee, but I'm not about to ask. I don't need any more reminders of how long I've been celibate by choice.

"Let's go in. Hopefully the gossip about our arrival has died down."

He snorts. "Not if my cousin's here. River is going to smirk and interrogate me."

"Maybe he won't have time."

"According to my watch, we have fifteen minutes until the meeting officially begins. He'll make every second count," he sighs and tunnels his fingers through his hair.

"You just gave yourself horns."

He tries to smooth it, but it only makes things worse. "As much as I think it suits you, let me help. We don't want the good citizens of Willow Creek thinking their fire chief is a sloth."

I stand on my tiptoes and sift my fingers through the strands of sunset. It's like gossamer against my skin and I feel burned when I drop back to the ground.

Chapter Twelve: Take a Breath

Ian

I'M CONVINCED THE UNIVERSE is trying to kill me. I should have refused her offer to join her at the book club - but at least we won't be alone. I'm crazy for accepting her dinner invitation , because there won't be any barriers. It was obvious her kids were trying to set us up.

It's been two weeks since the hug and I haven't stopped thinking about it. I almost added lime and coconut air freshener to my pharmacy order because I missed the smell of her hair.

The chairs are fanned out in a half circle, and there are only two left that don't seem to be taken. I set my helmet on one and Luz sets her purse on the other one.

"I'm going to go talk to Emma," she says with a wave of her hand.

As soon as I set down my helmet and take a seat, River strolls over.

"Motorcycle, huh? Who was your passenger?"

"You know exactly who it was."

"Yep. I just want to watch you admit it."

"You're an asshole."

"Not an asshole, but seeing you tumble from your pedestal is a nice change."

"My pedestal?"

"You know. Rescuer of kittens. Slayer of fire-breathing dragons. Pin-up model."

"I am not a pin-up model."

"Roxie told me the calendar hanging up at Curl Up and Dye is still on your month."

"My month was March. Maybe they just got too busy."

"Nope. Roxie asked. Mabel told her that the way you had your arms crossed and were smoldering at the camera made her lady parts spring to life every morning."

"I did not need to know that."

"You're welcome."

He just laughs and elbows me.

A woman in a frilly blouse, giant hoop earrings and a boho skirt moves to the center of the circle. "If I could have your attention, " she says as she claps her hands. Like we're unruly kids.

The room settles down and she smiles. "Welcome to all of you who are new. We'll have introductions in a moment. This is my co-host and partner in crime, Sam Wright. He's the muscle behind the madness and he's only here to arbitrate disputes."

A tall guy in a blue button down and wire-rimmed glasses moves away from the shelves and takes a place beside her. She looks up at him adoringly, and I guess that he's the other librarian.

"Like Laura said," he places a hand on the small of her back. "This is her rodeo. If anyone disrespects her, you'll have to deal with me."

"Before we get started, let's introduce ourselves," she turns her gaze on me. "We all know you, Ian Montgomery, you're basically a fixture in Willow Creek. But why don't you introduce yourself anyway and tell us what the last book you read was."

I rise to my feet and clasp my hands. "Ian Montgomery. Willow Creek Fire Chief. Lord of the Rings." I sit back down.

"My that was efficient," Luz snarks from beside me.

"You seem to be acquainted with Mr. Montgomery, and you're wearing a Willow Creek Fire Department shirt, would you like to introduce yourself?"

Luz's knee brushes against mine as she stiffens, and I chuckle at her discomfort. She throws me a glare as she stands.

"I'm Luz Martinez. I went to high school here in Willow Creek, class of 2008. My brother is Dex Martinez. The last book I read was this one, and I'm excited for the discussion."

"At least I didn't give them my life story," I mutter.

"Welcome back to Willow Creek, Luz!" Someone calls out from the other side of the circle. She waves at them and sits back down.

"Does anyone want to begin with their thoughts on the hero?"

Luz's hand shoots into the air.

"Go ahead, Annika."

"Caleb's misgivings are flat out ridiculous."

"What makes you say that? He has a tortured past, after all."

"But it's a tortured past because he feels guilty about things he couldn't control."

"So you don't think his reasons for staying away were justified?"

She fiddles with the hem of her t-shirt. "I'm not saying that. I just think he could have come clean a lot sooner about the way he felt."

"Even if he didn't come clean, everyone could sense the tension between them. And he's been pining the entire time he's known her. That has to stir you to empathy," Luz speaks up.

The librarian turns to her. "So what appeals to you about Caleb's pining?"

Luz shrugs. "Just the fact he's doing it. He's such a goner and it's obvious from their first kiss that the only way he's going to resist her is if he stays away or acts like she doesn't exist. Guys are usually too macho to admit their weakness."

The wildflower farmer raises her hand again, and when the librarian nods she bites her lip. "The problem is that him ignoring her is affecting her mental health. All of her brazen behavior is false bravado and she's acting out because it's about more than who she is. She's trying to get him to notice her."

"So you think Sesily is affected by society's opinion of her and the nonchalance is nothing more than a mask?"

The woman nods vehemently.

"Do the rest of you agree?"

At least a dozen hands shoot into the air, and they hash it out for the next thirty minutes. The room is firmly divided between team "Caleb was an ass for ignoring her" and "Caleb had his reasons for ignoring her and he deserves to be forgiven."

I haven't read Caleb and Sesily's story yet. After today's heated discussion and condemnation of his "slower than molasses on a pile of cowshit" (according to Lillian Snead) claiming of the woman he loved, I'm not sure I'm ready for it. Not when I can still smell lime and coconut and the subtle citrus of her lemon verbena perfume if I tuck my nose against the shoulder she was pressed against on the ride over.

Luz Martinez is the kind of woman you fall for. Utterly and Irretrievably. Sharp around the edges like Sesily because she's had to hone her defenses and bite her lip instead of crying when the world gave her less than she expected. A woman whose greatest gift is her capacity to love and protect others.

I'm taking her home on my bike and when we get there I'm telling her goodnight and keeping my hands and my thoughts to myself. Dinner can happen another time, because I don't trust myself to behave if we're alone in her empty house. I can't stop thinking about all the versions of Twister we could play together. Versions that don't need a board or a spinning wheel.

Chapter Thirteen: High Hopes and Nightmares

Luz

THE MALEVOLENT STARES DIRECTED at my back as we left were like knives between my shoulder blades. And the gossip that happened after we left was probably even more intense. That new-girl-in-town feeling is still shivering over my skin, like a blanket of fog, as I fasten the helmet. He just shakes his head as he watches me, like he can see all the stuff swirling behind my eyes. There isn't any judgment in his gaze - maybe because he's feeling uncertain too.

The ride to the cabin takes us straight toward the sunset. Everything is soft and muted beneath its rosy glow, hazy and beautiful. Like an Impressionist painting. As soon as we're past the outskirts of town, he accelerates. The pavement is a smooth black ribbon beneath us, the wind a dull roar and the purr of the bike throbs under my seat. I wrap my arms around him even tighter, and wish I could feel the open air on my skin and in my hair, and hear the chirp and bustle of the spring night as it settles over the countryside.

When the sun sinks below the horizon with a final burst of red, we pull into the winding driveway that leads to the cabin door. The crunch of gravel beneath the wheels as we come to a stop reminds me who I am. Luz. Mom and employee of the man I have my arms wrapped around. The thought flusters me and I'm hopping off as soon as he sets the kickstand and turns off the engine.

He dismounts too, and lifts the helmet from my head without giving me a chance to protest. The careful way he does it makes me catch my breath and I step back to cover my confusion. I should have insisted on doing it myself, but I didn't. Because I wanted to feel the rough pads of his fingers brush my cheek.

"Tell me again, Luz, why you're here in Willow Creek. Tell me why you applied to become a part of my fire station." There's something brittle and desperate in his voice. The lone call of a whippoorwill breaks through the chorus of tree frogs and trilling songbirds, yearning and plaintive. I can smell the wild honeysuckle blooming at the edge of the woods.

"I've told you why."

He steps forward and catches my jaw, sliding his fingers into the sweaty strands of hair plastered to my cheek by the helmet. "You haven't told me all of it. Firefighting is dangerous and I want to know why you chose it. Maybe it'll make it easier for me to protect you if I understand why you're here."

I don't like the feeling of helplessness that always overcomes me when I remember why I chose this path. I take a deep breath and plunge ahead. "I'm here because I've seen what fire can do. How fast it can take away everything you've worked for and leave with nothing."

His expression turns grim. "You've experienced it yourself."

I nod shakily, and cup my elbows because my hands suddenly feel like ice. "The trailer the kids and I lived in burned down while my husband was gone. The only reason I'm standing here, the only reason my kids are alive, is because we had an amazing dog that woke us up and dragged us out."

"You didn't have a smoke alarm?" He sounds pissed. It's hard to tell if it's because of the situation I was in or because he thinks I was neglectful.

"It must have been defective - because I made damn sure I replaced the batteries every three months."

"I believe you. Sometimes they're defective. I'm just glad you and the kids were able to get out in time."

"That's why I wanted to fight fires. Because I've seen what it can do and I want to prevent it from happening to other people."

"I respect that," he says as he hangs the helmet dangling from his grip on the handlebars. He's clearly not going anywhere.

I look between him and the helmet and raise my brow. "Do you want me to invite you in for a cup of coffee and that thank you dinner?"

"I promised to tell you my story, and I owe it to you even more now because you just told me a part of yours. You deserve to know why I'm here too, what brought me back to Willow Creek."

I don't know if I'm ready for his confessions, but I dig my keys out of my pocket anyway. "Come on."

He reaches into the saddlebag and swings my purse over my shoulder. "Don't forget this - unless you were looking for an excuse for me to show up tomorrow?"

I shrug, "Nope. Just have a lot on my mind." When I push open the door, he's right behind me and I'm ambushed when I turn toward the side table to set down my keys.

His hand brackets my face and his grip is suddenly wound up in my hair. "What..."

The kiss stops the flood of words in my throat. I've been craving this for days, and I don't know why he's letting his control slip, but I'm not going to complain. His lips press softly against the corners of my mouth, as his thumbs stroke my cheeks. He tastes like cinnamon because of the flavored toothpicks he always has, and the warmth of his palms against my ears feels sinful.

"I just needed to know if you'd be as sweet as I imagined, Luz. I've been dreaming about your kiss since that damn Twister game," he says as he rests his forehead against mine. I count the thud of heartbeats between us. *One. Two. Three.* Somewhere between three and four he drops his hands and steps back.

I'm flustered and speechless for a second. And then I'm annoyed with him for teasing me. "That's all? After the way you've been eating me with your eyes for weeks?"

"If I give into my base instincts, I'm going to press you into the wall and you'll have beard burn all over you, Martinez," he emphasizes with a thump of his fist against the plaster.

I swallow hard and push down the urge to beg. "Well, we can't have that," I mutter over my shoulder as I head for the kitchen.

He's right on my heels. "We both have too much baggage, and you know it. And neither one of us is good at poker face. If we give in and sleep together, everyone's going to see it."

"Everyone already knows you want something from me. Your brother asks me every day if you've made a move. And you're an asshole for calling my kids baggage," I tell him as I put the filter in the coffee pot.

He grunts. "Jack needs to mind his own business. He's not exactly winning at the game of love, either. And I wasn't calling your kids baggage. I was talking about our relationships and the way they messed us up. Mine messed me up and I know you've had shitty luck too. Your kids are probably one of the few good things from all that, right?"

"Yeah. I was young and crazy and would've followed Ben anywhere. When I left Willow Creek, I was determined to never return. But I'm back because this is what's best for my kids - a new beginning and a stable home we can make our own."

"I left too...about ten years before you. We both have long, complicated stories and that's going to make anything that happens between us even more complicated."

"This thing between us," I wave my hand like I'm swatting at mosquitoes. "It's never going to be complicated. I don't have any space in my life for complicated things - just orgasms that make me forget for a little while about all my responsibilities and obligations."

He rakes his hand through his hair. "I'm not looking for complications either, but that doesn't matter. If we lean into how much we're attracted to each other, it's going to get complicated. It's inevitable and there's nothing we can do to stop it."

"Jack said you changed after the first calendar was released. That you turned into even more of a workaholic. What happened?"

"Let's talk about the other hard stuff first and then we can tackle that."

"Okay," I agree as I flip the switch. Once the smell of coffee fills the air, I take down two stoneware mugs.

"You don't have to wait on me, Luz," he says and grabs one of the mugs.

I flush. I'm used to waiting on other people. Especially men. My ex-husband was very traditional and would never have considered pouring his own cup of coffee or washing dishes or changing a diaper. "It's no bother," I demur.

He mutters something unintelligible and grabs my wrist. "It's a bother to me. Sit down. You've been on your feet almost all day. I know you helped detail all the trucks today, and then you made dinner for all of us before you tackled the supply order. Take a break - you've earned it. I'll pour our coffee."

He pushes me into one of the chairs.

"Are you one of those men who actually believes in equal rights and division of labor?" I never would have guessed - especially based on his chauvinism about hiring me.

"I am. My mom would give me a swirlie or something worse if I acted entitled to special treatment because of my gender."

"So why were you such an ass about hiring me?"

"That's my own personal trauma. Which I'm about to dump on you in all its nitty gritty detail. As soon as I pour our coffee."

I let him take over because it's clearly not up for consideration. Watching him putter about in my kitchen is surreal. He dominates the space, and a couple of times, almost bangs the top of his head against the open cabinet doors. "Okay, I give up," he finally says. "Where's the sugar?"

"I don't use it. There's local honey from Emerson's on top of the fridge, and there's almond milk in the door if you need it."

He grabs both and sets them on the counter. "How much of each for you? I've never seen you get any at work."

I rest my chin on my hands. "That's because I bring a huge thermos from home. The coffee you guys purchase is questionable."

"Don't wrinkle your nose at me. Blame Jack."

"You guys can drink the swill, I'll just keep energized via the private stash in my locker."

"What else do you have stashed in your locker? Any Girl Scout cookies?"

I laugh. "Nope. Rosie was in the Brownies, but I couldn't convince her to stick with it. I have some Stroopwafel in there though."

"I'll trade gossip for it."

"I'd rather have more of your secrets. And besides, I've never heard you gossip."

He shrugs and grins over his shoulder. "It was worth a shot. So do you take your cream with a little coffee or vice versa?"

"Neither. Straight up black. Like my heart. I don't want anything to ruin the flavor."

"Your heart isn't black - you're one of the kindest people I've ever met."

I shake my head in denial. "Not true. I turn away stray dogs."

"Only because your kids would have a menagerie if you didn't."

"It's funny how quickly you caught onto that."

"I may have heard through the grapevine about your weekly trips to the kennel, and you told me about the dog that saved you. I figured they were animal lovers and they got it honest."

"Yeah, I'll tell you about Knocks after you tell me about the fire Jack mentioned. And your super secret life as a smokejumper."

He slides my cup over and takes the seat across from me. He peers into his mug and the silence stretches for ten minutes before he raises his head. There's a sheen in his eyes, and I know this story isn't at all what I thought it was going to be. When I reach over, his hand latches onto mine.

"I was barely twenty when I went through smoke jumper training. My parents were already furious that I turned down a baseball scholarship to train as a firefighter out west in Missoula, and when I told them I wanted to become a smokejumper, none of them understood why. Even my dad - and he was a fireman too."

"Why'd you do it?"

"It's going to sound crazy, but you know the scene in Lonesome Dove when the prairie fire destroys the ranch?"

"I've never seen it."

"Well, it's my dad's favorite movie. And mine too. The fire destroys everything in its path and they don't really have a way to fight it. The devastation from that scene, and the emotional toll it took, even though it was on actors, stuck with me. And then I saw a documentary on the National Geographic Channel about wildfires when I was seventeen and the men and women who fight them. I didn't tell anyone about my plans, I just decided that's what I wanted to do."

"So are you going to make me watch the movie so I have a better understanding?"

"Absolutely, Martinez," he smiles and strokes his thumb over my wrist. "The next time we're on shift together I'm holding you hostage every minute we're not sleeping or responding to an incident."

"As long as there's plenty of popcorn, I promise not to complain. What happened after you went to smokejumper school?" I ask and squeeze the fingers he has wrapped around mine.

"I met a girl."

I smile wistfully. "That's how all the best and worst stories begin. Boy meets girl. Girl meets boy."

"I thought it was going to be the best story. She was a few years older than me, and a single mom."

"You have a type," I observe.

He shrugs. "Maybe. But it's not about the kids. It's that a woman who has all that on her plate knows who she is," his thumb strokes my wrist again. "Justine knew who she was, and to a twenty year old kid still trying to figure out who he was, that was really attractive. I grew up with a strong-minded mom, and I've never been afraid of confident women."

He pauses to sip his coffee and I withdraw my hand. "That explains a lot, Chief." Now I want to meet his mom and pick her brain about what he was like growing up. If he was always closed off or if that's a newer development.

His shrug speaks volumes about him as a person and how much he cares about what people think. If he has the choice not to care, he's not going to. "Justine was the most determined person I'd ever met. She made you second guess how competent you were at things, and how well you thought you knew yourself. She was spinning me around from the moment I met her. When I finally convinced her to go out with me, it felt like I'd planted a flag on the moon," he flushes at my raised brow and holds his hands up. "I know, I know. Territorial. But that's how I felt. In my defense, I still wasn't mature enough to have a fully rational reaction. Tristan was two years old when we started dating."

"You were both wildland firefighters? That must have been hard on her, leaving her kid with other people for three months out of the year."

"She had really supportive parents and Tristan spent fire season with them. Even when it started to stretch for longer and longer periods. We both started out doing the basics. Like being pack mules and shoveling dirt. We were always competing. I became a sawyer first and she was so jealous," he smiles at the memory. "She said she wished all of the units would recognize women were just as capable as men of doing every single job on the squad."

"Did she ever become a sawyer?"

"About six months after me. After that, she got transferred to another crew with a base closer to home, because Tristan was starting second grade and having problems adjusting to her absence. We lived together during the off season, but sometimes we'd go months without seeing each other because we were fighting fires thousands of miles apart." He takes another deep breath. "I haven't talked about this with anyone, not the details anyway, so give me a minute."

I nod and brace myself for whatever revelation he's going to make. "Take your time."

He gulps down the last of his coffee and pushes the mug to the side. When he lays his hand on the table and opens his palm, it's an invitation. Asking me to lend him some of my strength so he can tell the full story. I tangle my fingers in his again.

"So, we lived like that for about ten years. Together but apart. Snatching every minute we could to be a couple. To make it work. When we both got transferred to the Eastern Basin, I knew it was finally time to pop the question. I'd always been there for Tristan, a second father. And Justine and I may have fought every once in a while about stupid shit, but we always made up and came back to each other."

His eyes close, and I know what's going to come next broke him and his confession might break something in me too.

"The fire shouldn't have become what it did. It started out as a brush fire on the north slope, and when we dropped in to fight it, the wind was dying down. The weather forecast was the best we could expect that time of year based on the temperature, the relative humidity, the wind and the likelihood of storms and lightning. We were relying on the Hanes Index and didn't know then that it wasn't designed to predict atmospheric instability or plume fire growth. The storm came out of nowhere and suddenly we were dealing with a pyrocumulonimbus." His hand tightens on mine as my eyes widen.

"Those are fast and increase the risk of burnover." Burnover is something anyone who's studied wildland firefighting has heard about. It happens when a crew gets trapped by the fire on all sides and their only chance of survival is the emergency shelter they carry in their backpacks.

His expression is grim as he nods. "There was no way out. Everything was crackling and roaring all around us, with only the little ditch of dirt behind us. We all knew there was the possibility we wouldn't make it. Justine and I had only been in our cabin about six months. It was in this beautiful valley, and the meadow was carpeted in columbine. When we weren't on duty, she used to pick it in the mornings and put it in mason jars in every room. I think she knew I was going to ask her to marry me soon, and she'd started talking about leaving the fires behind her and being there permanently for Tristan before he left for college. And having another kid - with me."

I squeeze his hand. "Go on."

"I was the superintendent, but that day the fires were so numerous, everyone who had a red card was asked to step in. We were on the same crew that day, with her as a squad leader and me as the incident commander. Like I said, we were on the north slope of the canyon, when the fire generated a tornadic vortex. The flames were swirling above us, and the ones behind us were shooting almost two hundred feet into the air. I gave the order for everyone to get out their emergency shelters and huddle underneath them while the fire passed over us."

I hold my breath, because I sense what's coming, and he's gripping my hand like it's a life preserver.

"There were nineteen of us when I gave the order. By the time it was over, there were only sixteen of us left."

"And Justine wasn't one of them."

He blinks away the tears. "No," he hoarsely agrees. "She was in the shelter next to mine, and when I heard her panicking, I tried to calm her down. When she left it and started running, I was shouting at her to get back under it because it was the only chance she had. I was supposed to protect her."

"You did everything you could to protect her. You couldn't have predicted that the situation would trigger what sounds like a symptom of post traumatic stress disorder. She wasn't thinking rationally, because she had the same training you did."

"I know that. I knew it then. But it doesn't change the way I felt like I'd failed her, or make the guilt go away. And she wasn't the only one who died that day on my watch. Two other crew members panicked. One of them left the shelter and sucked air into his lungs. It killed him immediately. One of the other guys ran away like Justine and couldn't escape the spotfire that erupted at his feet. I can still hear him screaming as he was burned alive."

"You still haven't forgiven yourself."

His laugh is bitter. "I don't know if I ever will. Her son never will."

"Her son blamed you for what happened?"

He nods, and the hurt flashes over his face. "Yeah. Tristan told me I was the one who promised to take care of her and I broke that promise."

I want to hug him again, because now I have an even deeper understanding of what he's carrying around and why he didn't want to hire me. "You don't ever want to be in that position again. That's why you didn't want me on your squad and why you're determined to keep your distance - no matter how much you're attracted to me."

"I can't ever be that man again. The one that stands there and gives that news to a kid whose world revolved around their mom. That she's gone because of me and they have to finish growing up without her."

"What happened wasn't your fault," I say it again and hope he'll hear it this time. "Her panic had nothing to do with you and there's no way you could have stopped it. If you'd gone after her, you wouldn't be sitting here."

"I should have seen the signs and made her stay behind. We lived together, and I should have seen the cracks."

I shake my head. "If she was good at hiding them, if the cracks were already there for you too, her behavior would have seemed normal. You were both impacted by the brutality you experienced on a daily basis, and I bet there were times that no matter what you did, Mother Nature won."

"Mother Nature won a lot. Not as often as she would have if we weren't doing our job, but a lot."

"So you had trauma too. My therapist says that healing from a traumatic experience is a journey, not a destination. It means you have to be patient and compassionate with yourself - give yourself grace. After the fire, I was forced to confront the ways I'd failed myself. I was so wrapped up in trying to survive, I never took the time for self-care. It's why the fissures became so wide after the fire. I'm still on that journey, but it's a much gentler one now."

Chapter Fourteen: When I'm Not Strong

Ian

Luz Martinez is wise and earnest, and truly cares. I can see it in the way her eyes coast over me, filled with empathy. Her empathy makes me feel even more broken and I want to push it away. Push her away.

I stretch my arms over my head with an exaggerated, completely manufactured yawn. I don't lie easily, but I need to do it now. "I have some projects I need to get an early start on tomorrow."

"More fence?"

"No, stuff at my own place." I'm in no mood to endure my cousin's ribbing about what happened at book club tonight, or the fact he saw me leave with Luz.

"So you're taking a raincheck on dinner?"

I nod, because I don't trust myself not to blurt out that I want her. Not spaghetti or casserole. The banquet of her, like a dessert laid out in front of me.

She gets up too. "Okay, I'll walk you to the door."

I shake my head because if she walks me to the door I'll be tempted to kiss her good night. There's a good chance I won't be able to stop at a kiss. "There's no need. You're tired too."

"I might be tired, but I'm wound up too. I don't get many nights to myself."

"The kids aren't coming back tonight?" I don't want to think about her in this house by herself. Where I could be with her - no interruptions.

"Nope. They're having a sleepover at my brother's house since his fiancee isn't on call this weekend."

There's no chance of interruption if I end up doing more than kissing her and that means I need to make a run for it before I do something I'll regret in the morning.

"You really don't need to see me out," I repeat and hope I don't sound like an asshole.

"I'm walking you out. It's the least I can do."

I swallow my sigh. "Okay."

When I reach for the door handle, she sets her hand over mine. "Thank you for sharing your battles with me tonight. Dealing with the things we talked about can be really hard, and it always helps to share them with someone."

I don't know if she's talking about me or herself or both of us. "I haven't talked about the fire with anyone else. Not even Jack," I tell her as I clear my throat.

Her brows dip into a vee. "Not even a therapist?"

"No," I say with a rough laugh. "If I go to a therapist there's a possibility they're going to make me take a break. I need this work, Luz. It's one of the only things holding me together."

"Ian," she gives me a pleading look and tightens her grip on my hand. "You can't keep carrying all of this around by yourself. You need to speak to someone who can give you the tools you need to come to terms with your trauma."

I need to distract her from this line of conversation. That's what I'll blame my lapse of judgment on later.

I let go of the handle and circle her wrist. When I step into her she starts backing up, her gaze wary. Her shoulders hit the wall with a soft thump and there's nowhere else for her to go. Nowhere for her to retreat or hide from what I think she knows is coming. "I know you're trying to distract me," she warns.

"I don't care if you know," I tell her as I circle her other wrist and press her manacled hands into the wall above her head. "Just let me know if it's working."

The hitch in her breath is all the confirmation I need. She turns her head aside and I graze the stretched tendon of her neck with my teeth, taking full advantage of the elongated arch of her body. "Even your skin smells like coconut and lime," I murmur. She's like a summer day, and I want to trap her warmth against the cold nights and loneliness that are my only company.

"You're breaking all your own rules..."

Her raw protest dies in her throat when my mouth lands on hers. She winds her arm around my neck and clutches at my shoulder, her ankle twining itself around my calf. Her body is giving up her secrets - that whether it's against her better judgment or not, she wants to throw away the rulebook too.

When I slip my tongue inside her mouth, she chases it. I can taste the hazelnut notes from the coffee we just shared, and my whole body wakes up to her sudden surrender, like a shot of espresso. She moans into the kiss when I press her into the wall, every inch of us so aligned, we may as well be plastered together with super glue.

My hand slips to the hem of her shirt and I brush my fingers over the soft cotton of her long sleeved tee. I can feel the elastic waistband of her joggers, and fight the desire to drag them below the swell of her hips.

"Tell me what you want, Luz. What you need."

She tilts her head to the side, breaking the kiss so she can look up at me with hazy eyes. "You already know the answer to that question, Hotshot. Stop denying us both."

I want to forget the weight of my past, lose myself in the haven of her body and her sweetness. I want to be that twenty-year-old kid again who was so full of hope and determined to make a difference in the world. This could be an escape for her too - so she can forget, just for a handful of stolen minutes, about all the other people she has to be strong for. I can't let us have all of it - because I'll never be able to let go. Maybe a piece of that forgetting will be enough to sustain us.

"You asked for this, and I want it too. But our clothes stay on."

Her answering smile is dreamy and mischievous. "Mmm, dry-humping against a wall. Very nostalgic of you, Hotshot. But not all of our clothes." She balances herself against me and reaches behind her back. She twists her arms and wriggles out of her bra, then flings it to the side.

I don't know how I feel about her new nickname for me, but I know how I feel about the way her lips purr around the syllables, and the way she circles her hips against mine when she says it. My hand finds its way underneath the waistband of those infuriating joggers, and slips over the ripe curve of her ass. She's lush, but that curve is almost solid muscle under my grip, and I haul her leg around my waist so I can hold on.

My dick is is so hard, the cage of denim is painful. I fumble with the button fly of my jeans, desperate to relieve the pressure, and groan in frustration when it slips from my grasp.

"Let me," she hums along my jaw. Her touch is deft and swift, and when she pushes the jeans down to my hips with a firm jerk, I surge forward in relief.

When her fingers go to my boxer briefs, I push them away. "No," I mumble as I bury my nose in her hair. "Too dangerous."

"It wouldn't really be dry-humping then, either," she smiles wickedly as she loops her arms around my neck again. "Now show me what your teenage dreams were made of, Hotshot."

"This is more than a teenage dream, Luz. More like finally confronting the poltergeist that's been haunting me."

She drops her head to my shoulder and bursts into merry laughter. "I don't think I like being compared to a demonic spirit."

"Hold on, little demon," I tease as I hook her legs around my waist. When she locks her ankles in the small of my back, our bodies are finally flush against each other.

When I surge forward this time, every inch of me scrapes against her. Her head hits the wall with a thump, "Oh my god," she moans.

"It's been a really long time since I felt anything but my own hand around my dick, so I'm not gonna last very long."

Her eyes are half-veiled, shimmering smoky quartz when she raises her head. When she licks her lips, I chase her tongue back into her mouth. I'm hungry for this, for her.

"It's been a really long time for me too."

Her soft, raw confession floats between us. Reminding me this isn't a dream, or a haunting, but a woman, warm and real in my arms. A woman I can't stop thinking about. I need to make this as good for her as I know it's gonna be for me. "Hold on," I repeat with a growl as I thrust forward.

I can smell the salty musk of her arousal, like sunrise over the ocean, hot with promise. The circle of my hips as I tease us both draws the shiny material of her joggers tight over her thighs, and when I look down, it's a three-dimensional freeze frame of her spread over my girth. Like a fucking banquet. "Demon," I say again as I chase her mouth with mine. I suck her tongue, showing her all the ways I want to make her forget about the world. Her nails dig into my shoulders and her response is savage as she bites my tongue and then my bottom lip. I slide my palm under the waistband of her pants and cup the curve of ass I couldn't stop staring at that first day. I wish I could see the way her panties skim over it, and bite its lush bounty. When I grip her cheeks in my palms and nuzzle her collarbone, she gasps, "You're the demon," and bows her back as much as the wall will allow.

I've been hard for weeks, imagining this and more, and I'm going to make the most out of every second without taking us somewhere we can't afford to go. "Am I the only one?" I groan against her skin.

She whimpers. "No, I've been craving this too. Please touch me everywhere you can reach."

I lift a hand from her ass and skate it over the loose cotton hiding her breasts. I flick my thumb across one furled nipple and her answering moan is all the encouragement I need. I thrust between her bent knees, and dip my head.

The warmth of my breath is all I give her at first. She trembles when the direct stream of air hits her skin, and her nipple pebbles behind the material like a ripe cherry. Her moan echoes through the kitchen when I envelop it. When I use my teeth and tongue and lave it into a sweet little bud against the roof of my mouth, she bows her body nearly in half. One of her feet digs into the small of my back as she circles her hips. "Holy shit," she breathes, and I feel her body shiver against mine as she moans. It's long and quiet and I know she just found her release.

I've been holding back for so long, even from giving into dreams of her while I have my own hand wrapped around my dick, this is going to end way too soon. I fist my hand in the waistband of her pants, and pull them tight enough that I can feel every slick inch of her slide over me as I thrust forward and drop my forehead to the tangled mess of her hair.

My breath sounds like a freight train in the span of millimeters between us, and when she clenches the skin of my shoulder in her teeth, I lose control.

I surge against her, my head thrown back, my arms braced against the wall on either side of her body, and come so hard I almost black out.

The tinkle of her laughter is muffled against my shoulder. "Are you still hungry, Hotshot?"

"Yeah," I wryly admit. "But not for food."

Her hand lands in the middle of my chest as she lowers her legs from around my waist. "I'm not hungry for food, either."

My regret must already be showing, because she shakes her head. "Fine. We'll act like none of this happened."

I hitch up my jeans and re-fasten them, determined not to look at her. "It can't happen again. As much as I might want it to happen again, I can't let it. I took advantage of you just now."

She tightens her jaw and taps a nail between my pecs. "You didn't take advantage of me. I needed it too. Don't turn this into a power play, Hotshot."

"I'm not. Just stating a fact."

"You're seriously giving me whiplash. Go. Before I lose my temper completely," she tells me as she crosses her arms and glares.

"Going," I mutter and resist the insane urge to drop a kiss on her forehead.

Chapter Fifteen: Treading Water

Luz

I WENT TO THE dock after he left. Sitting under the stars, dipping my toes in the water was the first thing I wanted to do when I saw our cabin on the lake. That hasn't changed - but there never seems to be time for it. I took deep breaths and leaned back and waited for my heart to stop racing and the hurt to subside. Because when he kissed me, I knew how it was going to end - with him walking away. Probably regretting his loss of control. I kept telling myself that I spent my whole life without knowing the weight of Ian Montgomery's chin on my shoulder or the sight of him ruined.

It's been four nights and three days since he left me standing on my porch, and this is the first time since then we've been on shift together. I've kept my distance from him today. There was only one awkward moment - when we brushed past each other in the narrow hallway. He gulped, and his eyes followed me, but he didn't bother making any more excuses. He probably sensed I was ready to stab him with one of my bobby pins if he opened his mouth.

When I hear the iconic eighties rock anthem, I smile. I don't know who left the radio on, but I'm singing along as I make my way to the locker room to turn it off. I've only been in there once, when I was on clean-up duty, but I know it's empty. I volunteered to catch up the logs and buff the floors. Everyone's sleeping but me.

The sight that greets me when I round the corner isn't at all what I expected. Or the sound.

Ian Montgomery is standing in the open shower stall with his hand fisted around his cock. The water's sluicing over his shoulders and a lock of his hair is lying across the sharp blade of his cheek, darkened like a question mark dipped in blood.

He just groaned my name. That one hoarse syllable was unmistakable and the roughness of it arrowed straight to the part of my body I've been determined to ignore since our sweaty goodbye.

I should turn away and run as fast as I can in the opposite direction. This is way beyond the temptation of what happened when he walked away and left me with soaked panties and shattered nerves.

His head is thrown back and his eyes are closed, but I must make some sound or he has a sixth sense he's being watched, because he braces his free hand against the wall and turns toward me.

His eyes flicker before widening in surprise. There's a spark in their depths as his gaze roams over my face. But he doesn't stop what he's doing.

The chorus swells around us and I want to do exactly what it says. Pour sugar over him. And lick away every tiny crystal from his washboard abs and thick thighs. Chase every crumb of it across his shoulders and down the divot in his chin. Smear it over the dark lines of the tattoo above his heart.

It's the first time I've seen him without a full beard and he has a cleft that accentuates the strong line of his jaw but softens it too.

I lick my lips and his eyes glint with determination as they lock with mine. My gaze devours him as the tendons in his wrist flex and his head tips back again.

Like he can't help himself, or he's inspired by my gaze on him.

I'm rooted to the spot, turned to stone. Like I looked into Medusa's eyes.

"Do you want me to leave?" I croak. "I think I should leave."

He shakes his head and braces a hand against the wall as the water pours over him and pools around his clavicle and hip bone. "Stay," he commands in a voice that sounds like the low rumble of an engine. It should sound like one of our sirens - screaming danger and disaster. Because whatever the hell I walked in on is something I should walk away from. I should be bleaching my eyes out instead of wishing there were less shadows.

"Okay," I shakily agree as I struggle to keep my gaze on his face.

His mouth quirks, and even from twenty yards away, I can see the blazing heat in his eyes. He gives me an obnoxious, loaded grin. "You should watch everything, Martinez. It's what I was imagining when you walked in."

"What you were imagining?" The words almost strangle my throat.

His eyes skate over me and he sinks his teeth into his bottom lip. "You, Martinez. I was imagining your hand here. Like I wanted it there four nights ago."

"My hand?" My whole body feels tight and strung, like I'm standing on the edge of a cliff.

"Yep," he confirms with a rough stroke. "Your hand."

"How long have you been imagining my hand, Hotshot? Since the wall? Or since Twister?"

"Way before that, Martinez. Almost from the first second I saw you. And since you're standing here instead of running like you should, you're going to watch."

I toss my head and try to act haughty. "What if I don't want to watch?"

He throws his head back and laughs. "Oh, you want. I just saw you stick out that little pink tongue and lick your lips. You can deny you want it, but I know better."

"I shouldn't want it." My protest sounds halfhearted.

"Neither should I. But I'm getting really tired of denying my reaction to you. And I thought I had a moment of privacy to revel in it."

"I'm not interfering with your revels."

"The hell you aren't," he rumbles. "You're just making them more realistic."

"Well, obviously I didn't know you were in here doing that," I gesture toward the flex of his wrist like I'm affronted instead of turned on. "I just came in here to turn off the music."

"Hmmm," he murmurs with another flex of his wrist.

Chapter Sixteen: I Need You Like God Needs the Devil

- -

Ian

I KEEP MY EYES on her as I stroke harder and faster, the soap making the path smooth. Her hands are still in her pockets.

"Wanna give me some real-life inspiration?"

She shakes her head. "Someone could come in," she protests.

"Come on, Luz. Take off your shirt and let me see the tits I've been dreaming about. Those hard little nipples I tasted through your t-shirt."

When she bites her lip and takes her hands out of her pockets I know I won.

She whips the cotton over her head and I groan. She's not wearing a sports bra. Instead, she's wearing black satin and the fullness of her breasts almost spills out of it. I need to know what color her nipples are. If they're bronze or coral or soft pink. Or the dark amber red of ripe cherries.

"Let me see them," I hoarsely plead.

She blushes the color of one of our trucks but reaches behind and unclasps the bra. She slides it over her arms and when she goes to cover herself, I almost step out of the shower. "I've had three kids, Hotshot. My body isn't like one of those calendar spreads the guys keep in their lockers."

"Let me see, Luz, fuck, let me see. You don't have to do anything, just stand there and let me look. I already know you're perfect."

When she arches her back I give her a feral grin. "Just like that."

"I'm not an exhibitionist," she grumbles. "And in exchange for this, I get a better look at that tattoo later."

"You don't have to be an exhibitionist. This is the first and last time I'm gonna ask you to do this."

Her heavy breasts are topped with dark red tips, her hard nipples like maraschino cherries. I want to feel them against the roof of my mouth. I savor the thought of what her skin will taste like- how I'll breathe in the scent of summer mojitos when I bury my nose in her cleavage. Her body is ripe and lush - a humbling reflection of the lives she brought into this world. I want to trace every etched silver line she's trying to hide from me with my tongue, cup the full weight of those gorgeous tits in my palms.

When I open my eyes again, she has her bottom lip between her teeth. I know her well enough now to know that's her tell. "Are you turned on, Luz?"

"I've never watched something like this."

"Then you were missing out on being reminded how much power you have." I grip my base almost brutally, staving off my release. "You did this, only you. It's how I always am around you. I don't even have to see you. It can just be the wake of your perfume in the kitchen, or the sound of your laughter."

"I don't know why I'm the one who does this to you."

"I know why. Because you see me, Luz. Even when I want to hide who I am and what I'm feeling. It's scary as hell, but it's liberating too."

I let my release take over, and grit my teeth when I come even harder than I did during our teenage dream session. I watch it swirl down the drain before I shut off the water and turn to her.

She has her hands cupped over her breasts, and I can't tell what she's thinking from this far away. I don't bother with a towel when I stalk toward her. There's a trail of wet footprints and stray droplets when I come to a stop. When I stroke her collarbone with my wet finger, she inhales, like she can't find enough air to fill her lungs.

"Do you want me to take care of you?"

She shakes her head.

"Why not, Luz? Everyone's asleep and no one needs to know. I can be fast. I just want a taste."

"You didn't even look back."

Her voice is raw with hurt.

"Not because I didn't want to. Because I didn't trust myself not to turn back around and worship you all night long."

"What happened to just this one time, Hotshot?"

I laugh bitterly. "I knew when I said it I was lying to myself."

"Then why bother tormenting us both?"

"Because I'm trying to be a good person, Luz. I'm trying not to pressure you or make you uncomfortable. But let me take care of you the way you deserve to be taken care of."

"I told you whatever we do will be nothing more than me chasing the orgasms I've been missing, so maybe I should let you take care of me."

"Then you'll let me touch you? Taste you?"

Her nod is almost shy.

"Take off the rest of your clothes, Luz, and go sit on that bench," I tell her and point behind me to the bench along the back wall.

She obeys with shaky fingers, and drops everything in a pile. Once she's naked she walks past me, trailing her fingers through the water still dripping down my chest. She sits primly down on the bench and crosses her ankles.

I stalk toward her and when I'm standing in front of her, I stroke my already-hardening cock before I drop to the floor. I press the outer edges of her thighs until she spreads her legs and let my knuckles drift over her cleft. She shudders when I graze her clit, and her arousal coats my hand when I stroke her again. The scent of it, like a damp spring morning, fills the air.

I push one of her legs up, so she's open to me, her foot planted on the edge of the seat. I hold her there with a hand on her hip, and touch her again. This time, I crest the hood of her clit, and flick it roughly against the pad of my thumb. She closes her eyes and jerks toward me. I swirl her arousal through her curls, let it paint the length of every one of my fingers. When I bring them to my mouth and lick away her juice, her eyes darken. She hasn't said a word, but she hasn't moved either.

"Do you want this, Luz?"

She lifts her hand to my face and nods shakily. When I raise a brow, she tightens her grip, tangling it in my beard. "I want it," she confirms.

"Thank fuck," I mutter and scoop an arm beneath her hips. I lift her to my mouth and take one long, slow lick. The sound she makes starts with a wheeze and ends in a bellow. Completely feral. She grips the base of my neck and presses me harder, until her thighs are clenched around my head and we're fused together. I skate the edge of my teeth over her clit and give her an even slower, more sumptuous lick. She's the most decadent thing I've ever tasted.

She bucks her hips and tosses her head. Her hands dig into my scalp like sharp little claws, and if I didn't have an almost bruising hold on her waist, she'd be thrashing. When her writhing body snaps up, she's almost strangling me. I sip the juice from her soft, wet cunt and coast the pad of my thumb over her swollen clit. She moans and I do it again, scissoring two fingers inside her dripping entrance.

"Do you like it when I eat your pussy, Martinez?" I rumble into the crease between her thigh and hip.

"You're a champion pussy-eater, Hotshot," she gasps, all bright and sassy, all her shyness gone.

She tastes so good I'm getting hard all over again. Like the way I lost it in the shower didn't even happen. "Need you, Martinez." The confession escapes me before I can take it back.

"Take what you need, Hotshot," she says as she scrapes her nails across my nape and over my scalp.

I can't take everything I need. I need to wrap my hand around my cock and feed it to her, watch her lick the crown and inch it down her throat. I need to see the way she takes me deep and hard, in her mouth, into her body. I need to see the way her hair tangles around our bodies while we're sleeping, and the drowsy, sated look in her eyes from the night we've spent together. The look she has on her face when she's waking up - before she has her morning coffee.

I slide two fingers back inside, and twist them in and out, stroking her g-spot while I suck her clit against the roof of my mouth, rolling it over my tongue and letting it brush the edge of my molars. Her strong thighs surge against me as her heels thrum against my back. When she finally lets go, I groan and drop a hand to palm my dick. I lap up every drop of salt and sunshine, let it coat my tongue and my throat like I'm parched from a trek through Death Valley.

When I sit back on my heels, I cup her jaw in one hand and tweak one of those cherry nipples with the other. "You're fucking addictive."

"So are you, Hotshot." Her eyes are half-lidded and I bet this is the way she looks when she wakes up in the morning. Rosy and hazy and the most delicious thing I've ever seen. I stand reluctantly. Even though I told her not to worry, that everyone else was asleep, we weren't exactly quiet.

"We should get dressed."

She nods. "Help me up? I don't think I can stand on my own right now. And you're not allowed to cover up that tattoo until I get a better look at it. We had a deal."

I pull her to her feet, even though I'm wobbly too, and she twines her arms around my waist. Our skin sticks together as she leans against me, and I inhale the smell of our mingled musk and sweat. I lay my cheek on the crown of her head and close my eyes, just relishing the way it feels to hold her.

"This really shouldn't happen again," I murmur.

She giggles. "The last time you said that, you couldn't stick to it longer than three days."

I hold her tighter and groan, because she's right. "I'm your boss. I'm eleven years older than you are. I'm grumpy and jaded and I don't really like people."

This time her giggle coasts over my neck as she rises to the tips of her toes and plants a kiss on my jawline, just in front of my earlobe. "You're all bark and no bite, Hotshot."

"At least where you're concerned, I am. What are we gonna do, Luz?"

"We're going to see where this leads and not take ourselves too seriously. We both have a lot going on and maybe this is exactly what we're missing."

She steps away just far enough to slide her hands over my shoulders and chest. Her brow wrinkles as she peers more closely at my talisman. "Is it supposed to be fire?"

I've never explained why I got it. Not to anyone. "Yeah. It's the Celtic rune for fire. I got it after the canyon fire."

Her eyes flood with tears and understanding. I knew she'd get it.

"To remind you?" She whispers roughly.

I nod. "Yeah. It reminds me that fire can cleanse and kill. That it's to be respected and feared. It's to honor the people on my crew I've lost too."

"That's beautiful," she murmurs as she skims her nails over it again. "Mine's just the kids' initials."

"I showed you mine, are you gonna show me yours?"

She smacks me in the chest. "I showed you other things, and, like you said, we need to get our clothes on."

Chapter Seventeen: Rhetorical Questions

Luz

IT'S BEEN TWO DAYS since I caught my boss in the shower, and I still feel the glow of what happened afterwards. I'm in the best mood I've been in for months. Actually, probably the best mood I've been in for years.

We're over at Dex and Mari's for a combination late Cinco de Mayo and Memorial Day barbecue, when my brother corners me. It's a tradition we've kept up whenever we're together. Our parents and grandparents were an important part of the Chicano activist movement in the sixties, and in defiance of the way it was commercialized to help the alcohol industry,

I've made sure the kids know that we're celebrating the Mexican victory at the Battle of Puebla and all it stood for, not Mexican independence from Spain. We have photo albums full of pictures of our grandparents in reenactment costumes, and the kids are finally old enough to understand what it all means and how important it is to preserve our culture. The kids are chasing fireflies and Dex and I are finally relaxing on the porch to try his latest brew.

"You didn't tell me you went to book club with Ian Montgomery."

I should have known someone would rat me out and an interrogation by my protective older brother was inevitable. I shrug. "I wasn't hiding anything."

"Come on, Sis," he scoffs. "I know you better than that. If you weren't hiding anything you would have at least casually mentioned it. That was almost a week ago."

"There was nothing worth mentioning. My car needed a new starter, I needed a way to get to book club, and he had enough room on his motorcycle for two."

"And your kids were conveniently sleeping over at their aunt and uncle's house."

"It wasn't like that."

"It's the second time he's been over there."

"How do you know that?" I cross my arms.

"Your kids tell me everything, Luz. Especially stuff that involves Twister. And Rosie confessed to Mari that she thinks he has a crush on you because of your spaghetti."

"My kids need to keep quiet about things they don't understand."

He leans against the porch railing and surveys me over the rim of his beer. "He's not taking advantage of you, is he?"

When I sigh, I hope he can hear how exasperating I think his question is. "I'm a grown woman, Dex. I've worked too hard to let anyone take advantage of me. And I don't need my big brother stepping in every time he thinks I'm making a bad decision."

"That's not what I'm doing, Luz." He sounds just as exasperated as me.

"Then explain to me exactly what you think you're doing."

"I'm watching out for you, Luz. Because it's my job. I wasn't there for you when you needed me, and I'm damn sure gonna make up for it now."

I lay a hand on his arm, because I know his intentions are honest and he isn't trying to be overbearing. "You should never feel guilty about anything that happened to me while you were deployed, Dex."

He shakes his head in frustration. "If I hadn't been so dead set against taking over the body shop, I could have given you a place to stay when you left that asshole."

"I know you never liked him, but he gave me three beautiful kids. They're the one part of that journey I'll never regret."

"I love being their uncle, and I wouldn't change that for anything," he reaches over and throws an arm over my shoulder. "But your judgment in men leaves a lot to be desired, Luz."

"Not all of them can be big, protective cinnamon rolls like you. And Ian Montgomery's nothing like Benito Alvarez."

"Maybe not. But I think his demons are a lot worse."

"Neither one of us wants anything serious, so stop worrying about me."

"I can't help it. Just promise you'll be careful with your heart?"

"I'll try. But he's a lot easier to like than I thought he would be."

***

That night, after the kids are snug as bugs in their beds, my phone buzzes. It's a number I don't recognize, but I accept it because it might be the firehouse.

"Luz speaking," I quietly say as I step onto my porch.

"Hi Luz."

His voice washes over me like the moonlight filtering through the trees.

"Is something wrong? Do you need me to find someone to watch the kids and report to the station?"

His laughter is low - rusty and slightly reluctant. "No, we were all over at Sunset Lavender for a cookout and I missed you."

His admission catches me off-guard. "You missed me? We just saw each other yesterday."

"Yeah, but there were too many people around. I couldn't kiss you."

"There were probably too many people at the cookout too. People you'd also have to hide our kissing from."

"Yeah," he sighs and I hear the scrape of his nails against his bristle. "It doesn't make any sense, but I can't help the way I feel. I decided to do something about it today."

I swallow hard and hold the phone to my ear like it's a life preserver. "What was that?"

"I'm going to coach Rico's ball team. Because even if I can't kiss you, at least I'll be able to see you in something besides your t-shirt and coveralls."

"So whatever this is, it's still a secret?"

"Until we both decide otherwise. I know that Twister game was a ruse from Rosie, but I don't want to give your kids the wrong idea. It's probably hard to explain your relationships to them."

I laugh harshly. "I haven't had any relationships since I got pregnant with Rubi almost seven years ago. And that was with my ex-husband."

"So you've never had to navigate how to tell them mom needs a life too."

"There's never been any room for me to have a life of my own, Hotshot. I was married. And then I wasn't. But I had three kids to take care of and we were living with my parents."

"This is something neither one of us was expecting."

"No, you weren't in my plans, Ian Montgomery."

"You weren't in mine either, Luz Martinez."

He's quiet for too long after his confession, so I take a deep breath and the question spills out of me. "So why'd you really call me?"

"I told you. Because I've been thinking about you all day. About the way you felt in my arms when you laid your head against my chest. I want to see where we go."

"Starting with Rico's games?"

"Starting with Rico's games. The first one is in a week, right before the town ice cream social. Which you and the kids can come with me to. We can all go to the drive-in afterward that just opened afterward."

"Now you don't care who sees us kissing?"

"It won't be anything more than a peck on your cheek or forehead in public. But I was hoping we could hold hands."

"I got roped into being one of those booster moms that runs the concession stand."

"Good. Then I can pull you under the bleachers and give you a real kiss when we win the game."

"I've never necked under the bleachers, and I want to hold your hand too."

"Then it's settled. It's a family date. Do you want me to ask the kids' permission to date their mom?"

"If we're going to date, you should make sure Rico and Rosie are okay with it. They're the ones who knew their dad the best, and might have misgivings."

"Maybe I can stop over tomorrow and take you for a ride? There's a place I want to show you."

"If you show up on your bike, I might be tempted to re-enact that scene from Erin Brockovich."

His laughter rumbles through the phone. "The one where Julia Roberts asks him exactly what number he wants?"

"Yes. It's iconic. And trust me, the kind of thing most single moms experience when they try the dating thing."

"I don't have a problem with your kids, Luz," he somberly tells me. "In fact, I think they're adorable and I can't wait to get to know them better. I bet they're just as lovable as their mom."

"You're really not a porcupine, are you? You're more like a big, cuddly teddy bear."

"Don't tell anyone. Is it okay if I show up tomorrow afternoon around three? I have to make an appearance at my parents' for Sunday dinner first."

"That's perfect."

"Sweet dreams, Luz. Don't let the bedbugs bite. I'm the only one who's allowed to do that."

When he hangs up, I'm still smiling.

Chapter Eighteen: Every Time I Think I've Lost My Way

Ian

WHEN I PULL INTO her driveway, I hear her and the kids laughing in the backyard. The sight of Luz chasing the kids with the water hose makes me grin. There's a slip and slide and a kiddie pool and they're all shrieking like hyenas. They're all in bathing suits, and I let the sight of her in a coral red bikini soak in. One of the side ties is loose, and the ends are trailing down her wet thigh.

She has her hair pulled back in a long ponytail that just grazes the top of her ass.

Mom asked me to help dad plant some more bulbs after dinner, and when I told her I couldn't because I had somewhere to be, her eyebrows crawled almost all the way up to her widow's peak. "Where are you going on a Sunday afternoon, Ian Montgomery?" She'd demanded to know.

When I told her I was taking a friend for a bike ride, Jack interrupted us with a guffaw. "I knew it," he said as he doubled over with laughter.

I'd thrown him a look and dropped a kiss on Mom's cheek. "I'll tell you everything when I'm ready," I'd promised.

Now, as I watch them all running back and forth, completely oblivious to my arrival, something starts to knit back together that's been gone since I lost Justine.

"Do you have room for one more?" I call out as I step toward them.

Luz whirls around and loses her grip on the hose. It snakes into the air, and drenches all of us. Including me. She covers her hand with her mouth, "I'm so sorry."

The kids all start clutching their stomachs and cackling. Even I'm-too-grown-up-for-this eye-rolling Rico. Rubi topples over and rolls in the grass, kicking her feet in delight, her eyes closed.

I'd believe Luz's apology, but I can see the grin curling the edge of her mouth. "No, you're not," I say, as I stride toward her and yank my now drenched shirt over my head. She blushes and steps backward.

"Do you wanna play Marco Polo too, Mr. Montgomery?" Rubi excitedly interrupts.

My gaze meets Luz's and she shrugs.

I turn to Rubi. "Sure. Tell me the rules."

"Well, first you need a bathing suit," Rubi explains.

"Mr. Montgomery doesn't have a bathing suit," Rosie says. "And he doesn't need one to play."

"Fine. You can wear your clothes. Next you have to close your eyes while we go and hide. You have to count to one hundred."

The kids take off running and I turn to Luz again. "So tag I'm it?"

"Yep. And I mean, I'm not gonna complain if you want to strip down to your underwear."

"Seeing you in that bikini might have made that impossible."

She cackles. "When you get drenched with cold water again, it'll go away. Here, take this," she says as she hands me the hose.

I twist the nozzle to slow the stream of water. "What's the water hose have to do with the game?"

"It's a really long one, and you drag it with you. When you find them, you spray them with it until they say Marco Polo."

"That is not the game of Marco Polo I grew up with."

"There wasn't a neighborhood pool, so we made up our own version."

"If I get to see you in that every time we play, I could get used to the Martinez family version of the game."

She smiles mischievously. "I have a blue one too."

"You'd better go hide, if you're going to play."

When she saunters away, she blows me a kiss over her shoulder.

I count to one hundred, and when I'm done, I head in her direction first. There aren't that many places to hide, mainly behind the trees and under the balcony. I stroll toward the big oak at the edge of the woods.

I smell her before I see her. Coconut and lime. I think it's her shampoo and it's stronger because her hair's wet. Just as I'm about to turn the hose on her, she yanks me behind her tree and pulls my head down to hers.

The kiss is all-consuming. Her mouth is hot and the lycra and nylon of her bathing suit is cold where it's molded to her curves. I run my hands over her ass, and slide one of the bikini straps from her shoulder so I can chase the droplets of water from her shoulder to her cleavage.

"I like seeing you wet for me," I growl.

"I am wet for you," she admits. "And we have about four minutes before the kids come looking for us."

I slip my hand under that half-undone trailing tie at her hip and flick her navel. "Mmmm," she mumbles and tilts her head against the trunk.

When I dip a finger inside her and pinch her swollen clit, I know she wasn't lying. She's soaked at the thought of what she wants me to do to her, and my cock stirs behind my jeans, desperate to find out how she'll feel clenching around it.

I kiss a trail from her collarbone to her jaw. "This is torture. Not having enough time to savor you."

She nods vigorously in agreement. "My kids will get ideas. We need to stop until we know we're going to be alone for a while."

I remove my hand and drop my forehead to hers. "I can't take much more of this."

"Me either. But I helped you make the schedule and I know neither one of us has a free night for two weeks."

I lift my head and grin as I tuck her hair behind her ears. "Not until after we all go out for ice cream and movies."

Her eyes search mine.

"If we do that, my kids aren't just going to get ideas. They're going to make assumptions. Are you ready for that?"

"Luz, ask me what number I want," I say as I cup her nape.

She gulps and her gaze flicks over me again. "What number do you want, Hotshot? I got numbers comin' out my ears. We'll start with six - that's how old my youngest is. Do you wanna hear the rest of my numbers?"

Her hands grip the waistband of my jeans as I nod.

"The next number I have is twelve. That's how old Rosie is. And then there's Rico. He's fourteen. The last number I have is eighty-seven. That's how much money I have left in my bank account every two weeks when I finish paying bills and buying groceries. If you're still interested, the number you're asking for is eight zero four five five five, zero zero five six."

"Oh, I'm still interested. In those numbers and the numbers you didn't tell me about. Like how many times someone's walked away when you told them those numbers, and how many times you had to be strong for other people instead of crying like you wanted to. How many times you wished you could start over again, and how many times you've thought about me and touched yourself in the dark. I wanna know all those numbers too," I admit as I kiss her softly.

She shakes her head. "You could wreck a woman, Ian Montgomery."

When I swipe her bottom lip with my thumb, she nips it. "There's only one woman I wanna wreck, and she's standing right in front of me."

"I think we'd better go find the kids- before we get distracted again."

I drop a quick kiss on the tip of her nose and grab her hand. "Come on. We'll find them together."

She stoops to scoop up the discarded hose and slips it in my empty hand. "You're forgetting the most important part."

I can't resist another kiss. "No, I'm not," I tell her when I come up for air.

We look behind every single tree, expecting the kids to pop out squealing at any second. They're nowhere to be found.

"I'm not going to worry, yet. Let's check inside- maybe they got tired of waiting."

"Let me grab my shirt."

I don't really want him to put it back on, because I've been surreptitiously drooling over the flex of every single muscle, but I pick it up and toss it at him.

He slips it over his head and reaches for my hand again.

When we stroll into her kitchen, Rico is stirring a pitcher of red Kool-Aid. The girls are seated on the bar stools, kicking their legs.

"Hey, Mom," Rosie greets us with a grin that seems too innocent.

Luz stacks her hands on her hips and gives her daughter a stern look. "Don't hey mom, me. I was starting to worry. Why aren't you guys still hiding?"

"We were hot and we got tiwed of waiting," Rubi pipes up.

"Rosie said we needed to leave you alone so you and Mr. Montgomery could kiss. I told Rosie and Rubi I'd make some lemonade and you wouldn't care if we got some popsicles from the freezer."

Her son's frowning down at the pitcher instead of looking at us. I have a feeling he's the one I really need to convince I'm not going anywhere if I decide I want Luz for good.

"So what are we having for dinner? Or did you bambinos fill up on grape popsicles?"

Rubi slides off the stool and throws her arms around Luz's waist. When she looks up at her mom, you could park an air carrier on her bottom lip. "Can we have pizza, Mommy?"

Luz's expression is troubled. "There isn't any pizza. You ate the last one we had in the freezer on Friday to celebrate the start of summer vacation."

"Can't we order one, Mom? Please?"

They all have hopeful looks on their faces and I remember what she said about the eighty-seven dollars. Spending twenty-five dollars to have pizza delivered will put a serious dent in her bank account. "If you guys let me help you eat it, I could get us some pizza."

Their mom gives me a sharp look. "My kids can do without what they want for one night, Mr. Montgomery." She crosses her arms and turns back to them. "Sing the song."

There's a chorus of sighs..

"Come on."

Rico rolls his eyes and clears his throat. "Fine. You can't always get what you want. You can't always get what you want. But if you try sometime, you'll find you get what you need."

"Exactly. And what the three of you hooligans need is food. It doesn't have to be pizza."

I'm between awe and hilarity at the fact she taught her kids the chorus of a Rolling Stones song to teach them humility and keep them from being spoiled.

I don't know if what I'm going to propose will piss her off, but I'm willing to take the chance. "But what if I'm the one who wants pizza and I need someone to share it with?"

Rubi starts jumping up and down. "Pweeze, Mom! Can Mr. Montgomwy get us pizza?"

She narrows her eyes at me. "If he promises to take the leftovers home."

"Cross my heart," I tell her and do just that. "I know Gus delivers out here because he delivers all the way out to Sunset Lavender, and you're closer than that."

Her glare incinerates me as I dial the number and I know I'm going to have to beg forgiveness for stepping in when she was trying to parent. "Why don't the three of you play frisbee in the backyard until the pizza gets here? I'll be out in a sec."

They shuffle to the door and then break onto the lawn in a dead run. She shakes her head and smiles softly.

Hopefully, their exuberance mellowed her a little bit.

"As for you," she grinds out as she steps toward me and pokes me in the chest. "What the hell was that? You interfered."

I throw my hands in the air. I was right, she's pissed. Honestly, she has every right to be. "I was thinking about one of the numbers you gave me."

"Which one?"

"The balance in your checking account. That's partly my fault because I'm your boss, and if your kids want pizza and it'll mean a night you don't have to cook, I'm going to pay for it."

"Of course you'd give me the one right answer," she grumbles. "I really didn't feel like cooking tonight."

"And you won't have to do dishes either. Gus knows to add a stack of paper plates to my order."

"I should probably give you shit for being so prepared, or being such a guy that you have a standing order for paper plates, but the one thing I miss about living with my parents is their state of the art dishwasher."

I slide my hands around her waist and haul her closer. "My mom refuses to buy one. She says they use too much water and she likes making her grown children show her they appreciate her cooking by volunteering to wash the dishes."

"Do you ever volunteer?" She asks as she loops her arms around my neck.

"All the time. I like showing the women in my life how much I appreciate their sacrifices."

"What sacrifices do you think I've made?" Her teasing tone has an undercurrent of sincerity.

"I think you've made almost too many to count. A mom at nineteen. A marriage to someone who couldn't, or wouldn't, support your dreams. Balancing the demands of putting food on the table and spending time with your kids. Your life is all about sacrifices and selflessness," I conclude as I kiss her cheek. "So don't be mad at me for ordering pizza."

"I should be, but that was a pretty awesome apology, Hotshot," she concedes.

I realized something today - Luz's support system is paper thin. Justine was lucky because her parents basically co-parented Tristan. I don't think Luz has ever had that luxury. Even when she and her kids were living in Florida. It makes me ache for her and respect her strength even more. It amazes me that she's honed her capacity for patience and kindness instead of losing it.

Chapter Nineteen: I'm in this With You

Luz

AFTER THE KIDS HAVE completely demolished one of the pizzas, Ian pushes his chair away from the table. "Rico, I promised your mom a ride on my bike tonight. Will you watch your sisters for thirty minutes?"

Rico's chest puffs out at Ian's request. I just started letting him babysit about three months ago, but never for more than a quick trip to the gas station a few miles away. I'm always afraid something's going to happen while I'm gone - like a house fire or a natural disaster.

"Sure."

Ian gives him a sharp nod, one man to another. "I'll be counting on you to hold down the fort. Your mom's going to change into long sleeves and pants, and then it's all yours."

I slide away from the table too. "I'll be right back."

I stand in front of my closet for at least five minutes because a lot of my clothes are still in boxes or sitting in the dirty laundry. My denim jacket is crammed on a hanger in the very back, so I slip it on over one of my t-shirts and shimmy into a pair of comfy jeans. When I emerge from my bedroom, he's waiting in the hallway and I slip my hand in his when he stretches it in my direction.

"I'll have my phone with me, so there's no excuse not to call me if anything comes up," I warn Rico as we head for the door.

He rolls his eyes at me. "Mom, I love you, but you're a worry wart."

"Rico, your mom has reason to worry. Bad things happen all the time and she's just doing her job. Watch your sisters and be glad you have a mom that worries about you instead of leaving you to your own devices."

"There aren't very many places we can go that are thirty minutes round-trip."

He smirks as he tugs me outside. "Oh ye of little faith. I know you grew up here, but I think you've forgotten a lot."

I snort. "I haven't forgotten that there aren't that many places to hang out but the lake and the woods. And when you're a teenager, going to those places is just an excuse to make out."

"Maybe that's where I'm taking you because that's what I want to do. I even bought an extra helmet," he says as he pulls it out of one of the saddlebags and hands it to me.

"Then you lied," I tell him as I fasten the helmet under my chin. "Because you gave me the impression you were showing me one of your secrets."

He taps my cheek. "All I said was that there was something I wanted to show you. You took away that impression all by yourself."

"Well, the clock is ticking and Rico's probably already started a countdown. So let's go."

He tweaks my chin again. "You're adorable when you're being sassy. Hop on behind me once I have it revved."

Obediently, I scramble up behind him once the engine's purring. This time, I splay my hands over his thighs and cradle his body. If I'm going to be plastered against him, I'm determined to get my money's worth.

The bike speeds forward with a tiny lurch and before I can blink, we're following the shimmering ribbon of road along the lakeshore. Spring settles over me like a mantle, and the slight chill of a breeze from the west skims over my exposed knuckles. It's a gentle caress that carries the perfume of the blooming redbud and dogwood trees that dot every hillside with bursts of color. It stirs the leafy branches that reach over the road, and when I take a deep breath all the things weighing on me are less of a burden.

He slows down when we get close to one of the gravel pull-offs I've passed hundreds of times. I have no idea why it's there and I'm always too busy, on my way to somewhere else, to explore. Once the bike is parked, the engine dies and he removes his helmet. "Are you ready for an adventure, Magnolia?"

His question is muffled through my helmet, and once I take it off, I lay a hand on his shoulder. "Did you call me Magnolia?"

A flush creeps over his cheekbones. Like two twin flags of red glowing over his bearded jaw. "I couldn't keep calling you demon."

"But why Magnolia?"

"It's my favorite tree. Those big, blowsy blooms that make everything smell like heaven. It sounds crazy now, but the way you smell, and your smile, they're basically my version of heaven. And when I'm around you, everything else gets cancelled out."

I'm a little rattled by his confession. "The grumpy fire chief I know doesn't say stuff like that."

"I'm not grumpy, Magnolia. Just barricading myself against the pain of the world. You stepped over all of my defenses like they were nothing more than a stack of paper."

He dismounts and then holds his arms out. When I swing my leg over the backrest, his arms envelop me. His embrace feels like the hug in my kitchen that happened last week. Too essential. Too much like something I could learn to depend on.

"It's from that movie Steel Magnolias, too. It's one of my mom's favorites. She says it shows how women bend without breaking. You're one of the strongest women I've ever met, Luz."

A pack of coyotes starts yipping in the distance and I step away. "Show me before the creatures of the night ambush us."

"Follow me," he says and grabs my hand.

The trail curves through the woods, and I pull out my phone so I don't trip over any roots or step on anything slimy.

When we've gone about a hundred yards, the trees start thinning.

"Not much further."

"Good, because these woods look creepy at night. Especially when there isn't a full moon. And I'm not too keen on meeting a black bear or a pack of coyotes."

"I have bear spray in the pocket of my jacket, Luz. We'll be fine."

He comes to a stop at the foot of a giant poplar. "You wanted to show me a tree?"

He breaks into laughter and tugs me into him. "Not just any tree, Luz. This is the kissing tree."

"The kissing tree? I've never heard of it. Especially out here in the middle of nowhere."

"My grandfather told us it was more than three hundred years old. Look," he shines his flashlight on a patch of bark about halfway up the tree. There's a heart with four words carved into its center.

My Spanish is rusty because the kids and I don't speak it at home as much as we should, but this looks like it could be a romance language. "Guance dolci and gatta selvatica," I read aloud. "What's this mean?"

He rubs his hand over the grooved wood. "They were my great-great-grandparents. My great-great grandfather was Italian-American and these were the nicknames he and his wife had for each other. My granddad still speaks it a little and there's this family legend that her nickname for him was how she thought you said sweet cheeks in Italian. She was wrong, and it cracked up her husband."

"So that's the top nickname? Sweet cheeks?" He nods. "Then what's the second nickname mean?"

"It's wildcat in Italian."

"That's sweet, but I still don't understand why you brought me up here."

He covers my eyes with one hand and tugs me around the tree. "Look down," he tells me as he takes his hand away.

When I do, the whole town is laid out in the valley below us. All you can see from here is a bunch of lights, the shadowy steeple from the Presbyterian church and the outline of the clock tower at the top of the courthouse.

"I used to come here all the time when I got back," he rasps. "It grounded me, to see it all laid out like this. Coming back here wasn't what I wanted, but it's what I needed. I like to think that's why my ancestors stayed here too - because these mountains and this town gave them things they knew they couldn't find anywhere else."

What he's telling me settles in my chest. Maybe Willow Creek holds more of the things I needed than a support system. Maybe I should use it like one of those trampolines that launches you into the air instead of one that catches you when your life is at a crossroads. "Is your name on that tree, Hotshot?"

He pulls me into him and wraps his arms around me from behind. "No, Magnolia. I wasn't ready for any of that when I left town all those years ago. And I haven't really explored those options since I got back."

I gulp. "What's different now? You said you'd tell me about the calendar your brother keeps hinting about."

"You're what's different, Luz. You get it. That being a firefighter isn't about the suspenders and the boots and women who want me to carry an ax or show them my firehose."

I'm shocked into laughter by his surly explanation. "They did not say something that corny."

He shrugs behind me. "A couple of them did when they propositioned me after the first calendar came out. The last straw was the woman who called the firehouse because her kitty was in a tree and specifically asked for me because she said I'd helped her before. When I got on the scene, there was definitely a pussy in the tree and it was not of the feline variety."

I bring a hand up to cover my mouth. "She was naked?"

"Not just naked. She was aiming for her coxys and superglued the fake tail to her asshole instead. An emergency room visit was required."

I touch one of the hands he has wrapped around me. "I'm sorry. That must have been so awkward and mortifying. Did they usually proposition you in private?"

He grunts. "Kind of. Every once in a while they'd show up randomly at the station looking for me. So I could autograph my picture."

"They didn't harass the other guys?"

"Nope. Just me. My name was the only one on the calendar, because it said to contact me if anyone who bought the calendar wanted to make an additional donation. It listed my email. I had to change it because there were so many invitations in there I couldn't even find the information I needed. Of course my brother thought it was hilarious."

I brush my thumb over his knuckles. "But you're a private person. I don't know Jack well, but I don't think he's ever had a private thought in his life."

His answering laugh is more relaxed and I breathe a sigh of relief. The tension and anger he still feels about what he calls the calendar fiasco was seeping through his embrace. "I think you're right about Jack. I wanted to show you this because I think deep down you need a home too, Magnolia. A home that's more than four walls and your kids. Somewhere you can feel the vines twining around you, holding you in place and giving you gravity."

"I think you're right. Thanks again, Hotshot."

The air stirs as he plants a kiss just behind my ear. "Now that you know it's here, you can visit whenever you need to."

I dip my head in a silent yes.

"We should head back to the house," he murmurs as he strokes my arm.

I sigh in agreement. I may have grumbled about the journey, but the destination was worth it. Especially feeling his warmth wrapped around me beneath the stars. I'm standing on more than the precipice of a valley. "Okay, let's go."

This time, I lead the way. The clouds finally floated away from the full moon, and the yipping coyote pack sounds far away. His hand is curled in mine, and his chest brushes against my back every few steps. Even though I'm not as nervous as I was on the trip up the hill, his nearness is comforting.

I want to hoard the tiny moments pressed against him on the bike, the ripple of wind inside my jacket, and the way his thighs are solid between mine as we lean into the curves. We're slowing down in front of the gravel driveway before I'm ready to let go.

After he hangs my helmet on the handlebars, he twists around in the seat and cups my jaw. "Can I have a goodnight kiss?"

"It's going to be an awkward one at this angle, and I just saw the curtains flutter. I think we have an audience."

He snickers. "They're probably in there high-fiving each other."

"I know Rosie's happy about whatever's happening, but I think Rico's still on the fence."

"That means I need to work harder at winning him over."

"I thought this thing between us was just a way to blow off steam."

He peers at me in the dim circle of light from the porch. The yard's fringed by trees, and mostly in shadow. "It's always been more than that for me. Guess I never figured on being the one that had to do all the convincing."

My breath suddenly constricts my lungs. "I'm a package deal, Hotshot, and I have to protect my kids from fallout."

His thumb strokes my cheek and he tips up my chin. "I know, Magnolia. You're the real deal."

When his lips land on mine, I'm overwhelmed. The soft, slightly chapped texture of his lips, the bristle of his beard, the tickle of his mustache. The way the locusts are humming in the trees and the sound of whippoorwills calling to each other through the night air. The perfume of the redbud and wild honeysuckle blooming on the edge of the yard.

He tastes like cinnamon and hazelnut, like he dumped it in his afternoon coffee. I have a flashback to the way he stirred the milk into his mug after our book club foray.

His lips mold the outline of mine, and swallow the gust of breath I exhale before he nips the corners of my mouth, like he's demanding entrance. Our tongues tangle together and suddenly both of his hands are cupping my face, holding me still. It feels like I'm suspended and spinning from a single rope, weightless and dangling over the ground, his hands sure and strong the only thing anchoring me.

The kiss gentles and slows until we're just swaying with our foreheads pressed together.

"I'll see you at the game," he tells me as his hands slide from my hair.

This time, as I watch his taillight disappear, I don't feel cold.

***

The girls bolt away from the window when I ease the door open. Rico stands there, glowering, arms crossed. "Are you dating him, Mom?"

Rosie rolls her eyes. "Duh, Rico. We saw them kiss."

Their interrogation flusters me, because I think I know the answer to that question, but I'm not sure. "It's complicated, Rico."

"It's a yes or no question, Mom."

"Then the answer is yes."

"He's my coach, Mom. It's embarrassing. And we don't need anyone else hanging around."

How am I supposed to explain to my kids that even though I love them, I need someone for myself?

"Ian and I will do our best not to embarrass you, Rico."

"Good, because otherwise I'll get nothing but shit from the other guys on my team."

"Rico, language. What have I said about using vocabulary instead of profanity?"

"That only lazy people use profanity when they could be expanding their vocabulary instead," he grumbles. "But I've heard you swear."

"I'm not fourteen years old and I've had plenty of time to expand my vocabulary."

"You're supposed to set a good example."

His tone is belligerent and I know this whole conversation is really about the fact that he's feeling replaced. I walk over and set my hand on his shoulder. "Rico, I do everything I can to show you and your sisters how to be strong individuals who make the world a better place just by being in it. Even those kinds of people swear every once in a while. What's this really about?"

"Rico doesn't want anything to change," Rosie explains.

"He said we don't need anybody," Rubi pipes up.

"It's not about changing our family or whether we need somebody else. Sometimes life is about opening up your heart when you least expect it."

Rico throws his arms around my waist. He sprouted up like a weed last year, and he's almost as tall as I am. "I'm sorry, Mom," he mumbles.

I run my hand over his tousled head, enjoying his moment of vulnerability. He doesn't let me see very many of them. "It's okay, baby boy."

He pulls away, scowling, the moment lost. "I'm not a baby."

"You'll always be my baby, Rico. Even when you're all grown up. Get used to it."

"Just not around my friends, Mom. Okay?"

"Sì, bambino," I tease.

"I'm bambino, not Rico," Rubi pouts.

She giggles when I swing her into my arms. It's her little baby giggle and I haven't heard it much since she started kindergarten. I rub our noses together. "You're my bambino too. And so is Rosie. You're all my bambinos."

Rubi throws her arms around my neck and plops a kiss on my cheek. "I love you, Mommy," she sighs happily into my neck.

***

Today's Rico's first game.

When Dex proudly presented me with the matching gear he ordered for all of us, I was touched. Rico deserves to have his own cheering section and hopefully we won't embarrass him. I'm rounding the corner of the bleachers so I can lean against the fence and wave to Rico, and a hand snakes around my waist from behind. I know what the solid weight of Ian's arm feels like now, warm and familiar.

I smile up at him when he twists me around and brings me closer.

"You have on a team jersey."

He pecks each of my cheeks before he kisses me softly on the lips. The crowd is still weaving past us and climbing into the bleachers, and I seriously doubt our canoodling went unnoticed.

"Dex ordered them for the whole family from some online store. They all have Rico's number on the back because he said it would make my son feel like he was a superhero."

He grins even wider. "It will make him feel invincible. Which we'll need against this team, so I'm grateful."

"Who's this?"

I've seen the guy around who's interrupting us, but we've never been introduced. He sticks out his hand.

"I'm Alex McIntyre. Jess's dad. I think our kids are chemistry lab partners."

I take his hand and shake it heartily. "Rico hasn't said anything, but you know how teenage boys are. I'm Luz."

"It's great to finally meet you. My fiancee, Vanessa, is around here somewhere. She's been dying to talk to you."

"We've met?"

He chuckles. "Nope, but she said she's never seen her brother so distracted." He casts an amused glance at the man standing rigidly beside me. "She also said she's never met any of his girlfriends."

"But, I'm not..." I trail off as Ian squeezes my hand.

"We're still pretty new," he tells Alex. "So maybe warn my sister to control her excitement."

Alex's brows fly toward his hairline. "I'll make sure she knows to keep her cool," he says as he shoves his hands in his front pockets and rocks on his heels.

The silence becomes more awkward by the second until the guy who's suddenly become my boyfriend thrusts the clipboard he;s been carrying in Alex's direction. "Why don't you get the team lined up for the first inning? The batting strategy's on the first page. I'll be over there in a minute."

He lifts my twisted hands and plants kisses over my knuckles. "Relax, Magnolia, it'll be okay."

I try to tug my hands away, but his hold is unbreakable. "I'm in this thing with you - no matter where it takes me. I don't care who sees me holding your hand or kissing your cheek. Or lifting you up," he finished as he wraps his hands around my waist. He twirls me in the air and even though no one's looking directly at us, it feels like we're the center of attention.

"People are watching," I protest.

"You're a magnolia. You don't care if people watch. I bet you dare them to watch. And I don't care if they are, so why should you?"

"You were moving like a reluctant turtle, denying whatever this thing is between us, and now you're moving at warp speed. You're making my head spin."

"I just figured it was about time I leaned into something."

"You could have warned me before you did an about face," I grumble.

He just chuckles. Nothing like the thundercloud I met on my first day. At least not toward me. "I know you have to report to your concession stand duties, find me when the game's over?"

"You find me. I know I'll get stuck on clean-up duty."

"Fine. I'll find you. Save me a pretzel," he says as he plants a kiss between my eyebrows.

I step away and head for the concession stand. When I look over my shoulder to wave, he's rooted to the spot, watching me walk away like I cast a spell on him.

As soon as I get to the concession stand the other mom I'm paired up with backs me into a corner. "We can't figure out how you got him to notice you," she hisses. She has spiral curls, like those nineties perms, and when she purses her lips you can tell she's a smoker. I bet she's a bitter former mean girl and I'm not going to let her bully me.

"Well, I wasn't chasing him. Maybe that's why he noticed me."

I knew this was inevitable. Because everyone's been telling me Ian Montgomery doesn't date. And a whole bunch of people saw him kiss me before he strode into the dugout.

"Bless your heart," she sneers, and I know she means exactly the opposite. In that condescending eat-shit-and-die, you-just-fell- off-the-turnip-truck way some Southern women have. "Don't get your hopes up about anything that lasts, darlin'."

"We're just seeing each other and I don't expect a ring."

"Best not. That man isn't interested in settling down. We've all been tryin' to get him in the sack since he came home and he isn't takin' the bait. Why would he want some illegal instead of one of us?"

I'm not an illegal, and I know she knows that. I wouldn't be working for the fire department if I didn't have citizenship. She's just trying to get under my skin and make me lose my temper. Because she's jealous. I take a deep breath. "I'm not an illegal. I grew up here."

"You still don't belong. And Lord knows what you get up to in that firehouse with all those men."

I clench my fists. "I get up to my job. Which I was hired to do."

She sniffs again. "Yeah, sweetheart. We all know what that job is. No wonder he's with you."

Ian Montgomery and I might want to bang each other's brains out, but that's none of her business. Or anyone else's. "Let's just agree to be cordial, okay? We're here to help raise money for our kids' team, and it's not going to make the afternoon go by any faster if we're rude."

"I'm not tryin' to be your friend," she snarls.

Her hostility is exhausting. "I didn't say you were. I'm not either. Let's just play nice, okay?"

She shrugs as she turns away. "I know how to keep my mouth shut."

I don't think she does, but I know better than to argue. A tiny part of me feels sorry for her because her bitterness has to come from somewhere. "Great," I say as I bend down and open the cooler. The booster president told me all of the hotdog stuff would be in it, and the sodas were in a crate ready to be stocked in the fridge.

Once we have everything set up and the hotdogs are in the warmer, I breathe a sigh of relief. My partner hasn't said a word since her snide comments, and I'm grateful. Even though I can feel her animosity, she hasn't acted on it again.

I'm relieved when we run out of everything but the chips and soda because the card reader stopped working after the first half hour and I've been calculating change in my head since we had to go to cash only transactions. There was a lot of grumbling because if they wanted to eat they had to go to the ATM, but it was manageable.

We win the game - and my son is the one who sends the pitch into the far corner of the outfield and gives us the homerun that takes our team over the top. I watch from my perch on the sidelines while his teammates all high five him and then lift him in the air in a victory carry. My heart aches with pride and relief because this feeling of belonging and coming into his own is what I wanted for him.

My fellow mom ditched her duties about ten minutes ago, and honestly I'm glad of the peace. I'm sweeping the concrete floor when a pair of arms snags me around the waist from behind.

"Rico won us that game. And it's all because he has a mom and a family that show him every day they have faith in him and are proud of him," he murmurs into my hair.

Tears spring to my eyes, because that's exactly the kind of parent I want to be. "Thanks, Hotshot," I croak.

He twirls me around so I'm facing him. "Are you crying, Magnolia?"

I sniff and brush my hand over my eyes. "No, not really. That's exactly the kind of thing this single boy mom needed to hear right now."

"Well, you're a great mom and you're doing a fantastic job. Anytime you need to hear it, let me know. I'll give you all the affirmation you need."

"I wonder sometimes if the sacrifices I've made are worth it, if my teenage kid is going to hate my guts for the next four years," I tell him as I slide my hands up his chest.

He catches my chin and tips it up. "Your kid talks about you all the time. He's proud of you too. Just maybe no more forehead or cheek kisses in front of his friends."

That makes me cackle. "Little does he know how grateful he should be that I don't embarrass him the same way my mom used to embarrass me."

"There's no way your mom was as bad as mine. Grace Montgomery asked my freshman girlfriend if she wanted to reserve a spot in the family crypt we were building. And every year she and my dad dress up like Morticia and Gomez for Halloween. Except they wear nothing but those costumes for a week."

His parents sound both creepy and awesome. "You have a family crypt?"

He rolls his eyes. "No. It was her idea of a joke because she couldn't stand Ashleigh. It worked, because she broke up with me the very next day."

"I think you win. The most embarrassing thing my mom ever did was yell my full name across a parking lot and tell me to make good choices and always use condoms."

"The whole always use condoms thing is pretty obnoxious."

I groan and bury my head in my hands before bursting into laughter. "You're right. Needless to say, I was a virgin until after I ran away with my ex-husband."

He grins conspiratorially. "High school was a virgin experience for me too. I had two one night stands before I met Justine, and then it was only her. I like monogamy."

His confession warms me up from the inside, like a slice of apple pie straight from the oven. "Ben's the only person I've ever done anything with besides you. And my toys," I admit with a blush.

"Your toys?" He sounds far too intrigued.

"I'm not ashamed," I tell him sternly. "I'm a single mom who's had no time for dating and worries that bringing a stranger around will result in irreparable psychological harm to her kids."

He drops his head and nips my earlobe. "But I'm not a stranger, Magnolia. And maybe I want to see how you use your toys."

"Some things just need to stay in a drawer, Hotshot," I tell him with flaming cheeks.

He strokes my hair. "It looks like neither one of us is what our parents would call worldly."

I nod. "Physical intimacy should mean something. I can't be with someone I don't already feel a connection with."

"I agree. Which is why all these things I feel for you have me in a tailspin. I do have a question, though."

"Should I be scared?"

He smiles and shrugs. "Probably. I just want to know if you've opened that drawer since you caught me in the shower. And if you have, did you open it because you were thinking about me?"

"I'm not answering that."

"You just did," he whispers smugly. "I'd take you between these buildings and show you just how much I like your non-answer, but people, especially your kids, will come looking for us soon. Will you settle for a kiss under the bleachers?"

"There's no jumbotron to worry about, so yeah, I think I can agree to that."

"So that's the only reason you'll kiss me under the bleachers?"

I loop my arms around his neck and press a kiss to the cleft in the middle of his chin. "Maybe not the only reason, but definitely the most convincing one."

He swats my butt and picks me up. I'm hanging over his shoulder, squealing and pounding my fists against his back when he lopes back to the field.

He sets me on my feet when we come in sight of the bleachers and presses soft kisses all over my face that make me giggle. "The jumbotron spotlight isn't usually reserved for those kinds of kisses," I tease.

"No, it's not," He says and backs me up against one of the columns. His head drops to my neck and he inhales. "I can still smell the lime and coconut - even though it's mixed with popcorn and ketchup."

"The other mom was basically useless. I'm surprised I don't smell worse."

He lifts his head and frowns. "Do I need to say something to someone?"

"No, Hotshot. I can take care of myself. Besides, if you intervened that would only add fuel to the fire."

"Was she harassing you?"

"Nothing I'm not used to. It was for a different reason than it usually is, but still something I'm used to dealing with."

"Like what, Luz?"

"Comments about illegal immigrants and how they take things away from the people who deserve them."

"Tell me her name, Luz."

I shake my head. "Nope. Not worth it, Hotshot. If I let every single petty comment and ignorant person get under my skin I wouldn't be able to sleep at night."

"Why did she think she had the right to make those comments?"

"She saw us and got jealous. She wants you for herself."

He tips my chin up. "Well she can't have me. I think I already belong to someone else. Or at least it's starting to feel that way."

My big sister's words echo in my head. *You shouldn't hesitate to claim a chance at happiness because you're afraid of the potential consequences.* "I'm beginning to feel the same - and it scares the crap out of me."

"I'll be careful with you and your kids, Luz. I promise."

"Things happen, Ian. I'm just going to take each day at a time and see where this goes."

The kiss he plants on my forehead feels both fragile and steady. "I'm honored you're taking a chance on what we could become, Magnolia."

His endearment curls around my heart when he takes my hand and leads me toward the dugout.

Chapter Twenty: Working on a Feeling

Ian

I WAS ON SHIFT last night and none of us got very much sleep. There was a pile up on the interstate when a tractor trailer jack-knifed around a curve, and there was a fire in the mobile home park last night. The driver of the semi-truck walked away with only a mild concussion, but the families from the park now have nowhere to live. Zane called everyone on the ice cream social organizing committee this morning, including my mom, and told them all the proceeds from today would go toward helping those families instead of buying something for the town. Willow Creek is a close-knit, compassionate community, and I don't think anyone will have a problem with it. Now I'm running late because Mom asked me to help load up her Expedition with clothes and all kinds of other stuff for the now homeless families.

I'm exhausted and caved and bought an energy drink because I want to experience every moment today with Luz and her kids.

When I texted Luz to let her know I was running late she sent me the hand over the face emoji - I don't think her morning went as planned either. The girls are sitting on the porch eating orange popsicles when I get there, and the screen door slams as soon as I turn off the engine.

"Mom!" Rico hollers. "He's here! Stop primping and let's go."

"You didn't make your bed, Rico! You know that tomorrow's laundry day. Get your butt up here and strip the sheets."

When she steps onto the porch, I swallow. Hard. She's wearing a bright red t-shirt and cutoffs. She's wearing a pair of black tennis shoes and she has her long hair tied up in a ponytail. She looks like everything a summer day should look like and it's suddenly hard to breathe.

"Hi, Hotshot."

I shake my head to clear it. "Hi, Magnolia. Are you and the gang ready to go?"

"They've been ready for hours. I gave them popsicles so they'd stop asking when you were going to be here every three seconds."

"Sorry. Dad couldn't lift the boxes down from the attic Mom wanted, and she said she doesn't trust him on the rickety ladder anyway."

She meets me halfway up the steps and presses a quick kiss to my cheek. "I heard about the fire, and that it took you guys half the night to put it out. Are you sure you still want to do this? You're probably exhausted."

"I wouldn't miss it. I can't wait to see Rico with the old-fashioned ice cream maker. I'm a little tired, but I'm off for a couple of days, so I can catch up on the sleep I need."

She taps me in the middle of my chest. "You shouldn't make a habit of that, Hotshot. Your body needs sleep."

I flick the end of her ponytail. "I know. And I promise I'll get the rest I need."

"You should take naps like me, Mr. Montgomery," Rubi pipes up.

"It's too bad the grown-up world doesn't think I need them, Rubi," I say as I drop to a crouch and pat her head.

Her little snub nose wrinkles up in response. "My teacher Miss Jones says everybody needs naps and quiet time."

"Miss Jones is right. Maybe I need to make some changes."

"Mommy leaves her phone in her purse and shuts the door when she doesn't want us to bother her."

"Only when you pester me every fifteen seconds and make me forget what's on my to-do list."

I rise to my feet and bend over her shoulder so I can whisper in her ear. "Am I on your to-do list?"

She smacks me in the arm and turns to her daughter. "Rubi, go wash off your face and hands. They're sticky from your popsicle. You too Rosie," she calls over her shoulder.

Rosie, who's been avidly watching but hasn't said a word, hops up and grabs her little sister's hand. "Come on Rosie. If we don't get cleaned up, Mom won't let us go."

Once the screen door bangs shut behind them, their mom pulls my head down to hers. "You're at the top of my to-do list, Hotshot."

"Do you have a babysitter for tomorrow night, Magnolia?"

"That's not our mom's name," Rubi interrupts.

We were paying so much attention to each other, we were oblivious to the kids coming back outside.

"Hush, Rubi," Rosie says. "People give each other nicknames all the time. Like when Mom calls you Manzana because of your cheeks."

"But Mommy calls me Manzana because she loves me. Does Mr. Montgomery love our mom?"

Rubi might think she's speaking in a whisper because she has her hand in front of her mouth - but she's not.

"I'm sorry," she whispers out of the corner of her mouth.

"It's okay, Luz," I say as I grin and drop to Rubi's level. "Your mom and I are just friends, Rubi."

Rosie crosses her arms and makes a hmmmph noise. It makes me wonder how much of the goodnight kiss they saw before we crept around the side of the house.

We all hear Rico thundering down the stairs like a herd of elephants and I stand. He's frowning when he stops a few feet away. "I think I should sit in the front seat with you," he says as he crosses his arms.

I shrug. "It's up to your mom. If she's willing to give up riding shotgun, I'm okay with it."

"It's fine with me," she calls out.

As soon as I hit the unlock button, the kids make a beeline for my truck.

"Rubi, I need to grab your carseat!" Luz yells after them.

"I'm not a baby anymore, Mom!"

"No, but I want you to be safe. If you want to go with us instead of being dropped off somewhere, you're going to sit in that car seat."

"I'll grab it, Mom," Rosie tells her and heads for the garage.

"Are we making you late?" Luz asks.

I lean forward and swipe the crease between her brows with my thumb. "No, babe, you're not," I reassure her. "It doesn't begin at a set time."

When Rosie emerges from the side of the garage with her sister's booster seat, Luz takes control. "Rosie hand me that, and you get in behind Mr. Montgomery's seat. Rico, if you're going to sit up front, you're going to help Mr. Montgomery man the radio or whatever else he needs you to do so he can pay attention to the road. Rubi, come here so I can strap you in."

The ride is uneventful except for Rico's questionable dee-jaying. I don't think it's what Luz had in mind when she told him he was in control of the radio. My phone's blue-toothed, so he's using my streaming service. First it's some song about gummy bears. Then Rubi asks him to find the Barbie song. And we listen to it four times before we get to the park.

I've never been so relieved to get somewhere and shut off my music.

"Let me give you some change to buy your cones," Luz says as they swing the car doors open, ready to scramble out. Even Rubi. She unfastened her car seat and she's hot on Rosie's heels.

"I've got it, Mom," Rico tells her. "I've been saving my lawn mowing money."

"Well thank you for treating your sisters, Rico," she says. He waves his hand over his shoulder in acknowledgment.

"You'd think they've never had ice cream before," I laughingly say as her kids make a beeline for the striped awning and picnic tables.

"You'd think. Dex told them it was homemade ice cream, and it was a thousand times better than Dairy Queen. This'll be the first time they've tasted it and also their first exposure to a famous Willow Creek tradition."

"When I was growing up, it always meant summer was officially here. My mom's been on the organizing committee almost every year for as long as I can remember."

She takes my hand and navigates her way over the running board. "I don't think we ever came as kids. Dad always had the shop open on weekends and the three of us, me, Perdita and Dex, were always helping out somehow."

"Dex and I played football together, but he was a freshman when I was a senior. I don't think we ever actually had a conversation."

"Well he had plenty to say about you."

"That sounds ominous."

"He said you were a grouch and I couldn't let you intimidate me because I deserved to be here."

"You know the couple I was telling you about?"

"Sweet Cheeks and Wildcat?" She asks with a smile.

"Yep. She got arrested after one of these ice cream socials and he had to get her out of jail."

"Ooh!" She exclaims. "That's some juicy family history."

"She was a suffragette who liked to bend the law to her own devices. A very strong woman. Kind of like someone else I know. Maybe that's the weakness of the men in my family," I say as I squeeze her hand.

"You don't seem to mind."

"I don't. It means you won't be afraid to tell me what you want tomorrow night."

"What if all I want is peace and quiet and a foot massage?"

"Then that's what you'll get. You deserve a break, Luz. And don't worry about asking your brother to watch the kids - I'm going to ask Alex and Ness. Alex's daughter just started babysitting and she's very responsible."

"If you insist."

By the time we make it to the front of the line for the ice cream, the container looks empty. "Is there anything left?"

One of my mom's friends leans over the table. "I saved some for you, but only enough for one cone. Maybe you can share your ice cream cone with your new girlfriend?'

"She's not my –"

"Shush," Jenny Jones tells me. "It's no use denyin' it - anyone with eyes in their head can see you're crazy about her. This one's on me." She digs a five dollar bill out of her pocket and drops it in the tip jar.

When I turn to Luz, she's hiding her smile behind her hand.

"It's not funny. And we're the furthest thing possible from a secret now."

She snorts. "You're obviously hallucinating if you don't remember the kiss you gave me in front of the bleachers for the whole town to see."

I grab her hand and squeeze it. "It's cute that you think even half the town showed up for the baseball game. As for today, though... the tongues will be wagging."

The kids staked out one of the picnic tables and are halfway through their cones by the time we sit down across from them.

I take Luz's hand out of sight, under the table and tip my cone in her direction. "I don't mind sharing my ice cream with you."

She leans forward and braces our clasped hands on my thigh with a sultry smile. "Aren't you generous?"

I feel the press of every single one of those slender fingers as she swipes her tongue around the bottom of the melting scoop. "Demon," I mutter under my breath.

"What happened to Magnolia?" She murmurs back as her grin widens.

I stroke my thumb over the glimmer of her dimple and lift it to my mouth. "You had a speck of chocolate," I explain when her smile disappears and her eyes narrow.

"Mommy, you should have got a napkin. It's gross to let people clean your face with their spit."

Rubi's disgusted expression makes all of us burst into laughter.

"Mr. Montgomery didn't really clean my face with his spit," Luz protests when she finally stops laughing.

"Mom, he stuck his thumb on your face and then stuck it in his mouth. That's basically the same thing," Rosie proclaims.

"No it's not," Rico finally jumps in. "But he should have used a napkin." He shoves his own napkin across the table, his glare leveled in Ian's direction.

Luz claps her hands to get their attention and dispel the tension. "There's a water balloon contest happening, there's a dunking booth, and I have it on good authority that tug-of-war will be happening soon. Why don't the three of you find your friends and have some fun?"

Rosie gives us a salute and takes Rubi's hand. "Come on, Rubi, I've got you. Let's go clean off and then we'll find the go fish game."

"The go fish game?" Luz asks. "Rubi's still learning to swim."

Rosie rolls her eyes. "*It's not actual water, Mom.* One of my friends, Emily, is running it. There's a little fishing pole with a magnet and whatever you pick up with it behind the booth, you get to keep."

Luz reaches over and flicks Rosie's arm. "There's no reason to be so sassy," she reprimands her oldest daughter with a stern look. "Keep Rubi with you at all times. Mr. Montgomery and I will be over by the dunking booth. Meet us there at four-thirty."

"My friends are over there," Rico points toward the volleyball net.

"Go. Just meet us at the dunking booth later."

After the kids scamper off, I reel her in. "I can't stop thinking about the way you taste."

"Well, my kisses are yours anytime you want them, Hotshot."

My mouth charts a path up her cheekbone. "You know those kisses aren't the ones I'm talkin' about, Magnolia," I growl in her ear.

The goosebumps that suddenly appear on her upper arms are exactly the reaction I was looking for. "Those kisses are definitely yours anytime you want them – in the time and place that are appropriate."

I snag her hand in mine again. "Come on, let's head for the dunking booth before you distract me so much I haul you into the woods so I can remind you of all things I can do with my mouth."

Jack volunteered to be the dunking booth sacrifice this year, and I can't wait to pay him back for all his meddling. A crowd is gathered when we get there and we sidle our way to the front.

A slight woman in a baggy t-shirt and cargo pants is hurling the balls like missiles and everyone is cheering her on.

"Tell him what this one's for!" One of the women in the crowd shouts.

She curls her body like a major league pitcher and lets the ball fly toward its target. "This one's for assuming every woman wants a piece of you!"

Her aim is true and Jack tumbles into the water when she hits the bullseye. He was dripping wet before that, but now his clothes are plastered to him like a second skin.

"Who's she?" Luz asks in fascination.

"I think she's the woman who ghosted him after their blind date. He hasn't exactly been quiet about how that date went and she probably heard through the grapevine he's been running his mouth."

"Jack's usually so easy-going."

I snort. "Apparently not when he's been spurned."

"Doesn't anyone else want a turn?" Jack grumbles to the crowd.

"Nope!" A woman calls. "It's about time someone showed you what happens when you carve a path through Willow Creek with your flirting!"

"Uh oh," Luz giggles.

Uh oh is right. Jack's day of reckoning has been waiting impatiently in the wings, and it looks like it just made its debut. "My brother is kind of a himbo," I tell her.

"Oh, I know. Remember how he propositioned me with a cup of coffee within three minutes of meeting me?"

"Yep," I say as I squeeze her hand. "And I also remember what a shit he was when I warned him off."

She lays her head against my shoulder and I'm oblivious to the insult that preceded my brother catapulting into the water this time.

"You must have warned him off pretty early."

I shrug. "The look I gave him didn't require words. He knew I was staking my claim and telling him to keep his hands to himself. In case my message wasn't clear, I made sure there was no doubt that night at family dinner."

Chapter Twenty-One: You Came Without a Warning

Luz

"It's hard for me to believe you showed your hand like that." The thought of him baring his teeth and growling "mine" shouldn't intrigue me. He's usually so self-contained and hard to read.

"That isn't really what I did - but Jack probably saw straight through my warning." He gives me a sheepish grin. "I told him I knew he wasn't ready to play for keeps and I didn't want an emotional mess in the station."

I flinch. "That was a little harsh."

"Maybe. But maybe there's a reason that woman has dunked him nine times in a row."

I tap my chin. "Hmmm, maybe. But I think there's more to him than he leads people to believe. Sometimes we're too close to the people we love to see they're hurting and doing a damn good job of covering it up so we don't ask too many questions."

"Jack's always been the sunny day in our family, and I've always been the thundercloud. If he is covering something up we'd never know it."

"So maybe go easy on him? We had to handle Dex with care when he got back from Landstuhl."

"Landstuhl? Where's that?"

"It's the military hospital in Germany. He was flown there after the IED wiped out everyone on his team but he and Mari. He became an amputee, and watching him learn to navigate life again was really hard for our family."

"So he and his fiancee knew each other before she took the job at the clinic?"

"Yeah. They were in love, but he pushed her away when he was discharged because of his injury."

"I don't think Jack's trauma is that bad, but I think you're right. I think he's definitely struggling with something."

"It probably has to do with her or whatever it is might be the reason she's so angry with him."

"I'll have Ness try to get him to spill whatever's going on. Our sister's good at that. And she's relentless - we tell her all the time her high school guidance counselor is coming out and we're not moody teenagers."

"I bet you and Jack are totally like moody teenagers when you're brooding over something."

"I hope I grew out of that - but you might have to ask my mom. Who hasn't started pestering me yet, but I know it's inevitable."

"What's inevitable?"

"A dinner invitation. She'll probably pull you aside and make it today."

"That's exactly what I was going to do, Ian," a tall woman with Ian's lean features and dark red hair calls as she makes her way toward us. As soon as she's in reach, she extends her hand. "I'm Grace Montgomery and I am so pleased to meet you, Ms. Martinez."

We shake and I'm relieved. I can sense her warmth and acceptance. Some mothers don't want their sons to date single moms, but I don't get those vibes from Grace Montgomery and her enthusiasm seems genuine.

"It's lovely to meet you, Mrs. Montgomery."

"Please, call me Grace. It feels like I should be on a first name basis with the woman that finally convinced my oldest son becoming a recluse won't make him happy."

Ian groans. "Mom, not all of us are social butterflies like you."

She taps him on the arm with the fan she's carrying. "I don't expect you to be a social butterfly, but you should remember your manners every once in a while, and respect the fact that as your mother I'm entitled to worry about you."

It's hilarious to see her chiding him. "I agree, Grace, your son can be somewhat frosty at times." I want to giggle when he sneaks his hand under the hem of my shirt in the back and pinches my hip. Not hard enough to bruise - just enough to let me know he doesn't appreciate me commiserating with his mother.

"That's the perfect way to describe his attitude. But not frosty like the friendly snowman," her eyes are gleaming with amusement and she shares the bracket of a dimple her oldest son has in his left cheek.

"Why don't you go pick on Jack and leave Luz and I alone?" His exasperated question is full of affection.

"Your brother is already being picked on." She narrows her eyes in the direction of the dunking booth. "And I'd love to know exactly what he did to deserve that girl's anger."

"Ian says you know everyone in town. Do you know who she is?"

She smiles brightly at my question. "As a matter of fact, I know exactly who she is. Her name is Ophelia Daniels."

"That's the woman who ghosted him? She's definitely not his usual type."

"I'm told her sister is a famous clairvoyant. And Ophelia had a reality show on the History channel until very recently. She was a haunted tour guide and explored the most famous graveyards in America."

"That's a very unique job."

Grace nods enthusiastically. "Isn't it macabre? She only recently hung out her shingle here. She does haunted house explorations, cleansings and exorcisms."

"Exorcisms?" Ian huffs in disbelief.

"Yes, Ian. Exorcisms as in the banishment of evil spirits. You shouldn't scoff at things you don't understand."

He shakes his head. "Mom, the fact you've read Stephen King for thirty years doesn't make you an expert on the occult."

"Perhaps not," she concedes. "But I do know that something about that unusual young woman has turned your normally unflappable brother upside down."

"Jack's never let anyone disconcert him that much. You're imagining things."

"I'm not. You'll see. But, meanwhile," she turns to face me again. "I'd love to have you and your children over for our family cookout on the Fourth of July, Ms. Martinez."

"We'd love to join you. What should I bring?"

She waves dismissively. "Just you and your delightful children. It's been far too long since we had this many little ones at one of our celebrations. Ian and his father will make sure the swingset is cleaned up and sturdy."

"You should ask Dad where he put the tire swing."

"Excellent idea!" She beams at him like he just won a gold medal. "I'll let the two of you enjoy the festivities- I just thought it would be remiss of me not to introduce myself."

After she's behind the raffle ticket booth again, I turn to Ian. "Is she always that disarming and bossy?"

He nods and looks after her with a rueful expression. "Yep. But we tolerate it because we know it comes from a place of love. She just wants us to be happy."

"How does your sister escape her attention?" I shield my eyes with my hand and watch her animatedly drawing in customers.

He guffaws. "Ness wishes she could be so lucky. Mom is in wedding planning mode and convinced my sister and her fiancee need to have a ceremony that makes all her friends green with envy. Come on, let's go sit in the shade." He leads me over to a bench situated underneath a spreading oak.

"That's not what Ness wants?" I ask once we're sitting down. Not only is there shade and a breeze, it's much quieter.

"Nope. She wants the exact opposite. Barefoot on a beach with maybe ten people."

"Why doesn't she say something?"

"In case you hadn't noticed, Grace Montgomery is a force of nature. And Ness doesn't want to hurt her feelings."

"Maybe they should just elope."

"I think that's what they'll end up doing. Mom just has binders - she hasn't dropped any money yet."

"My mom's an orchestrator too. Don't get me wrong, I love her - Rosie's her namesake. But she's very opinionated. She's a devout Catholic and doesn't believe in divorce. She still thinks I should run after the man who deserted me and my kids and make things work."

"Some people just aren't cut out for sticking around. Especially when things are hard."

"I think my ex-husband liked the idea of having a family more than the reality of it."

"That seems to happen a lot. People get into a relationship and don't understand the hard work that goes into it if it's going to last. Especially when kids are involved. That's why Justine was a single mom, and it sounds like that was your experience too."

"Yeah. I learned a lot - especially about my ability to stand up for myself. My dad is fond of saying hardship builds character. I agree, but I wish it wasn't quite so hard sometimes."

He scratches his hand over his jaw. "Maybe it's a generational thing? I swear our parents would be best friends."

"I try not to make my kids feel as judged as I felt growing up. Even if I'm tempted to say it sometimes, I bite my tongue every time the words *I brought you into this world and I can take you out of it* pop into my head."

"My dad used to tell us *people in hell want ice water* when we asked for a second helping."

"Mom never used that one, but she did tell us life wasn't fair every time we complained about something we thought was unfair."

"Our mom and dad used that one too."

We laugh in unison. "Maybe it is a generational thing."

"You don't ever slip up and say those things to your kids?"

"I think I've said life isn't fair. What about you? Have you caught yourself saying any of the things your parents said?"

"Every summer day when my dad got in from mowing the yard and popped a beer he said it was hotter outside than a fart in a skillet."

"Oh my god... I don't know if that's the most disgusting thing I've ever heard or the funniest."

"Jack uses it on his scale of ranking the fires we get called about."

"What are his other ones?"

He tips his head back and smiles. "One of his other ones is hotter than two rats fucking in a wool sock."

"What??" I splutter.

"Dad used to say that about the woodstove in our grandparents' cabin in the Poconos."

"Your dad was very creative."

"Mom called it crass, but we've caught her saying some of the things she told us she was going to wash our mouths out with soap for repeating."

"Mom used Ivory on Dex and me one time when she caught us calling the neighbor kids shitheads. We were doing it in Spanish and they didn't understand it. But she did."

"Your older sister wasn't calling them names?"

I roll my eyes. "She was always the goody two shoes - holed up in her room with a stack of books. We should've known she'd become a librarian."

"She still lives in Florida?"

"Yeah. I really miss her. Dex and I are trying to get her to move up here, but she feels guilty about leaving Mom and Dad down there all by themselves."

"I get it. Even though I was happy living out west, I felt guilty for leaving Jack and Ness here with my parents when I'm the oldest."

"Why'd you finally come back?"

"After my dad had his heart attack it just seemed like the right thing to do. I couldn't stop thinking about the burnover and coming back home felt like the right thing to do."

"Shouldn't you have been in counseling?"

His entire body tenses beside me. "I didn't need it. I just needed a change of scenery."

"I'm no expert, but I think you might need more than a change of scenery to get over something so traumatic."

"I've dealt with it."

I seriously doubt he's dealt with it appropriately, but it's not my place to contradict him. If his past ever comes back to haunt him and affects our relationship, I'll confront him about the need to seek professional help. Most of the men I know are stubborn about admitting they need that kind of help - like it stigmatizes them or means they turned in their man cards. Even Dex. He tried to be stoic when he got back from Afghanistan, but he finally had to admit he didn't have the tools to cope with his PTSD on his own.

"Okay," I say.

"I can tell you're withholding judgment. I promise I'm a fully functioning adult, Luz."

"I said okay."

He opens his mouth to argue, but we get interrupted by a sticky, sweaty six-year-old. She thrusts her cotton candy in my face. "Look what Rico got me! It's blueberry and cherry."

"You have to eat it all-even if it gives you a tummy ache- before we go to the movies."

***

The drive-in feature is *Encanto*, and my kids have memorized the entire soundtrack. Even Rubi. Rico is humming the melody under his breath, because apparently it's not cool for teenage boys to commit themselves to belting out Disney showtunes, but we can all hear him. Ian laid a blanket in the bed of the truck and the two of us have the rear window at our backs while the kids are on their stomachs with their chins propped in their hands. They've already gone through three buckets of popcorn, and after an afternoon of ice cream, cotton candy and funnel cakes, I drew the line.

I know they have stomachs of iron, but they're already buzzing so hard with sugar, it's going to be almost impossible to get them to sleep tonight. "It's a good thing you didn't have any plans for us tonight," I mumble against his shoulder.

"What makes you think I don't have any plans for you tonight, Magnolia?"

"Because you probably didn't get much sleep last night and we both know your decrepit bones can't hack it. The fire and the accident were all over social media last night."

"My old man bones?"

I giggle. "Yep."

"Oh, I'll show you how much my decrepit bones can handle. Especially my decrepit boner." He shifts restlessly.

"I love that you have everything on lock down right now, Hotshot." I wave my hand at the outline of the erection he just shifted to hide. "Especially that."

He raises a brow and catches my wrist, pulling it toward the lower half of his body. I'm horrified at what he thinks he's doing but can't seem to wrestle away. The kids are oblivious right now and my palm's itching to feel his length.

When our joined hands are only a few inches away, he moves them to his thigh. "The look on your face, Magnolia. I can't tell if it's disappointment or relief."

"Probably both," I grumble. "I'll see what I can do to tide you over once the kids are asleep."

We don't want to get stuck behind the long line of cars pulling onto the main road, so we leave right before the credits start rolling. Ian made Rico sit in the back with his sisters and the whole trip, he's kept my hand in his - even when he goes to shift gears.

When the porch light comes into view as we round the bend Rubi sighs from the backseat. "I'm tired,

Mommy. Do I have to brush my teeth before bed tonight?"

Maybe the sugar high is turning into a sugar crash and burn.

"You know what Mom's gonna say. If you don't brush your teeth before bed, your mouth is going to be full of rotten teeth by the time you're twelve," Rosie reminds her.

"And you'll just have to brush them longer in the morning," Rico chimes in.

This time, Rubi's sigh sounds like the wheeze of a hippopotamus. "If I have to brush my teeth, Mr. Montgomery will have to carry me upstairs to my bed."

Ian is squinting at the windshield and his whole body is shaking with laughter.

"If you brush your teeth, Rubi, your mom and I will read you a bedtime story."

"I want you to make one up about ice cream fairies."

He glances over at me, bewildered.

"Rubi decided last month that all the best things to eat were made by fairies."

"That's because candy is magic," she pipes up from the backseat.

"Sure, I can make up a story about ice cream fairies. But only if you brush your teeth first."

***

Rosie and Rico both trudged to their rooms like their socks were full of lead, and when I looked in on them, they were both snoring. Rubi fell asleep long before Ian got to the "and they lived happily ever after" part of the story. He's been yawning for the last fifteen minutes, like he's running on nothing more than fumes.

"I don't think you have the fortitude for a demonstration of how much you missed me," I say as I plop down beside him on the couch.

He rubs his eyes. "Maybe I just need to rest for a minute. You could snuggle with me on the couch," he says and waggles his eyebrows.

He flips over onto his back. I stretch out over him, tangle our legs and lay my head on his shoulder.

When his soft snore ruffles my hair, I ease away and grab one of the afghans my mom insisted I take. She spends all winter crocheting them, and the yarn is always the perfect weight for sleeping on the couch.

I drape the green and blue pattern over him and flick off the light. As much as I want to spend the night nestled on top of him, it might lead to awkward morning conversations with the kids.

***

Something wakes me up just before dawn. When I open my eyes, he's standing in the entry to my bedroom, one hand on the doorknob, and one arm braced against the frame.

"What are you doing?" I mumble groggily.

"I was just going to kiss you on the cheek and leave a note."

"Well don't stand there like a creeper, come here."

The thump of his boots is muffled by the plush throw rug as he makes his way over and stoops to plant a kiss on my cheek.

I twist my head so our lips meet and yank him down. He falls over me, but braces himself on his forearms. He tastes like minty toothpaste. "Did you use my toothbrush?"

"No. Our relationship hasn't reached the sharing toothbrushes stage yet. I used my finger and your mouthwash."

I turn my head. "Speaking of which..."

He drops a kiss on the end of my nose and stands. "I'll text you later and let you know what the plan is for tonight."

"Mmkay. I'm going back to sleep so I'm rested up for whatever you have planned."

"You do that, Magnolia, because I plan on wearing you out."

There's a goofy smile on my face as I drift back to sleep.

Chapter Twenty-Two: If You Want It

Ian

"I SHOULDN'T BE SURPRISED you opted for a quiet night - but you should know I'm not in the mood for a chili dinner. As far as I know that's the extent of your culinary skills," she tells me as she slips off her shoes. "Your sister told me she and Alex had a whole night planned of stuff to keep the kids occupied and nobody would mind if I had a sleepover."

I'm laughing when I wrap her in my arms. "I'm not ashamed to admit I called in reinforcements. Dinner is courtesy of my mom- her family's chicken alfredo recipe. All I had to do was warm it up in the oven. It's almost ready. And my sister has been trying to get me laid for months so she probably has an itinerary worthy of a five star general."

"I'm impressed, Hotshot. For someone out of practice, you know how to make a girl feel special."

"Your sarcasm is noted but I'd also like to point out I intend to make you feel very special later on," I smirk as I lead her to the kitchen.

"Good, because I'm tired of settling for an appetizer when I've had a taste of the main course."

"I don't trust myself to stop with an appetizer... why don't you set the table while I plate us up? The silverware's in the drawer by the fridge and the napkins are in a holder underneath the roll of paper towels."

Once she has forks, knives and napkins, she brushes a kiss along my jaw. "Your house isn't what I expected, Hotshot."

"Why not?"

"There aren't muddy boots by the door, a set of antlers on the wall, or buffalo plaid curtains. It looks like you actually had an interior designer steer you in the right direction."

I grimace. "I'm not completely without taste- but I did have Vanessa's help. The industrial shelving and neutral colors were her idea."

"So what part of this was your idea?"

"I designed the kitchen to be big enough for two people to move around freely -because I'm eventually going to learn how to make something besides chili and I might need my own personal sous chef."

"Are you making an offer?"

The blush I feel on my cheekbones probably gives away what my shrug doesn't. "You'd make a great sous chef."

"I'll keep your preference in mind," she notes as her lips sweep over my jaw again. I watch her walk into the dining area until the alarm on the oven interrupts my thoughts.

I'm not nervous about her being here. It feels natural. But the way I feel about her and her kids scares me. Just the thought of all of them makes the hollow place I've been holding in my chest for five years disappear. This woman didn't just kick down my walls, she blew them to smithereens.

My mom always cooks like she's feeding an army, and since I tossed a salad too, there's plenty of food leftover.

After she cleans her plate she rests her elbows on the table and leans forward. "No wonder you and Jack are Vikings. If this is what you ate growing up, I'm not surprised."

"I think that's genes, not my mom's cooking."

"Trust me, Hotshot. It's both."

"Well, I'm glad you appreciate my Vikingness."

She squirms in her seat. "Oh I definitely appreciate it."

"I'm going to get us some after dinner wine," I tell her as I scoot away from the table. "Feel free to snoop."

She gives me a thumbs up and hops out of her chair.

When I bring out the glasses of wine, she's rummaging through my record collection. "Some of those are from my mom's collection, some of them I've had since I was a teenager, and some are thrift store finds."

She holds up the *Just Once in My Life* album from the Righteous Brothers. "I've been obsessed with *Unchained Melody* since I saw *Ghost*."

I set the glasses on the side table. "Do you want to hear it?"

"Only if you'll dance with me."

"I'll dance with you." I take the record from her and put it in the player. Once I have the needle in the right place, I take her hand, swing the French doors open, and lead her onto my porch. She lays her head in the crook between my shoulder and armpit when I sweep her into my arms and I gather her close as the notes pour into the open air.

I've never been much of a dancer. Even when we were partnered up for square dancing in high school gym class, I could never get my feet to go where they needed to. But when I hold her in my arms, it makes me feel like I have wings. I tighten my arms around her, and we just spin under the moon and stars. If I close my eyes it feels like the moon is a giant disco ball and the stars are twinkly lights.

"This is nice, Hotshot."

"I think so too, Magnolia." Swaying with her on this porch makes me think about all the empty rooms behind us. When I started building, it was a way to focus on something more than my grief. Now I can imagine inhaling the smell of lime and coconut every time I turn a corner, and hearing the kids laugh as they slide down the banister.

When I slip my hand under her waistband, she reciprocates. She nestles even closer, her curves plastered against mine in an obscene ballet that makes me even harder than I was when I left her lying all drowsy and beautiful in her bed this morning. Harder than I was when she tugged me down and I finally knew how it would feel to have our bodies parallel but touching. This is nothing like square-dancing or two-stepping. Where we go from here is pure instinct.

Her lips trail over my bicep and shoulder and I scoop her up. "No more teasing, Magnolia. Legs around my waist."

One of my hands is cupping the round peach of her ass, and the other one is anchoring her lower back as I move through the doors again. I stop just inside the entry and press her against the wall. "Is this a repeat of our dry hump, Hotshot?"

"Not a repeat. This is the sequel."

I work the buttons on her blouse open one at a time, until the sides are gaping open, framing her black lace bra. She shimmies as it drops to one shoulder and when she stretches her fingers, it slides down her arms and flutters to the floor in a pile of paisley chiffon. I rub the silky nylon of her bra straps between my fingers and thumb before I push them down to her elbows. The lace doesn't move, and I push the cups down so I can cup the warmth of her in my palms. I roll her nipples until they're hot little bullets burning her skin. When I drop my mouth to her cheek, she twists her face and catches my mouth with hers. She clutches my nape, holding me in place and silently telling me that if I let go or slam on the brakes she's going to find me. "It's been so long, Hotshot. Show me what I've been missing."

I don't know if she's talking about being skin to skin with anyone or she's remembering the way my mouth felt on her body when I lost the battle after my shower three weeks ago.

She locks her ankles in the small of my back, and I hitch her higher against the wall.

"Hands on my shoulders so I can get you out of these pants." I roll the elastic waistband down her hips, until I reach her upper thighs. "Feet on the floor."

Her legs drop, but she clings to my shoulders for balance. I crouch in front of her and peel them all the way to her ankles. She closes her eyes when I lift her out of them one foot at a time.

She has on striped knee high socks, and now she's in nothing but those socks and a matching black lace bra and panties. My heart's thudding like I just ran a marathon, because she's the sexiest thing I've ever seen.

I press a reverent kiss to the side of one knee before I drape that leg over my shoulder. "The socks stay on," I whisper as I slide my nose up the curve of her inner thigh. The satin of her skin and the smell of her like ripe peaches and ocean mist fills my lungs.

"I need to taste you again, Magnolia. After you come on my tongue, we're going to the bedroom." The record is skipping now, and the needle hitting the spindle isn't the kind of background music I want right now. "But first, I'm taking the record off the player."

I stand and feel her eyes on me as I stop the rhythmic thud of the needle. When I kneel in front of her again, she stretches her arms over her head and drapes her left leg over my shoulder. "Make me your dessert, Hotshot."

I palm her over the black lace, swiping my thumb over her swollen clit before I tease the lace aside just far enough to plant a kiss in the crease of her thigh. I smooth the fabric back in place. and run my thumb upward, spreading her labia and circling the hood of her clit through the black lace triangle. She tosses her head and moans.

I repeat the motion, but use my thumb and forefinger this time. I trail my other hand up her chest and push up one cup of the bra so I can twist her nipple while I pinch her clit. When I tug both pleasure points at the same time, my caress just this side of rough, she lifts her hips again. "I'm making you my dessert, Magnolia. This salty, sweet, juicy little cunt is my buffet."

When she cries out and grabs a fistful of hair to press me closer, I flatten my tongue against her clit and flick it against the roof of my mouth, just behind the edge of my teeth.

I need her on my face and I'm tired of wasting time.

I was raised in the country, so I always have a pocket knife. When I extract it from my pocket her eyes go wide. "Shhh," I place my finger over the bow of her mouth. "Trust me, sweetheart." She nods shakily and nips my fingertip.

I slip the blade under the thin strip of material at her right hip and she gulps. I don't want it snapping back and stinging her skin, so I place two of my fingers under the strip when I slice it. The underwear falls to the side and she's fully bare to me. When I close the knife and send it clattering across the wood floor, her exhale of relief is just as shaky as her nod was a few minutes ago.

I grip her hip and stroke the skin that still bears the mark of the elastic waistband. "I'd never hurt you, Magnolia. I'd cut myself first."

Her grip on my scalp tightens. "Prove it, Hotshot."

The lower half of her body cants completely toward me when I lift her other leg over my shoulder. "Relax and enjoy the ride, baby," I growl.

I dip two fingers inside her and nip her clit like she nipped my finger. She bucks against my teeth and tongue, her body bowed as one of her heels thumps against my back.

The second I taste and feel the pulse of her release, I lift her legs away and stand. There's a condom stowed in my front pocket and as soon as I unzip and lower my jeans, I rip it open with my teeth.

When I shove down my boxers and palm my erection, she licks her lips. "I want to feel it before you put that on."

She drops to her knees and wraps her fist around the base. I groan when her tongue glides around the rim and strokes the underside. The humming noise she makes and the sight of her there on her knees, sends the blood rushing to my cock again. I'm the hardest I've ever been in my life, and I know every nerve and ounce of my blood is there at the mercy of her mouth. I stroke her hair and nudge her chin as I jerk my hips away. "No, I wanna be inside you."

She gives me one last, teasing lick and stands. "I want you inside me."

Her hand covers mine as I slide on the condom, her fingertips brushing every ridge and vein.

Once the end is tight around the base, she retreats, so her back's against the wall again.

"So you want a wallbanger, Magnolia?"

I'm flattening her against the drywall and scooping her legs around my waist before she's even done nodding.

There's nothing I want more than to bottom out and feel her clench around me. But I grit my teeth and hold back because I need to savor every inch of what it feels like to have her body open and willing. I slide just the crest of my dick into her, and set my thumb against her clit again. The house settles around us as I drop my forehead to hers, the rattle of our breathing the only sound. When she palms her breast, I push away her hand and replace it with my mouth, and glide forward another inch.

Our breaths are harsher now, almost in unison. I drop quick little kisses over the gooseflesh around her areola, and suck the tight bead of her nipple between my teeth. When I graze the edge and roll it against the roof of my mouth, her heels scrabble against my back.

It's quiet except for our staggered breathing and the slap of our bodies melding together, slick with sweat and arousal.

"Deeper," she pleads, her voice full of yearning and desperation.

"As deep as you can take me, little demon," I promise.

She angles her hips, and suddenly I'm all the way in. "Hurts so good," she moans as she tips her head back.

From this point forward, this is all I'm ever going to want to do. Like there's no before drowning in Luz Martinez and no after. Like she's the perfect sunrise I've been looking for and won't ever want to give up.

"You're perfect," I croon as I pull out and slam back home. I'm in so deep, the base of my cock strikes her clit with every thrust.

"This isn't going to be enough," she wails and I wonder if she's reading my mind.

I brace my hands on either side of her head so I can look down and watch myself sink into her. She's soaking me and I can see my dick glistening in the moonlight streaking through the windows. "Almost there," I groan as I drop my head to her shoulder.

"Me too."

Her body flutters around me, tightening, and she keens like one of the banshees my Irish grandmother used to talk about.

I'm right behind her, and the roaring I hear in my ears probably sounds like a pissed off grizzly bear. I empty inside the condom, until I'm sagging against her and she barely has us propped against the wall.

"Maybe we should clean up for round two?"

The very thought of moving right now is painful. "I only have one condom, so clean up and then snuggle," I say as I hold the edge of the condom and pull out.

"You had a pocket knife but you only have one condom?"

I shrug bashfully. "I didn't want to assume."

She grins. "You know there's this thing my mom says..."

"Yeah, probably the same thing my mom says. Assuming makes an ass out of you."

"So this isn't a one-night-stand?"

"It's the furthest thing from a one-night-stand possible. You're not getting rid of me, Magnolia."

"I wasn't trying to —- just preparing myself in case I misunderstood the situation."

She sighs when I brush a kiss across her knuckles. "I'll be right back."

I'm not always thankful for my interfering sister, but this is one of the times I am. She insisted on fluffy, upscale, color-coordinated wash cloths and towels for both bathrooms and I know Luz will appreciate the softness.

When I stroll back into the foyer with both, her eyes light up. "No buffalo plaid curtains and you have decent towels. Definitely not the bachelor pad I expected."

"Ness can be a pain in the ass but I guess I should be grateful she insisted on doing the whole make-my-brother's-lair-cozy thing."

She takes the wash cloth from my outstretched hand and swabs herself clean. "And this smells like non-abrasive soap too."

"My skin's really sensitive, so it's just mild Ivory."

"Good, that means it won't cause a yeast infection." She turns bright red as soon as the words leave her mouth. "Oops, sorry. TMI."

I shrug. "Not TMI. I lived with Justine for over ten years. Yeast infections and the things women have to do to prevent them are just a part of life. You don't have to censor your thoughts around me because you think I'm going to be revolted or turned off. When you're final-ly comfortable enough to let one rip wide open in my presence, I'll know you're finally being fully yourself," I tell her as I scoop her into my arms.

She just shakes her head and this shy, soft smile creases her cheeks. "It will be a long time before you hear or smell my flatulence, Hotshot," she says as she flops onto the bed.

When I curl around her, she flexes her foot and slides it up the back of my calf before tangling our legs together. "Stay the whole night," I say and kiss the top of her head.

"I'm not going anywhere, Hotshot."

I don't know what time it is when I wake up, but I'm covered in cold sweat, the chill of it on my skin like an ice bath.

I haven't had a nightmare in weeks, but this time when I found myself back there and crawled from my tent, it wasn't Justine running into the fire. It was Luz.

My hands are shaking as I circle her ribs. She's safe for now, nestled in my arms.

Chapter Twenty-Three: Not Scared of the Stories in Your Scars

Luz

THE LAST FEW WEEKS of build-up to the Fourth of July holiday have bombarded the station with calls about fireworks accidents. Ian's doing a safety class at the community center later today about things you should and shouldn't do, and we've all been encouraging people to come out and see the official show we're putting on for the holiday. The town's been taking donations all year long and since Jack's the only one with the certification, he picked up all the ones we'll need.

Tomorrow is the Fourth of July cookout at his parents' house. I'm more nervous than I've ever been in my life. Most of the Southern mothers I know don't think any woman is good enough for their son. Especially a woman with brown skin and three kids. I didn't get the impression his mom was judging me, but a syrupy sweet invitation can disguise a lot of venom.

When the phone rings and I see it's Mari, I pick up, because she usually texts me. "Hey soon-to-be-sister-in-law."

"Hey Luz. I'm sorry to call you so early, but I wanted to catch you while the clinic's still quiet."

"I was just sitting on the deck with my coffee while the kids watch Disney. What's up?"

"Ramon's birthday is next weekend- he would have been forty-one. I'd like to visit his grave at Arlington and wondered if you'd mind coming with me? Dex isn't quite ready yet."

"Of course! I can have Ian's sister Ness watch the kids if Dex isn't up to it."

"He has his own way of grieving, and is working on a special project he hasn't shared yet. So yeah, it's probably a good idea to ask Vanessa to look after the kids."

"Rico's technically old enough to watch his sisters, but he can't drive yet and I know he has practice that morning."

"How's he doing with the fact you're dating?"

I sigh and rub my hand over my eyes. "Ugh. He's being very bossy and protective."

"Well, he's been the man of the house for a long time and he's used to it. That must be awkward since Ian is his coach."

"It definitely is. I can tell he looks up to him - especially since they've won every single game and there's a good chance they'll end up in the playoffs. But I think you're right - he got used to being the man of the house and he's feeling usurped."

"Ness is the guidance counselor, right?"

"Yeah. She's been at the high school for about twelve years."

"I'm sure she's seen this situation before. Maybe ask her to talk to him if she has the chance next weekend."

"You're brilliant. I trust her experience and I don't think he'll suspect anything since Ian's her brother."

"What about you and Ian?"

"I never thought I'd feel this way again and it's scary. It feels like I'm standing on a ledge. Or a high-rise diving platform. And I'm nervous about being around his whole family tomorrow."

"I've heard about the notorious Montgomery clan Independence Day barbecue."

Now my palms are sweating. "What have you heard?"

"That there's every picnic food imaginable, Ian's dad makes the best ribs in town, and there's always a flag football game after dessert."

"You haven't heard anything about his mom?"

"She has her hands in everything, but I've never heard anything bad. What are you worried about?"

"I'm worried she's one of those Southern boy moms."

There's a brief silence and I can almost hear her wincing through the phone. "I know exactly what you're afraid of. Has he dated anyone else in Willow Creek that could give you a heads up on what to expect?"

"Apparently I'm the first since he moved back five years ago."

"I'm impressed he was celibate for that long. Or smart enough to take care of business outside of Willow Creek. Since there's no one you can ask, just hope for the best and expect the worst. Fingers crossed you'll be pleasantly surprised and she'll welcome you and the kids with open arms."

"Do you know any of his family besides Vanessa?"

"River hangs out with Dex and the guys, and I'm friendly with his fiancee, Roxie. She's an introvert and hard to get to know."

"I'm just going to take your advice. His mom said not to bring anything, but that's not how I was raised. I have to bring something."

"You have your mom's chalupas recipe, right?"

"I'm already nervous about our cultural differences - I don't necessarily call attention to them."

Mari snorts. "Well if you guys are serious, his mom's gonna have to get comfortable with your complexion and your culture. Make the chalupas."

Her vehemence makes me laugh. "Okay, I'll make the chalupas. Let me go round up the kids so I can get to the farmers' market."

"You'd better set some aside for me! Dex brags about them all the time, but every time we plan a trip to see your parents so I can taste them, something happens."

"I'll save some for you."

"Thanks, Luz. And thanks again for being so gracious about next weekend."

"Mari, you're an unofficial part of our family and you brought Dex back from the edge. You should never hesitate to ask me for anything."

She blows me a kiss and after we hang up I head to the living room. Rubi loves the petting zoo at the farmers' market, so I know I have at least one kid who won't complain about spending Saturday morning there.

***

I'm balancing the plate of chorizo and chicken chalupas in my lap. I made two dozen -twelve of each. Ian said there are usually about twenty people there, so I hope that's enough. When I told him I was making something, he reminded me his mom said it wasn't necessary. And I reminded him that the way I was raised you always bring something besides yourself to the party.

He's been sneaking glances at the plate since we got everyone buckled up in his truck.

"I take back what I said about you not having to bring anything, because whatever you made smells amazing."

"It's a surprise."

"Mom made –"

I raise my brow at Rosie in the rear view mirror and she mimes zipping her mouth shut and throwing away the key.

"You almost got in trouble," Rico chortles.

She glares and pinches his arm and I'm getting ready to ask if we need to pull over so I can straighten some things out, when Ian speaks up.

"People who fight in my car get strapped to the roof. Or the bumper."

They don't know him well enough to know he's teasing, and they immediately square their shoulders against the upholstery and sit up ramrod straight. They even clasp their hands in their laps. I can see his mouth quirk sideways, and I can tell he's holding back his laughter.

"I never fight," Rubi primly asserts.

Ian and I share a loaded glance, because of the three of them, Rubi can be the most ruthless. She knows just where to pinch and when she kicks you in the shins it feels like tiny hammers. We bite our lips to hold in the laughter the entire remaining four miles. When we pull in the driveway, the garage door is open and Ian's dad is filling up balloons with a helium machine. Rubi's eyes are as wide as saucers when I lift her out of the truck.

"Mom, are those the floaty balloons?"

"Yes, bambino, they're the floaty balloons. If you want to keep one, you'll have to tie it around your wrist."

Grace Montgomery is wiping her hands on her apron as she opens the door. "Come in, come in! The food isn't quite ready, but make yourselves at home."

I lift the plate of chalupas in her direction. "I made one of our family's traditional recipes."

She beams and the lump of dread in my stomach starts to dissolve. "I'm sure it's wonderful and I can't wait to taste it. Why don't you take it into the kitchen and set it up? Ian can show you the way."

I nod and he puts his hand in the small of my back. "Come on," he murmurs in my ear. "She loves kids, so don't worry."

"Your name is Rubi, isn't it?" She asks my youngest daughter. "Ruby is my birthstone so I think we're going to be best friends. And Rosita, you're named for my favorite flower. As for you, Mr. Rico, my son Ian says you're one of the best batters he's ever seen."

"She's a pro," I say in awe as I glance over my shoulder and watch her melt my kids into preening puddles.

Ian chuckles. "She's been a Sunday school teacher for forty years - she can charm anyone."

"Was having you check over the swingset part of her ploy?"

"I wouldn't put it past her," he chuckles as he takes my hand and curls his arm around my lower back. He's so gruff at the station, I never imagined he'd be the kind of man who hugs like it's his favorite thing to do. There's something about being sheltered in his arms that makes me feel safe and brave.

"What other activities do I have to look forward to?" I mumble against his chest.

"I have a whole list."

When I tip my head up, he's waggling his brows. "I meant day-time activities - specifically barbecue and keep-my-kids-occupied activities," I clarify with a laugh.

"Oh, I know what you meant, Magnolia. Besides the football game, Jack's bringing about a hundred sparklers, and Dad has a super soaker water fight planned. My sister's bringing her four kids, and our cousins are bringing their broods too."

"What's going on right now?"

"Right now, you're going to let me sample whatever you brought for the potluck, and we're going to sneak a slice of Mom's signature dessert."

"You're awfully sure of yourself. Why should you get first dibs?"

"I should get first dibs because the smell permeated my truck and my mouth's been watering ever since.

There's a stack of paper plates on the counter behind you."

He's incorrigible and I love it. I press my hands to his shoulders. "Go sit down."

When he obediently takes a seat at the table in the corner, I shake my head.

I finished the chalupas this morning, and the aluminum foil kept them warm. I slide one from underneath the covering, plate it and set it in front of him. The flatware has to be in an obvious place, but there are about a million drawers. I turn around to ask him where the forks are, and realize he doesn't need a fork.

He's holding the chorizo chalupa in his hand, his eyes closed in bliss. There's a huge bite missing. "This is amazing," he garbles around a mouthful of food.

"So you think people will like them?" I clasp my hands to camouflage how nervous I am.

His eyes flicker open in disbelief. "Like them?" He asks as he swallows the bite. "Like them? Luz, they're going to love them."

He finishes it in four bites and sets the plate aside. "Come here."

I approach cautiously and when I'm close enough, he wraps his hand around my hip and tugs me onto his lap. "Anyone could see," I protest.

"There's nothing to see, just a man who loves the way his woman knows her way around a kitchen," he says as he smooths my hair behind my ears.

I roll my eyes. "You sound like a caveman."

"Not a caveman. A man who's thoroughly whipped by a woman who can cook, tie a tourniquet, defend her kids and do things to my body and my heart that make me think about her all day long. Now it's your turn to sit while I get us that slice of cake."

He sets me in the other chair and I watch as he crouches in front of the fridge and the cotton of his cargo shorts celebrates the curve of his ass. I look away and peer at the ceiling when he stands.

"You were ogling my butt, weren't you Martinez?"

"No comment, Montgomery."

He plates a thin slice of what looks like cake and slides it in front of me.

I lift the fork to my mouth and the flavor of summer explodes on my tongue. "What is this?" I ask around a mouthful of the dessert.

"It's mom's strawberry cake. She refuses to share the recipe with anyone. She said she might consider sharing it with my future wife since it's a closely guarded family legacy. I bet she'd trade it for your chalupa recipe."

I grin around the forkful of food. "That's a lot of pressure."

"Yeah, Vanessa's been trying to copy the recipe for years. She watches her like a hawk every time mom makes it, but it never turns out the same."

"Your sister's so competitive I bet that drives her nuts."

"She said she was going to tackle me for it when Mom finally relents."

"Speaking of tackles...tell me about the Montgomery family football game. It's flag football, right?"

He takes the other seat and leans forward. "Are you going to share?"

I'm tempted to tell him no, but offer him a forkful. "Here. Now tell me about the notorious game."

He tips his head back and rubs his stomach. "It's flag football and as much a Montgomery family tradition as the cake you're eating."

"Is it just the adults that play?"

"Nope. Kids are welcome. No tackling is allowed, so they won't get hurt."

"My brother taught me to throw a pass, so you'd better bring your best game, Hotshot."

His laugh surrounds me as he reels me into his arms and presses me against the edge of the counter. "I was a baseball player, not a defensive lineman, so I think you need to be on my team."

"If you think I won't distract you," I tease as I bracket his jaw.

"Oh, you'll definitely distract me - but it's totally worth it."

He kisses me gently on the temple and my heart flutters. "We should get back in there before my kids say something that will either embarrass me or incriminate me."

"We should. But I want to just stand here and enjoy this hug. Just for a minute."

***

Grace Montgomery motions us over when we emerge from the kitchen. "Ian, since Jack isn't here yet, will you help your father finish setting up the tables? And Luz, if you don't mind, I could use your help with getting everything out and finding all the serving spoons. "

"Of course. I just want to make sure the kids aren't up to any mischief."

She waves a hand and laughs. "They're fine. My husband gave them popsicles from the freezer in his garage and gave them each something to do. Rico's setting up the croquet and Rubi and Rosi are picking flowers from my garden for the tables."

I smile, because those tasks are perfect for them. Rico loves to be in charge of things, and the girls are always bringing me bouquets they've picked. Ian presses a kiss to the top of my head. "I'm gonna go help Dad. Holler if you need anything."

Grace watches him stride through the sliding glass doors with a faint smile. "I believe my son is wholly smitten."

When she turns to me, her eyes are clouded with tears. "Thank you, Miss Martinez. I haven't seen my son this at ease and content since he came home to us five years ago."

"I haven't done anything," I say, uncomfortable with her praise.

"On the contrary," she says as she takes my hand. "The shadows behind his eyes are nearly gone. And that is all because of you."

"Your son isn't what I expected," I confess.

Her smile this time is proud. "My son has always been a man of few words, but fierce and loving to those he claims as his own. He's exactly like his father in that way."

"He and Jack are so different," I muse aloud.

She nods in agreement. "They are. Jack's always been what I call happy-go-lucky. Very little fazes him and he's an eternal optimist. He's like Ian and their father, Ethan, though about the people he loves. Honey badgers are known for fighting to the death to protect those they love from harm."

The thought of Jack Montgomery as a honey badger is hilarious. "I won't be able to unsee that description," I laughingly tell her.

Chapter Twenty-Four: We Are Golden

Ian

LUZ AND MY TWO sisters, Ness and Laney, are sitting at one of the shaded picnic tables with a margarita pitcher in easy reach. Laney lives about thirty miles from us, and she's rarely able to make it to Wednesday or Sunday family dinners. Her husband is a pharmaceutical sales rep, and travels a lot for his job. That means she's stuck at home with the kids and I think her life pretty much revolves around them - especially now they're all pre-teens.

Her decision to leave her chemical engineering job and stay home with them surprised all of us.

We've all been worried about her because when we look in from the outside, it looks like she's trying to do everything and doesn't have a very robust support network. We help out when we can, but it never feels like enough. It's good to see her laughing with Luz and Ness.

It's been a long time since I heard her laugh.

I'm heading for their table when I hear Jack. "Dude, I knew you weren't warning me away because you were worried about that station dynamics bullshit. I could see it in your eyes."

"I'd just met her. There was nothing to see."

He lays a hand on my shoulder. "The day you realized you had no choice about hiring her- I've never seen you so conflicted."

I feel my body tense. "There were plenty of reasons for my reservations."

My brother snorts. "Yeah. Reasons you won't talk to anyone about."

"I don't need to talk about them."

"You're my brother and I love you, but the fuck you don't." He shakes his head. "And you're never going to. At least not with me."

My gaze strays to Luz. "No, not with you."

Jack's gaze follows mine. "Nope, not with me." His tone is full of resignation, and he sounds hurt. "I get it. I'm not the kind of guy you have serious conversations with."

I grab his arm, but he shakes it off. "It's not like that."

"Whatever, Ian. You always wanted to be the hero."

He's wrong. I've never wanted to be a hero. I know a lot of people do dangerous jobs because they have a savior complex or they like the rush of adrenaline. I've never done them for either of those reasons. I did them because I wanted to make the world a better place. I know that's why she does it too.

I slide onto the bench beside her and throw my arm around her shoulders. "How many pitchers of this have you guys had?"

My sister Ness has flushed cheeks, and her eyes are sparkling. "We drank the pitcher Mom made, but it wasn't strong enough. I made this one."

Ness's love of tequila is well-known in our family and I bet this pitcher packs a lethal punch. I kiss the crown of Luz's head. "I guess it's a good thing I've only had one beer."

"And the kids and I are spending the night," Laney informs us. "I never have the chance to have more than one, so I'm taking advantage of it."

Luz nods and sits up, extending her red plastic cup in Luz's direction. "I'll toast to that."

Laney taps her cup against Luz's, "Me too," she says and downs whatever's left in one gulp.

"Are the three of you going to be too tipsy to play flag football?"

My voice is stern, but when Luz pokes me in the ribs, the ruse is up. "Whatever. You'd probably think it was hilarious if one of us puked in the field, or on Jack."

"I would think it's the funniest thing I've ever seen."

Laney props her chin in her hand and scans the yard. "He's different somehow."

I clear my throat. "Yeah. I think he's having an identity crisis. And maybe I'm to blame."

Ness and Laney's brows raise, just like our mom's when she's surprised.

"How could that possibly be your fault?" Demands Ness.

"Apparently, I set a standard as the oldest and he thinks he's always fallen short. He thinks no one takes him seriously."

Now Luz has a wrinkled brow too. "He said that? I never thought he'd use someone else as a scapegoat."

I shake my head. "I don't think it's like that. He's not making me a scapegoat - more like making me the apple of mom and dad's eye."

Laney smirks. "Well, I can't argue with that."

Ness tips her cup back and takes a long swallow. "Neither can I. You were such a paragon in high school. Sometimes, Mom made us feel like juvenile delinquents in comparison."

Luz is nodding in agreement. "I can totally see it. My sister Perdita is the same way."

"Is she the oldest?" Ness asks.

"Yep. And the one that picks up Dad's prescriptions, and makes casseroles and sticks them in the freezer. And if she dates, she never ever talks about it."

"Is she happy in Florida with your parents?" That kind of life seems so different from the one Luz has chosen.

"She's a librarian, and she has a little apartment about a block from her job."

"Would she ever consider moving?"

Luz sighs. "I think she would, Laney. But I think she feels obligated to stay there since Dex and I have chosen to make our lives here in Willow Creek. Our dad was overjoyed when Dex came off deployment and didn't re-up. He took over the garage, and Mom and Dad finally got a condo down there. Perdita went to college in Fort Lauderdale and was already there."

Ness scoots the platter of chips and guac closer. "They moved down there for the weather?"

"Yeah," Luz says as she grabs a chip. "Our mom always wanted to be close to the beach."

"Do you think they'll ever move back?" I ask.

She shakes her head vigorously against my shoulder. "Nope. Dad's the resident shuffle board champion and Mom's in a Red Hat Society."

"Maybe your sister will find someone down there," Laney comments.

Luz shrugs. "Maybe. But I think she gave up on dating apps a long time ago and I don't know how you're even supposed to meet anyone in the 21st century if you don't use them."

Ness flashes us an obnoxious smile. "Apparently, you can meet people in your place of employment."

I throw a chip in her direction. "We didn't plan it."

Laney smirks over at us. "You might not have planned it, but it's pretty convenient."

****

The margaritas didn't affect Luz's throwing arm. We won the game against my brother's team with two touchdowns to spare. Rubi insisted on playing too, and since she's the littlest person here, whenever we tossed her the ball, no one interfered with her. When it was over, she threw her arms around my legs and looked up at me with glowing eyes. "I won, Mr. Montgomery!"

I chuckled and ran my hand over her curls.

The kids were too exhausted to argue about going to bed, and I took Luz up on her offer of decaf coffee. She's perched on my lap, her arms around my neck. "You're exhausted too."

"I'm fine," she protests in the middle of a yawn.

"Let's get you to bed."

"Are you coming with me?"

I laugh. "I wish I could, but I don't think that would be wise. Today was the first day your kids really saw us together and I think it's a little soon for me to stay over."

"Fine. You can carry me up the stairs and tuck me in."

She closes her eyes as soon as I lay her on top of her comforter. When I take off her sneakers and socks, she stretches her toes and snuggles deeper into her pillow. She's immobile and snoring lightly as I shut the door.

***

I'm just pulling into my driveway when my phone rings. It's Mom. I shut off the engine and answer. "Hey, Mom. What's up?"

"Luz Martinez is delightful."

"And..." My mother never starts conversations with an observation like that.

"I'm just wondering why you introduced her to your entire family - unless you've changed your mind about settling down."

"Mom, I was never against settling down. I almost did it with Justine."

"You haven't shown any interest in dating since you came home, and every time your sister and I have tried to set you up you manufacture an excuse or find a reason to avoid it."

"Mom, it's not that I don't appreciate your concern."

She sighs heavily. "We worry about you, Ian. You won't talk about what happened to you when Justine died, and you refuse to seek professional help."

"That's because I've come to terms with it."

"I know you think you have. But I don't want you beginning something with her because you're trying to fill something hollow. I was scared when your father had his heart attack, because it reminded me of things from my past. For the first time in my life, I wanted to talk to someone who could be objective and give me the coping tools I needed to deal with my fears. I think you need to do the same."

"Do we really need to have this conversation right now?"

I hear the clank of ice in her glass as she takes a sip. "No, but promise me you'll consider therapy before you commit yourself to another relationship."

"Luz and I are taking things slowly."

"Ian, any time a woman has children whose feelings she needs to consider, that should be the course you take. But those children already seem to accept you. At least the youngest one, Rubi. Don't drag other hearts around."

"I promise I'll be careful. You should worry more about Laney and Jack - they both have things going on too they need to examine."

"Being a mother means you're always tethered to your children, no matter how grown they are."

"Is that why you're always trying to tell us what you think is best for us?"

"I just want the four of you to be happy."

"I know, Mom. But you should let us find our own happiness, like Ness has with Alex."

Chapter Twenty-Five: Take My Hand

Luz

IT'S HARD TO CONCENTRATE on what we have to do sometimes. Especially now the fact Ian and I are dating is out in the open. Even the casual brush of his hand against mine, or the way he tips his coffee, makes me feel like a live wire that's shooting sparks across the ground. I want to place my mouth in the exact same spot on the mug his lips just touched. I want to slide his suspenders down and kiss every one of the freckles dusted over his shoulder blades. I want to feel every one of his ribs against my fingers and count them as I drop to my knees and make him see stars.

Now that the rest of the crew knows we're involved, it's an endless stream of innuendo and pranks. Especially from Jack. When he barricaded us in Ian's office with a crowbar across the door yesterday, Ian was furious.

Even though we see each other almost every day at work, and he eats dinner at the house nearly every evening, we haven't had the chance to be alone together since the night I stayed over.

It's the middle of the month, and I'm catching up on the incident log, when I look up to see him hovering in the doorway.

"The rest of the guys are either asleep or playing euchre. We have about fifteen minutes."

I stretch my arms over my head. "Fifteen minutes for what, Hotshot?"

"You know for what," he says as he shuts and locks the door behind him.

I grin up at him as he kicks the chair away from the desk and pulls me into his arms. "I didn't want to be presumptuous."

"Are you okay with a quickie?" He asks as he slips a hand underneath my shirt to palm a breast.

When he flicks my nipple, I arch into his touch. "Make it good, Hotshot."

He steps away and unzips his station issued khakis. He tugs them past his thighs and yanks down his gray briefs. "Your turn, Magnolia."

I unfasten my pants and wriggle them below my hips. I brace my hands behind me on the desk and hop onto it. "Do you have protection?"

He raises a brow, like he's saying how dare I question him, and pulls one from the side pocket of his pants. "I'll even let you put it on."

"Let me, Hotshot? I think you like watching me do it."

I tug him closer and slide my hand over the hard ridges of his cock. He groans when I cup his balls and clenches his fists. "Hurry, before we're interrupted."

I don't make it a leisurely exploration, but I don't hurry either. When it's all the way on, he pushes me flat again and steps between my spread thighs. The fabric of his canvas pants is rough against the tender skin as he guides himself into me.

"Someday, we're gonna have the time for you to ride my face and my cock, Luz, but right now, I'm gonna ride you."

Every thrust of his hips sends him deeper, and the way he has his hand curled around one of my hips means I'll have bruises later. I twine one of my legs around his waist and the angle changes. Now he's brushing against my clit and my g-spot with every plunge, and I can feel the release building in my body.

He offers me the side of his hand. "Bite me so you don't scream."

"I'm not a screamer," I assure him.

He grins wickedly. "I'm going to make you scream, Magnolia."

My mind is like oatmeal right now, and I can't even think of a comeback. When he slips his hand between us and pinches my clit, my leg spasms around his waist and that's the thing that pushes me over the edge. I bite his palm so hard to cover the scream, it's probably going to bruise. My teeth on his skin must be his trigger, because he groans and his movements slow.

I'm gasping for air when he removes his hand. "At least no one heard me scream."

He drops his forehead to mine. "They probably heard the thump of the desk, though."

I flush because I didn't think of that. "Was it loud?"

"Yeah, but maybe the tv in the breakroom is loud too. Hopefully no one had their ear plastered to the door or came around looking for us."

He grabs a red bandana handkerchief from his other pocket and slips it between us. He gently wipes me off. "No soapy water?"

"No. I like knowing you smell like me, Magnolia," he says as he tweaks my nose.

"Are you coming over on your days off so we can take our time?"

"Nothing on the agenda but Rico's away game on Friday, and trying to twist us into pretzels and break all your furniture."

***

Our truck is the second one on the scene. Ian, Jack and Romero are already onsite because they were dispatched earlier for another incident. The fire is in one of the big abandoned tobacco barns the teenagers use for illegal parties in the summer and the wood is so dry it's nothing but kindling. We have to contain the fire because the structure sits just at the edge of the woods. If it ignites the trees, it'll scorch through them and the brittle grass and become uncontrollable. The new equine therapy facility is just over the ridge, and there are houses, crops and barns all along the path any brushfire would take.

It hasn't rained in weeks, and there's none in the forecast until after Saturday.

"How bad is it?" I ask Romero.

He shakes his head. "There aren't any fire hydrants and the hose doesn't stretch to the creek. That's why we called you guys. We're going to need all the water we can get."

"Did Jack call in one of the trucks?" The county water supply keeps two trucks on standby for remote fires like this.

"Yeah. There's one on its way. I don't know if they'll get here in time, though."

Ian comes to stand beside me. "We dug trenches around the perimeter and tried to remove all the dead limbs that will make it more powerful."

"That should keep it from spreading."

"As long as the wind keeps blowing from the south and doesn't speed up we should be okay. Fingers crossed."

When the little gray kitten creeps out of one of the second story windows, its mewl catches everyone's attention. "If there's one, there's more," Ian grimly observes.

"That roof is about to collapse, and you don't know what it's like inside. You can't risk it." He has this determined look on his face and I have a premonition something terrible is going to happen. When I put my hand on his forearm, he glances down at it, suddenly aloof. "Please don't go in there," I plead.

He shakes off my hand. "I have to do my job, Martinez."

"I might still be a rookie, but I don't think you should go in there either," Romero says.

"Doing our jobs means taking risks when the odds might not be in our favor. It means choosing not to let the fire take living things. Even kittens."

"It's unstable. You can tell from here."

"I'll be fast."

Romero and I watch as he pulls his helmet down and strides away.

"I have a bad feeling about this," Romero mutters.

I do too. And not just about the danger he's walking into. The way he brushed me off wasn't the caring, considerate man I've come to know. It was almost callous, and definitely a little arrogant. He sounded like a martyr and I wonder if he's always this obstinate and single-minded when he's in rescue mode.

The other end of the roofline just caught on fire and I breathe a sigh of relief when I see a dust trail and realize it's the water truck Jack called.

When the county guy gets out of the truck, I lead him over to the hose. He gives me a sharp nod and holds out his hand. "Burt Cross. You rescued my cousin's kids and I'm grateful."

"Briony and Cody?"

"Yep. Briony won't stop talkin' about you. Says she wants to be a firefighter when she grows up."

His story warms my heart. I think about Briony and her little brother almost every day.

I'm turning back to look at the barn when I see another gray kitten running straight for Romero. He scoops it up and even from here I can see him soothing it as its tiny claws scrabble against his shoulders. Romero looks panicked and I decide to rescue him, I just reach him when there's an ominous groan from inside the barn. We watch in horror as the ancient tar-papered roof finally catches fire and one side entirely collapses. Jack drops the hose he's pulling and sprints toward the building. The entire side of the structure is engulfed in flames now and my heart feels like a cannon just hit it. I watch as Sheffield grabs the edge of Jack's coat and hauls him back. From this distance, I can't make out what they're saying over the roar and hiss of the flames, but I know it's about Ian. One of us needs to rescue him before it becomes impossible. I decide it's going to be me because he might need medical assistance and I'm the logical choice. I pull down my faceplate and run toward them. "I'm going in after him," I relay over the radio.

"No, Luz. One of us should go. It's too dangerous. He's my brother, so it should be me."

Jack's tone is firm, but I'm not arguing about this. "If he needs medical attention, I'm the best person to retrieve him. One of you needs to call the ambulance and be ready to help me drag him into the yard."

Sheffield gives me a sharp nod. "She's right, Jack. Stop wasting time."

This is what I was trained for, and even though I'm scared, there's a sense of exhilaration too. Only a handful of moments have passed, but fire is unpredictable and he could be in there trapped or unconscious. Or both. I refuse to consider the other possibility because I just found him and I'm not going to lose him. The thought of it - when I've just begun to understand what he means to me and my kids sends my heart stuttering to a halt.

When I plunge through the barn doors, the fire is already creeping up one wall, and the smoke is hanging over everything like dense, impenetrable fog. I can barely see my hand in front of my face. Once I drop to a crouch, I spot him.

He's lying on the floor, his left leg pinned underneath a beam. He's still, and I don't know if he's dead or alive. *He's alive*, I vow under my breath. I kneel beside him and see his breath fogging the face plate. He still hasn't moved and when I place my hand on his chest and gently shake him, his eyes flutter open.

"What are you doing here?" His voice is weak and angry through the radio.

"I'm here to rescue you."

"Sheffield should have sent one of the guys in," he grumbles ominously.

"None of the guys are paramedics and I had the most oxygen. I volunteered and they agreed I was the best choice. Stop arguing with me so we can get out of here."

I struggle with the beam pinning him to the floor for precious minutes before I'm able to budge it enough to move him. "This is going to hurt, but we're running out of time."

His expression behind his faceplate is grim, and I know he's steeling himself. "I think my leg's broken and it feels like I cracked my ribs."

"Then let's get you out of here," I say as I wrap my arms under his shoulders from behind. He grunts and I grit my teeth, gathering the strength to start dragging him with the full leverage of my body.

He can still talk, which means his lungs probably haven't collapsed. But I can feel the heat of the fire at my back and thank the stars it's an old barn and they don't even use it for hay storage. Sheffield and one of the other guys have the hose aimed full blast against the side of the building now completely engulfed in flames, and Jack and Romero rush forward when I pull Ian through the arched doorway, and lift him so we can all get to a safer location, away from stray sparks. We're laying him on the ground about a hundred yards away when the entire roof of the barn comes crashing down. If I'd been a few minutes later or a few steps slower, he would have been crushed to death.

I unfasten his jacket and move the stethoscope Jack hands me all over his chest. He just took off his brother's boots and is rolling up his pants legs to check the break. His lungs and heart sound good, no rattling, and I think he'll be fine once his leg heals.

Jack glances over at me and shakes his head.

"Okay, Hotshot. According to the look your brother just gave me, your leg is definitely broken. We're going to splint it and wait for the paramedics."

Romero sets my medical kit in the ground and hands me a splint before he drops to his haunches beside me.

By the time we've eased Ian out of his heavy gear and helmet and I've splinted his leg, he's fading in and out of consciousness. I breathe a sigh of relief when I hear the wail of the ambulance.

*****

"How bad is it?" Dex's voice is grim.

"He's out of intensive care. No burns, and they don't think his lungs are permanently damaged. He was lucky."

"Or he had a guardian angel named Luz that dragged him out even though she could have died right there beside him."

He's angry, and I can't blame him. He lost so many people he loved while he was deployed, I'd be an asshole if I held the way he feels against him. "I had to do it. I didn't have a choice."

"There's always a choice, Luz. Think about what would have happened to the kids if you'd died. There's no guarantee Mari and I would get custody."

"There is a guarantee. You're the ones I have named in my will."

"But your ex-husband's still alive and he'd do it just to get the social security and the life insurance policy proceeds. Especially since he's behind on child support."

"How do you know he's behind on child support?"

"Because he's always behind on child support. Has he paid you a dime since they took his tax refund in 2022?"

"Ben not paying child support has nothing to do with this conversation."

"It has everything to do with it. Because you're always stubborn and trying to do things by yourself. Like dragging grown men from burning buildings."

"Dex," I firmly say to calm him down. "Now that the kids and I are settled in Willow Creek, addressing Ben's delinquent child support is the next thing on my to do list. I know you were scared, but I'm fine."

"Luz, I was scared shitless when Trevor texted and said he heard on the radio you went into a burning building to rescue someone. Hermanita," his voice breaks and I can hear him swallowing the tears, "I can't afford to lose you."

"I'm a firefighter, Hermano. I was doing my job. I had plenty of oxygen and all my fire gear. If I'd started to lose my air and the fire was too close for comfort, I would have found another way. I promise I'm as careful as I can be."

He sighs, and I know he just ran his hand over his buzz cut. It's what he does when he's exasperated. "I know you're grown now and there's nothing I can do to stop you, but for chrissake try not to give me any more heart attacks."

"Like I said, I'll be as careful as I can without shirking my duty."

"I guess I can't ask for more. What are you going to do about Montgomery? I can't believe you found someone even more stubborn than you."

I gulp, and now I'm the one swallowing back tears. "I still haven't seen him. His family was there and I didn't want to intrude."

"You work with Jack and haven't you met the rest of them?"

"Inviting someone to your house for dinner isn't the same as letting them in a hospital room. I'm not family, so technically I have no right to be there."

Dex scoffs. "You saved his life and you're in love with him. From everything I've seen I'm pretty sure he's in love with you too."

"We haven't said the words."

"The words aren't necessary when everything you do speaks louder than they ever will. You should make them let you see him, Luz."

"Okay, Dex. You've made your point. I'll let you know how things go."

"You'd better, Luz. You have a lot on your mind right now."

"Goodbye Dex, I love you." I hang up before he can give me any more commentary.

The screen door creaks open and I hear footsteps behind me. "Was that Uncle Dex?"

It's Rico.

"Yep. He was just checking on me."

He sits down on the swing beside me. "Are you crying because of Coach Montgomery?"

I raise my hand to my face. I didn't even realize I was crying.

"I'm not crying because I'm sad," I tell him as I wrap my arm around his shoulders. "I'm crying because I'm relieved. Your coach came pretty close to dying today."

"Just so you know, Mom, we'd all be sad if something happened to him. You seem so happy when he's around. Rosie said she's never seen you smile so much. More even than when Dad was around."

"I know it's hard for the three of you -seeing me with someone besides your dad."

"Rosie said she doesn't remember much, just that he wasn't around a lot and when he was, he made you cry.

And Rubi said she doesn't remember anything but him giving her suckers and telling her to be quiet, and not letting her sleep with Mr. Snoozy. I'm the only one who remembers what it was like before he turned into an asshole and you guys fought all the time."

"Your dad and I loved each other once, Rico. A part of me will always love that part of your dad, the one that was wild and crazy. But we want different things from life."

He lays his head on my shoulder- something he hasn't done in at least four years. "It's okay if you're in love with Mr. Montgomery, Mom."

"I think I might be, bambino. But I don't know if he loves me back or if he wants to live with us."

"Mom. You don't kiss people like that if you don't love them. He definitely loves you back. You should go see him in the hospital."

"How'd you know he was there?"

"It's all the guys at practice today could talk about. Coach MacIntyre had to make us all run laps to get us to shut up."

I press a kiss to the top of his head. "Thank you for being who you are, mijo."

He heaves a great sigh and leans away. "I love you, Mom. Even if I don't show it all the time. I just want you to be happy. If Coach Montgomery makes you happy, then I'm not going to make you feel like he shouldn't be part of our lives."

He stands up and I can't reply because my throat is choked with tears again.

"I'll make sure Rosie and Rubi brush their teeth. You should sit out here and watch the stars."

The screen door bangs shut behind him and it's like a chapter has just closed. The little boy I cradled in my arms when he was teething is becoming a man.

Chapter Twenty-Six: I Fall Apart Every Time

Ian

WHEN I WAKE UP, the woman who rescued me is sitting in the leather chair beside the bed. She tangles our fingers together as my eyes flicker open.

"Thank God you're finally awake. Mari said you had a concussion from the fall and we've all been so worried. Your parents just left, and Jack and Ness were here earlier."

"How long have you been here?" The words feel like marbles in my mouth.

"For about two hours."

Everything that happened comes rushing back. The kitten dropping safely to the ground, just past my reach and scampering outside. The weightlessness of falling when the support beam under the loft caught fire and I crashed to the dirt floor.

The memory of how it felt to know the end was near because I had less than ten minutes of oxygen. Losing consciousness to her voice, telling me I wasn't allowed to die on her when she'd just found me.

"You came in after me. You risked your life for me." The fury I feel at the thought of her sacrifice numbs me. "You did exactly what I was afraid you'd do. You were reckless and heedless and your kids would have been orphans." Everything that scrapes past my throat is raw.

She squeezes my hand- oblivious to the rage and desolation I feel. "Of course I came after you. We all saw the kitten run out the door and heard you yell when the floor collapsed. I had the fullest tank of oxygen, so it had to be me. I don't know that I would have let anyone else do it."

"How'd you get me out?"

"There was only one heavy beam on you-across your ribs. I was able to drag you away from it. And then I dragged you out."

"No one helped you?" Where the hell were my brother and Romero?

"They would have if I'd radioed that I needed it. But I didn't need it. We were lucky that you were on the side that hadn't caught fire yet, closest to the door. I went in first to scope it out and the guys were on standby."

She lifts the bag at her feet. "I brought you something."

"What is it?"

"Something to take your mind off things." She eases a dvd player out of the canvas and sets it on the ledge under the tv. Then she extracts what looks like a dvd bundle and props it up on my chest.

"Lonesome Dove?" I croak in disbelief. "I thought DVDs were getting harder and harder to find."

"I know you said we could watch it from a streaming service, but isn't this better? It might make it harder to binge watch, but I think that's a good thing."

I cup her elbow when she sets the dvd on the crowded table. "We shouldn't see each other again. Not like it was. Not even like this."

"Why? No one really cares about fraternization."

"It's not about that. It's too dangerous."

"Life is dangerous. An asteroid could hit earth, or we could die in an elevator accident."

"Those things only happen in movies."

She rolls her eyes before she plants her hands on her hips. "That's not the point. The point is that we only get one life and we should make the most of every single second. We don't know the hour or the day it's all going to come crashing down on us, so why live in fear?"

"I'm trying to protect you. When people love me, they die. You took a stupid risk because you think you're in love with me."

"I don't think I'm in love with you, Ian Montgomery. I know I'm in love with you. I wasn't going to let you die in that barn when I was there to save you."

"The last thought I had, when I thought that was going to happen, was about you."

She smiles triumphantly. "I knew you loved me back."

"Loving you will impair my judgment, Luz. I'll clip your wings because I don't want you putting yourself in danger. And what if one of my decisions leaves Rico and Rosie and Rubi without their mom? Rubi's only six."

"What can I say that's going to make you listen? I chose to do this because I know what it's like to lose everything. And I didn't want to lose you too. There is no world and no scenario that exists that I wouldn't do everything I could to save you. Especially when it means I'm doing the job I signed up to do."

"Luz, I thought I was ready for that, for this," I say as I wave my hand between us. "But I'm not. What just happened reminds me I'm not. I don't know if I'll ever be and you shouldn't put your life on hold waiting for me to be ready."

She covers her eyes, and until she moves her hand I think she's crying.

"You might be an idiot, Ian Montgomery, but I've been waiting my whole life for you. I'm not going to settle for anything less than what I found and I'll wait however long it takes for you to realize my kids and I are exactly what you need."

So she's not sad, she's angry. "You might be waiting forever, Luz."

"I might. And I might not. But I know that when you decide I'm right you're going to have to grovel to earn your way back into my life."

She pushes the chair away and stands. "Good bye, Ian. Come find me when you're ready to admit you're wrong."

***

They discharged me a week ago, and I haven't seen Luz or the kids. The baseball season was almost over - we only had three more games- and Alex said he could handle it. I've been hobbling around on crutches, and Ness and Mom took pity on me, so they filled my freezer with casseroles.

I've watched Lonesome Dove over and over with the gray kitten nestled on my chest. Romero brought her over because he said they couldn't find anyone to foster her. She's always either asleep or purring. Whenever I thought about getting a pet before, I always imagined adopting a German Shepherd or some other big dog. I never thought a tiny gray kitten with a white stripe down the middle of her chest and one white paw would completely steal the only piece of my heart left beating after I told Luz to leave.

I finally took my mom's advice and found a therapist. We're having online sessions until I'm cleared to drive again, but she's helping me work through all the trauma that's been stacked up inside my head. I didn't realize how much of it I was holding inside and burying until she made me start talking about it. The therapy made me realize something else too - just because I'm good at fighting fires doesn't mean I should be doing it.

Not when it's at the cost of my mental well-being and it's hard to let go of all the things I've been through.

I retired from it once, and it's time I found something else to do with my life. Even if Luz isn't part of it. I've been such an idiot, I don't even know how I'm going to make it up to her. I know she said she'll be waiting, but I don't want to win her back if I'm still broken.

I'm taking one of Mom's chicken noodle casseroles out of the oven when I hear the doorbell chime. My heart stops in my chest because it might be her.

When I swing open the door, it's not Luz who's standing there. It's my brother. We haven't really talked since the barbecue, and things have never been this tense between us. We've always had sibling rivalry, but I never realized his resentment went so deep.

"Come in. Even though I think we're fighting, I'm not going to leave you standing there."

He brushes past me as I close the door.

"You look like shit, Ian."

"I haven't had the easiest few weeks."

He snorts. "Yeah. I know. I was there when we pulled you out of that building, remember? I was traumatized too."

I head toward the kitchen and he follows me. "Do you want a beer?" I ask as I grab two from the fridge.

"I might need it for what I'm about to say, so yeah," he says as he takes it and pops the tab. "You might be older, but I'm smarter. I'd never let a woman like Luz, who for some unfathomable reason is in love with you, walk away. Why are you being such an idiot?"

I take a long gulp and set my beer on the counter behind me. "She risked her life for me."

"Duh. Because she loves you. It's what people do when they love you."

"She risked her life to save me and she didn't even think about the consequences. To herself, to her kids. This is exactly what I was afraid would happen. I can't be there to watch her take those kinds of chances. Especially on me."

"I know bad shit happened to you and you've been carrying it around since you got back home. But that's no excuse for the way you're ostracizing her and shunning everyone else in your life who cares for you. You need therapy."

"Mom kept telling me the same thing. I already signed up."

"Is it helping? You don't sound any more mellow."

"I'll never be as mellow as you."

His jaw hardens. "I'm not mellow, Ian. I just know when it's worth it to dwell on stuff and when there's nothing I can do to change it no matter how much I think about it."

"You act like a kid sometimes."

"And you act like a judgmental asshole sometimes."

We glare at each other over our beers before I finally relent. "Sorry. I don't know why I'm antagonizing you."

"I know why. Because you need to go and grovel to the woman you're in love with and you don't know how to do it."

"That's what she said. That if I wanted her back, I had to grovel."

He laughs. "I bet you've never had to grovel in your life. And you're not exactly the most romantic guy I know. This is going to be fun to watch."

"I can be romantic," I protest.

Jack levels me with a disbelieving look. "Can you? Have you and Luz even been on a real date?"

"We had one."

"Oh? And where'd you take her?"

I flush, because I'm realizing it wasn't really a date. "I made her dinner here."

"No you didn't. You can't cook anything but chili."

"Fine. Mom made the dinner and I warmed it up in the oven. I got the white wine Mom told me to get too."

"You're freaking hopeless. Did you give Luz a kiss goodnight?"

I feel my cheeks reddening again. "A little more than that," I admit.

"You banged on the first date? Didn't Mom teach you any class? Jeez. You're even more ridiculous than I thought," he says as takes another sip of his beer.

"Unlike you, I don't have that much experience wooing women."

He cocks his head to the side. "I'm just looking for the one, Ian. And trust me, when I find her, nothing's going to get in my way. Especially my own idiocy."

"So what am I supposed to do?"

He holds his hands in the air. "I can't tell you what you need to do. I'm just going to tell you that whatever it is, it should show her you see her and know what she needs."

I groan and rub my hand over my face. "I have no idea what that is."

He peers at me over the can. "I seriously doubt that. I didn't think I was that much smarter than you."

"What about her kids?"

"Oh, you're going to have to win them over too."

"Thanks for the vote of confidence," I mutter as I finish my drink.

"Can I ask you something, brother?"

"Ask away. You're determined to put me in my place tonight."

"Do you even like your job?"

I shake my head. "I'm always stressed and exhausted. I thought I could do something else when I retired from the Forest Service. Twenty years of fire and I thought I was done."

"Then Dad had his heart attack and you got stuck doing it again."

"My therapist thinks I should resign and I agree with her."

He surveys me closely. "You wouldn't have to worry about fraternization or human resources complaints."

"That's not why I'm doing it. I'm doing it for me."

"If you're doing things for you, then figure out how to win her back." He sets his empty beer down and gives me a salute.

"I will."

We give each other awkward one-armed hugs at the door and I sink back onto my couch, trying to think of a grand gesture that will convince her I'm willing to grovel.

Chapter Twenty-Seven: Ruins With You

Luz

"HE'S NOT COMING BACK."

I whirl around, because I don't want to believe what he's telling me. "Who's not coming back?"

"My brother, Luz. Ian isn't coming back. He resigned."

I'm gripping my coffee cup so hard, I'm surprised the handle doesn't snap off. "This is all my fault."

Jack shakes his head and lays a hand on my arm. "It's not your fault. I don't think it has anything to do with you. This job was eating his soul. You know him well enough to see that."

"What are we going to do?"

"We'll keep the station going. It's a good thing you know how to do the schedules and the paperwork too. There'll be a new chief soon - one of us will go from captain to assistant chief, probably Whitaker, and Sheffield will probably be the new chief."

"You're not going for it?"

"Hell no," he scoffs. "I like the level of responsibility I have as a captain just fine. I don't want my job to consume my life any more than it already does."

"What's Ian going to do?"

"He already gets retirement from the U.S. Forest Service because you're eligible after twenty years. And he's part of the blacksmith guild and has his general contractor's license. He can do whatever he wants."

"So you talked to him?"

He nods. "I went over there last night after my shift."

"Did he say anything about me?"

"Yeah, but not anything I feel comfortable telling you."

"I was too hard on him."

"I don't think you were. I think whatever you said finally woke him up from years of sleep-walking."

"I was thinking about transferring to the paramedics unit at the hospital. So things wouldn't be awkward."

"Well now you don't have to. And we need you here, Luz."

"I'm not going anywhere."

"Good. You should make my brother work for it."

"If he gets his head out of his ass long enough, I plan on doing exactly that."

***

I haven't talked to my sister in weeks. Our schedules never align and she's been working on some mysterious project she won't tell me anything about.

I dial and cross my fingers.

She answers almost immediately, and she looks exhausted.

"Hey Sis. Dex told me about the fire. How are you?"

"Just taking it one day at a time. It scared me."

"How's your fire chief?"

"He made it clear he's not ready to be mine. And he's not the fire chief any more."

"What happened?"

"His misplaced conscience. He thinks he makes my life more dangerous."

"Because he's your boss?"

"Apparently."

She scowls. "You're a grown woman."

"One who can make her own decisions."

"Are you going to wait for him to get his head out of his ass?"

I laugh bitterly. "I don't have a choice. Because he's in my head and my heart."

"Do I need to buy a cat burglar suit and make a trip up there? We're in the middle of murder mystery season at the library and there are lots of innocuous poisons I'd like to try out."

"I think Rico might beat you to it."

"How do the kids feel?"

"Rosie and Rubi haven't said anything, but Rico's ready to challenge him to a duel."

"Just keep your head up, little sis. I'll try to visit soon."

"Thanks, Dita. I miss you."

"Miss you too, baby sister."

Chapter Twenty-Eight: I'd Give Up Half of Forever

Ian

When she opens the door, she doesn't step away from the frame or invite me in. "What are you doing here?"

Her eyes are red-rimmed and her voice is hoarse and I know her misery is my fault. I deserve every bit of her anger for pushing her away when I needed her most.

"I needed to get myself right. To deserve you. It's where I've been."

She crosses her arms and raises a brow. "You expect me to believe you willingly sought out the therapy you so desperately need?"

"If I wanted you in my life, I didn't have a choice. I needed to make peace with my wreckage."

"I didn't want you to do it for me. I wanted you to do it for yourself. Because you're broken and you need help."

"I did it for me. Because you and your kids are the best thing in my life, and I want to be worthy of you. I want to show you I can learn from my mistakes and lean on other people when things get too rough for me to handle on my own."

She leans against the doorframe. "How do you plan on proving that?"

The kitten meows from the basket behind me.

"What's that noise?"

"The first step of me proving to you that I want this."

I step aside so she can see.

When she brushes past me, I close my eyes. I've gone too long without the scent of summer she always wears. She crouches beside the basket and peels back the lid. "A kitten. The kitten you risked your life to rescue."

I clear my throat. "Yeah. Phantom needs a soft place to land and so do I."

"So she's bribery disguised as fluff?"

"Bribery for Rico, Rosie and Rubi. I'm still trying to figure out how I'm going to bribe their mom."

"Why a kitten? Why this kitten?"

"I know you've been taking the kids to play with the dogs at the shelter, and I figured that was your way of appeasing them. That maybe you weren't ready for another Knocks."

She strokes the white stripe on the kitten's nose. "Her name's Phantom?"

I shrug. "It seemed to fit, so it's what I've been calling her. While Phantom was lying on my chest and I was watching Clara watch her ranch burn, I had an epiphany. We run into fires to save the things we can't live without. I shouldn't have pushed you away- I would have rescued you too."

She rises to her feet. "You would have rescued me because I'm one of the things you can't live without?"

I want to pull her into a hug, but the thread between us feels too tenuous right now. Like it could snap if I say the wrong thing or make a dumb move. "I think you are."

"I haven't heard a word from you in weeks and I had to hear from your brother that you're leaving the station."

"I thought you'd be happy I'm leaving the station?"

She crosses her arms again. "Why would I be happy about that? At least it's one place I could see you. Even if we were nothing more than friends."

I step toward her and unpin her arms so I can take her hands in mine. "We could never just be friends, Luz. Can we start over where we left off?"

Her eyes search mine. "I want to, but I'm scared to trust you again."

"Mom! Rubi spilled the Kool-Aid!" Rosie yells from somewhere inside the house.

"Thank God it wasn't purple this time," she grumbles. "Come on. And bring the cat."

I scoop up the basket and follow her inside.

Rosie has at least half the roll of paper towels layered over the kitchen floor, and Rico's struggling with a mop. Luz takes it from him. "Help your sister."

Rubi spots me first and her eyes widen. "Mr. Montgomwy, it's you."

"What's in the basket, Coach?" Rico asks.

His arms are crossed just like his mom's were. "A present," I say as I set the basket on the floor and lift the lid.

Phantom sticks one of her paws over the edge and Rubi squeals. "Mommy! It's a kitty!" She drops to her knees and scoots across the floor.

Rosie abandons the paper towels and drops to the floor beside her little sister. "Is she ours?"

"If your mom will let you keep her."

"Mommy, puhleez!" Rubi clasps her hands together and turns her most angelic look on Luz. There's no way she's going to be able to resist it, but I hold my breath anyway.

"Fine."

"Yay!" Rosie exclaims. "Can I name it?"

Luz raises a brow and I know that's my cue.

"She already has a name. Phantom."

"Can Phantom sleep with me tonight, Mom?" Rosie pleads.

"I want her to sleep with me," Rubi pouts.

"She can't sleep with anyone until she has a litter box and all the other stuff we need."

I stand. "I already have everything you need. All her stuff's in the truck."

"This really is bribery," Luz mutters.

"There's more. Because I had a feeling it would take more than the cutest kitten on the planet to get back in your good graces."

"Rico, can you and the girls take the kitten upstairs?"

"Actually, Rico, can you help me unload the truck so I can take your mom somewhere to talk while the three of you get Phantom's things ready?"

His gaze flicks back and forth between us and Luz rolls her eyes. "Go help your coach unload the truck and I'll finish cleaning up this mess."

Rico sullenly follows me outside and doesn't break his silence until we reach my truck. "You don't have crutches any more. Coach MacIntyre said you had to use them."

"Only until my leg healed. I just have a limp now and I can't put my weight on it."

"You made my mom cry."

"I didn't mean to. I was only trying to protect her. And you."

He snorts. "Well that was a dumb move, because now she doesn't want to like you."

"Will you watch your sisters so I can try to change that?"I ask as I hand him the litter box.

I hoist the litter and the bag of food and toys into my own arms.

"Only if you promise to be careful with her."

"I'll be extra-careful. I promise."

He gives me a nod, man-to-man. "We have to shake on it when we get back inside."

After we get back in the house and set the stuff down, I hold out my hand. "I promise."

I'm surprised at how firm his grip is when he shakes it until I remember what it felt like to be fourteen and trying to control how things affected me.

"I'll watch my sisters."

Luz glares at me ten minutes later when I hold the truck door open for her. "I could have done that myself."

"Not when you're with me," I tell her as I shut it.

She's quiet as I turn right out of her driveway. She's quiet when I park in the lot on the side of the road. Until she realizes where we are. "You already brought me here once."

"I have something new to show you."

"Fine." She clambers out the other side before I can open her door again.

I take a deep breath and remember Jack said this wouldn't be easy. "Follow me," I say and step onto the trail.

The only sign I have that she's actually following me is the occasional crunch of leaves. When we reach the tree, I turn to her. "Come here so I can show you."

When she comes to stand beside me, I point to the freshly carved bark. "This is what I wanted to show you."

She moves closer so she can read it.

"Hotshot plus Magnolia."

"In a heart. Because you have mine, Luz. Even if you don't want it."

She closes her eyes. When she opens them, they're full of tears.

"Shit," I say and search my pockets for a handkerchief. "I'm sorry. I didn't want to make you sad. Rico's going to murder me."

When she places her hand on my forearm I don't know what to expect. "I'm not crying because I'm sad, Hotshot. I'm crying because I'm happy. You have my heart too."

I wrap my arms around her, finally. And everything I've ever wanted is suddenly right there within reach. She cups my jaw in her hand. "Please kiss me. We need to seal the deal. No more apologies. We just go from here and take it one day at a time."

When she brushes her lips against mine, all the missing pieces and things I lost in a fire on the side of a canyon five years ago finally fall back into place.

Epilogue

IT'S THE TENTH ANNUAL Willow Creek Fire Department Charity Chili Cook-Off, and Ian and I have a joint entry. We experimented for weeks until we decided on a chili and jambalaya combination that's just the right amount of spicy and sweet. River boasted that he came up with his best concoction ever too, and Vanessa won't stop bragging about Alex's entry.

"Do you think you're going to win again?" I ask after the judges leave our booth.

"Even if I don't, I already did," he says as he raises my hand to his lips.

"What if the jambalaya seasoning made it too spicy?"

"It didn't. One of the judges had to drink a gallon of milk after he tasted my entry two years ago. And I still won."

The kids and I moved in with him two weekends ago, just in time to prepare for the upcoming school year and get on the bus route. Dex said he already had someone renting the cabin the first of the month, so I don't feel guilty about leaving it vacant.

Ian started a general contracting business last month, and he already has enough work lined up to fill half the year.

Fifteen minutes later, we all cross our fingers as the head of the fundraising committee steps onto the podium and motions for silence. "We have a unanimous winner."

"We'd better beat Jack and River," Ian vows darkly.

I rub my hand over his knuckles. "I have faith in us."

"And the winner is, for the sixth year in a row, Ian Montgomery. Let's give a round of applause for Mr. Montgomery and his partner, Luz Martinez."

I can't help squealing and jumping up and down. Ian pumps his fist in the air and picks me up around the waist to twirl me around.

"I think this calls for a special kind of acknowledgment."

Ian's mom is standing behind us with an envelope in her hand. She holds it out to me.

"What's this?"

"I know you'll take good care of it and pass it down to one of your kids."

"Is that what I think it is, Mom?" Jack calls after her.

I stare at the envelope.

"Did my mom just give you her strawberry cake recipe?" Ian sounds shocked.

I pry open the envelope and extract a hand-written recipe card. "She did," I say in amazement.

"Not fair!" Vanessa calls from Alex's booth.

"This is her formal stamp of approval, Luz," Ian says and gathers my hands in his. "Now you can't ever get rid of me. She'll never forgive me if I let you go."

I loop my arms around his neck. "You're stuck with me and my rugrats, Ian Montgomery."

"There's no one I'd rather be stuck with."

Sneak Peek at No Ghosts novella

Chapter One

IT'S HALLOWEEN NIGHT, AND someone always tries to break into the old house covered in ivy on the dead end street at the edge of town. My friends and I used to dare each other to spend the night there, but we always chickened out. One of mom's bunko buddies called the station and said she saw flickering in one of the windows and was afraid it was on fire. The rest of the guys are either off so they could take their kids trick or treating or at the six car pile-up that got called in earlier tonight. So when Mom called me, I told her I'd go check it out.

When I get there, I don't see any cars in the circular driveway. And there's a light moving past the windows on the first floor. I creep up the steps and notice the door's ajar. There's a wad of paper stuck between it and the frame and I pull it out as I push against the heavy oak. When it slams shut behind me, there's a gasp and a white figure comes hurtling toward me. I step backward and trip on the edge of a rug.

I go crashing to the floor with an apparition clinging to me. It starts beating my chest with its fists. "Why did you pull the paper out? Now we're stuck here until my sister shows up in the morning to get ready for her seance."

I recoil on the inside, because I recognize that voice. Ophelia. The only woman who's ever made me tongue-tied and awkward. The only woman who's ever ghosted me. The woman who dunked me nineteen times in a row at the ice cream social before she stomped into oblivion.

She pulls up a visor and I finally take in her ridiculous costume. "Are you supposed to be a ghostbuster?" I scoff.

She hops off me and glowers. "This isn't a costume, Jack Montgomery. It's my job. I'm a ghost-hunter. And you just interrupted the first job I've gotten in Willow Creek."

"You should have told someone you were going to be here."

"I did, you idiot! The owner. He said the door jams and I'd be stuck if I didn't wedge something in between it and the frame."

"Well how was I supposed to know? You're the last person I want to be stuck with on Halloween night. Especially since you acted like I didn't exist after our date."

"What else was I supposed to do? You were ridiculous."

"How was I ridiculous?"

"Are you for real? The last thing you said to me was, *Are you my little toe? Because I'm gonna bang you against every piece of furniture in my house.*"

Recipes Included in No Apologies

Grace Montgomery's Strawberry Cake

<u>**Ingredients:**</u>

Strawberry Reduction: 32 oz. fresh or frozen strawberries; 4 oz sugar; 1 T lemon juice; 1 t lemon zest; 1 pinch salt

Cake Ingredients: 8 oz unsalted butter at room temperature; 10 oz granulated sugar; 6 oz egg whites room temperature; 4 oz milk room temperature; 6 oz strawberry reduction room temperature; 2 oz vegetable or canola oil; 1 T lemon juice; zest one lemon; 1 ½ t strawberry extract; ½ t pink food coloring; 14 oz all purpose flour; 1 ½ t baking powder; 1 t baking soda; ½ t salt

Ingredients for Strawberry Buttercream Frosting: 4 oz pasteurized egg whites; 16 oz powdered sugar; 16 oz unsalted butter, room temp.; ½ t salt; 1 t vanilla extract; 4 oz strawberry reduction, room temp.

<u>Reduction Instructions</u>

1. Place your thawed strawberries into a blender and pulse a few times until they are liquid.

2. Pour the blended strawberries, sugar, lemon zest, lemon juice, and salt into a medium saucepan and bring to a simmer over medium heat.

3. Once bubbling, reduce heat to medium-low and slowly reduce until berries begin to break up and the mixture has reduced and looks like a thick paste.

This can take a while. Mine takes between 40-60 minutes! I know this sounds like a long time but low and slow is the best for keeping all the flavor. Just give it a stir every now and then.

Step 4 – Occasionally stir the mixture to prevent burning. You should end up with about 1 cup of thick strawberry reduction that looks like tomato sauce. Transfer to another container and let it cool before use.

Step 5 – You will use some of the reduction for the cake batter, some for the frosting, and the rest for filling between the cake layers for extra flavor

<u>Step-By-Step Instructions for Cake</u>

1. Bring your butter, egg whites, milk, and strawberry reduction to room temperature and prepare the rest of your ingredients. For the best success, use a food scale to weigh your ingredients. (Converting this recipe to cups could lead to failure)

2. Grease two, 8" cake pans and preheat the oven to 350°F/176°C.

3. In a separate medium bowl, combine the milk, oil, strawberry reduction, strawberry extract, vanilla extract, lemon extract, lemon zest, lemon juice, and pink food coloring. Whisk it together and set it aside

4. In a separate medium bowl, whisk together the flour, baking powder, baking soda, and salt. Set it aside

5. Add room temperature butter to the stand mixer with the paddle attachment and beat at medium speed until smooth and shiny, about 30 seconds.

6. Gradually sprinkle in the sugar, and beat until the mixture is fluffy and almost white, about

3-5 minutes.

7. Add the egg whites one at a time, beating 15 seconds between. Your mixture should look cohesive at this point. If it looks curdled and broken, your butter or egg whites are too cold.You must use egg WHITES for this recipe, the yellow from the egg could turn the inside of your cake peach.

8. Mix on low speed and add about a third of the dry ingredients to the batter, followed immediately by about a third of the milk mixture, mix until ingredients are almost incorporated into the batter.

9. Repeat the process 2 more times. When the batter appears blended, stop the mixer and scrape the sides of the bowl with a rubber spatula. If it looks like ice cream, you did it right!

10. Divide the batter evenly between the prepared pans. I use a spoon to make a divot in the center so that the cakes bake up flatter.

11. Bake cakes at 350ºF/176ºC until they feel firm in the center and a toothpick comes out clean

or with just a few crumbs on it, about 30-35 minutes.

12. Place pans on top of a wire rack and let cool for 10 minutes. Then flip your cakes onto the racks and cool completely.

13. Once cool, wrap each layer in plastic wrap and refrigerate before assembling your cake. Refrigerate for a minimum of 2 hours or freeze for up to 1 week.

14. Ice the top layer of each cake with buttercream frosting and stack them on top of each other.

Buttercream Instructions

1. Place egg whites and powdered sugar in a stand mixer bowl. Attach the whisk and combine ingredients on low and then whip on high for 5 minutes

2. Place pasteurized egg whites and powdered sugar in the bowl of your stand mixer. Add the whisk attachment and combine ingredients on low, then whip on high for 5 minutes.

3. Add in your softened butter in chunks and whip on high for 8-10 minutes until it's very white, light and shiny. It may look curdled and yellow at first, this is normal. Keep whipping.

4. Add in strawberry reduction, vanilla extract and salt and continue whipping until incorporated.

5. Optional: Switch to a paddle attachment and mix on low for 15-20 minutes to make the buttercream very smooth and remove air bubbles.

Strawberry Buttercream Notes:

1. Make sure your frosting is very light and white before adding in the puree. Give it a taste, if it still tastes like butter, keep whipping it until it tastes like sweet ice cream.

2. If your buttercream looks curdled, it's too cold. Take out ½ cup of buttercream and melt it in the microwave until it's just barely melted. About 10-15 seconds. Pour it back into your buttercream, and mix until creamy.

The Martinez Family Chalupa Recipe (Corn Tortillas Substituted for Homemade Chalupas)

1. Add about 1/4" of vegetable or canola oil to a heavy bottomed, medium-sized skillet and heat over medium-high heat.

2. When the oil is hot but not quite smoking, rest a corn tortilla onto the hot oil to fry (it will float like a boat).

3. Cook the tortilla for about a minute before spreading a few tablespoons of salsa onto the top and cook for 2-3 minutes until crispy around the edges.

4. (It's ok if *some oil mixes with the salsa*; however, you don't want to cover it entirely with the hot oil.

5. When the shells are crispy around the edges, use a slotted spoon or spider to gently transfer them to a sheet pan lined with paper towels to absorb the excess oil.

6. After the tortillas are fried, dress them how you

like. Traditionally, they use simple toppings, like queso fresco, scattered cilantro and shredded lettuce. Some queso fresco and cilantro make a perfect snack.

For a more substantial chalupa recipe try some of these combos after they've been fried with the salsa:

- Chicken chalupas – top with your favorite salsa and add shredded rotisserie chicken, diced tomatoes and cheese.

- Cheesy chalupa – Add grated Oaxaca cheese at the last minute they're frying. The cheese will melt and get oozy.

- Steak chalupa – Add thin strips of steak and guacamole to the just fried chalupas. Top with queso fresco and fresh cilantro.

- Beef chalupa – Brown ground beef with onion, cumin and chili powder (or use taco seasoning mix) and top the fried chalupas with a scoop of the beef mixture. Garnish with diced tomatoes, grated cheddar cheese and sour cream.

- Black bean chalupa – Saute diced onions and black beans in a skillet and season with cumin and chili powder, kosher salt and black pepper. Add several spoonfuls to the crisped chalupa shells and top with pico de gallo and queso fresco for a vegetarian chalupa recipe.

Luz and Ian's Dutch Oven Jambalaya Chili

Serves 6; Prep time: 15 minutes; Cook time: 1 hour, 15 minutes

- 1 tablespoon oil

- 1/2 pound andouille sausage

- 1 medium bell pepper, diced

- 3 celery stalks, diced

- 1/2 cup onion, diced

- 2 tablespoon tomato paste

- 3/4 cup water

- 1 (14.5-ounce) can diced tomatoes

- 1/2 teaspoon cayenne

- 1/2 teaspoon cajun seasoning

- 1 tablespoon chili powder

- 1 (15-ounce) can pinto beans undrained

- 1 cup shredded cooked chicken

- 1/4 cup chopped cooked turkey bacon

- 1/2 lb shrimp, deveined and cooked (optional)

1. Heat the oil in a dutch oven over medium heat. Cook the sausage, using a wooden spoon to break it up as it cooks, 5 to 7 minutes or until cooked through. Place the cooked sausage on a plate and set aside.

2. Add the bell pepper, celery, and onion to the pan; cook over medium heat until the pepper and celery are tender. Add the remaining ingredients and the sausage. Bring to a boil over medium heat, then simmer for at least 1 hour before serving.

Acknowledgements

As always, this book happened because I know what true love is. It's something my husband has been showing me since the moment we met and my four-year-old daughter's mischievous questions didn't scare him away. Thank you, my love, for giving me a solid foundation and wings to fly. Thank you for supporting me on every step of this journey.

Thank you to my ARC team and the incredible women I consider friends – especially Jen H., Whitney S., and Lindsay S. who have been with me since the very beginning, and Iesha A., Whitney L., RaeAnn, Brittany P., Juliann H., Meredith C., Heather M., Katy M., Lauren B., and Kathleen B – who read everything I send them so fast it makes my head spin, and whose kind words and belief in me make all this worthwhile.

Thank you to my amazing P.A., Sacha G. I am grateful every day that we met and cherish our friendship from the bottom of my heart.

Thank you to my incredible author friend, Nikki A. Lamers, a fellow indie author in the trenches with me who writes amazing stories and does everything she can to lift up and support other authors.

And last but not least thank you to every single one of you who is taking a chance on Luz and Ian's story and on Willow Creek.

Meet the author

Andrea is a two time H.O.L.T. Award-Winning Author (2023- Best First Book, No Regrets, 2025- Best Short Contemporary, No Excuses).

Andrea has been reading romance since she stole her aunt's copy of Ashes in the Wind when she was twelve. She loves writing sassy, independent women and complex, layered heroes who guard their hearts. She loves diving into obscure research and telling stories that readers don't expect to find. She believes in happily ever afters, soulmates, and the magic of love to heal invisible wounds. All of her stories have cinnamon roll heroes who do things for their partners without expecting anything in return - like make them breakfast and give them deep tissue massages. You can read her books on all digital platforms or borrow them from your local library via Hoopla and Libby. She also has several audiobooks you can find on Audible, iTunes and Amazon.

You'll find her on Substack, where you can subscribe to receive her newsletter, or you can connect with her on Instagram and Facebook via her author name. You can buy signed copies of her books directly from her website at andreajenelleromance.com

She loves hearing from readers! You can email her at authorandreajenelle@gmail.com

Other Books by Andrea

<u>Willow Creek Series (in order, but can be read in any order as standalones)</u>

No Regrets

No Surrender

No Promises

No Shadows

No Doubts

No Excuses

No Apologies

No Dreams (releasing October 2026)

No Strings (releasing June 2027)

Willow Creek Novellas

No Angels (Christmas novella in Kindle Unlimited)

Twelve Days & Twelve Nights (Christmas novella in Kindle Unlimited)

It Happened in the Library (novella in Kindle Unlimited)

The Princess and the Clown (novella in Kindle Unlimited)

No Ghosts (Halloween novella releasing in the One Dark Night anthology (KU) Sept. 2025)

No Christmas Spirit (Christmas Novella releasing October 2025 in Kindle Unlimited)

Snowflakes Fell in Silence (Christmas Novella releasing December 2025 in Kindle Unlimited)

<u>The Wainwright Sisters (Victorian era historical romance)</u>

When Araminta Greaves Traded Her Dignity for Bliss

How Frances Wainwright Learned to Love

Cece Wainwright's Christmas Wish

When Jess Wainwright's Curiosity was Satisfied

Handfasted in Haste (a holiday novella releasing November 2025)

How Gert Wainwright Spent Her Holiday (releasing Feb. 2026)

When Lavinia Wainwright Went Missing (releasing Feb. 2027)

Emily Wainwright's Exemplary Education (releasing November 2027)

<u>Sons & Daughters of Lir (paranormal urban romantasy inspired by Celtic mythology)</u>

Way Down We Go

Wither on the Vine

The Berserker's Daughter (prequel novella releasing August 2025)

Untitled Book 3 (releasing 2026)

Untitled Book 4 (releasing 2027)

<u>Starrlight Farms (a small town romance series set in Kentucky's Bluegrass region)</u>

Grace Above All (included in the Kentuckiana Romance Writers Anthology releasing in Fall 2025)

<u>The Terrible Trentons (a Victorian era small town romance series set in America)</u>

Spine of Steel (the first book in the Suffragette Uprising series, April 2025)

Nothing Compares to You (included in the Ordered Home Holiday Anthology, releasing Nov. 2025)

<u>Standalones</u>

What the Season Brings (a 1990s Christmas retelling of Jane Austen's Persuasion, rel. December 2025)

* 9 7 8 1 9 6 2 1 2 3 4 6 4 *